# Knightfall

C.L. Embry

Pendulum Publications

Cover Design by Moonpress, www.moonpress.co

Map by Dewi Hargreaves

Line editing by Kara Aisenbrey

ISBN: 979-8-9909883-0-9 (Paperback Edition)

ISBN: 979-8-9909883-2-3 (Hardback Edition)

ISBN: 979-8-9909883-1-6 (Ebook Edition)

First Edition Published October 2024

*He who grasps the truth of the Mental Nature of the Universe is well advanced on The Path to Mastery*

— The Kybalion

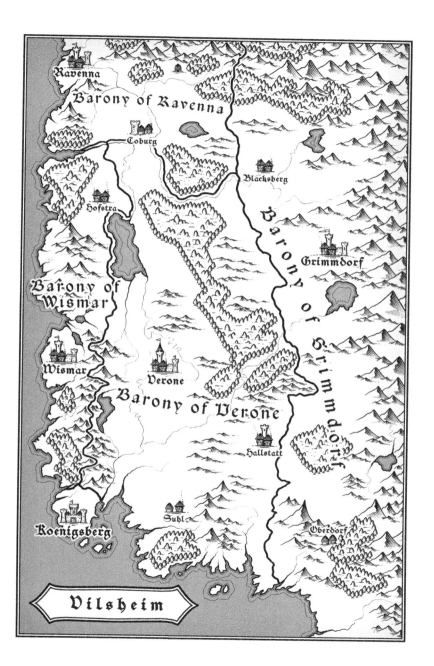

# Contents

# Chapter 1

## *Last Watch*

A brisk sea breeze swept through the Queen's Curtain, prompting Axel to wrap his fur cloak taut across his shoulders. The sky was clear, allowing the moon and stars to cast their radiant glow upon the shimmering surface of the harbor's still water. Amidst the darkness, the city lights sparkled, adorning the bustling taverns, brothels, and gaming halls that thrived at this time of night. The stunning panorama was deemed the most magnificent view in all of Vilsheim, and those who had the privilege of seeing it were lucky. But Axel did not feel fortunate.

He'd spent the last ten years atop Frostgarde's most formidable defense, watching for threats from land and sea. From its secure position atop the hill, surrounded by the great wall, the castle hadn't been at risk for hundreds of years, and there was little to keep a Watchman busy. Axel traced his hand along the weathered battlement as he strolled between the two towers overlooking the vast sea, every groove and sharp edge etched into the stone familiar to him. As far back as he remembered, he had been troubled by a weariness with his situation and deep dissatisfaction with his life. But tomorrow, everything would be different.

It was Axel's final night as a Watchman. His promotion to the BlackGuard meant a new assignment inside the keep, where his circumstances would improve. The keep was where everything interesting occurred, and he was looking forward to working in closer proximity to the king. Protecting visiting nobility while attending feasts and galas would allow him to overhear intriguing bits of gossip from around the realm. He couldn't ignore the twinge of anxiety settling in the pit of his stomach. As long as he maintained his composure and didn't allow the other knights to get under his skin, this would be a tremendous opportunity.

Before signing off, he embarked on his final patrol, knowing that he would soon celebrate with Stefan at The Badger and the Boar. He salivated, anticipating that first sip of ale tantalizing his taste buds, providing the perfect means to say goodbye to this phase of his life. He had to report to Commander Jurgen early in the morning, so he couldn't overindulge, and he weighed the need to unwind with his desire to excel on his first day. He could control his urges when something this important was at stake. Upon reaching the far-off tower, he gazed at the panoramic view one last time before heading back to his assigned position.

As he waited for his relief to report, he tended to the

fire, embracing the comforting warmth. How many years had he spent in this tower? The countless hours must add up to years. When the next Watchman arrived, he bid him farewell and raced down the stairs. Fifteen steps to the first landing, followed by another fifteen to the second, and then the last fifteen. As he descended, he slammed his ribs against the protruding wooden banister, a familiar annoyance that he had cursed countless times before. But this would be his final time. When he reached the bottom, he burst out of the tower with a sense of liberation he hadn't felt in years. A new chapter in his life was about to begin.

# Chapter 2

## *The Downward Spiral*

A xel lit up with a wide smile when he saw Stefan's towering figure waiting for him outside the Queen's Curtain. With his huge bald head and imposing physique, he was impossible to miss. They clasped forearms and slapped each other on the back before beginning the long trek down the hill from Frostgarde. The mammoth Boar's Gate, constructed of thick oak pillars and reinforced with forged iron beams, stood as the formidable barrier separating the castle from the rest of Koenigsberg. The Gatekeepers on duty saluted and inquired about their plans for the evening.

Stefan explained they were celebrating their promotions, prompting the taller Gatekeeper to eye them enviously. "Congratulations. I hope to make the BlackGuard one day. I'm sick of listening to sob stories when the king is holding court." Axel understood his sentiment, having started as a Gatekeeper twenty years earlier. Their role was to provide security for those wanting an audience with the king, and many turned away became unruly and violent. They bid their colleagues farewell and continued toward the tavern.

Axel relished in the familiar sight of The Badger and the Boar. A musty odor of stale brew and dank wood permeated the air. It smelled like home. He surveyed the room, relieved to find it wasn't crowded. A few off-duty Gatekeepers, still wearing blue tabards, were conversing at a table near the kitchen, and he gave them a polite nod as he headed straight to the bar and ordered two ales. After they'd received their drinks, Axel raised his tankard in celebration. "To our last night on that accursed wall. May better days lie before us."

They clanked their mugs together before taking a long draw. Stefan wiped his mouth and said, "I hope you get along with the rest of the BlackGuard. You're a good guy, but you have to dig through a lot of negativity to uncover it. When others want to get close, you push them away. I still can't believe how you blew it with Ysabelle. Why I bet—"

Axel slammed his tankard on the bar. "Enough. I'm trying to enjoy myself. I've moved on—I wish you would stop reminding me of her." He took another long drink, savoring the flavor as it settled in his mouth. He always enjoyed the initial euphoria he got from that first drink, all his cares and frustrations slowly drifting away. It put him in a good mood, making it easier to ignore the little things that annoyed him. However, when he drank too much, as was typical these past few months, that mood turned into anger. That was what worried Stefan. But

Axel wouldn't let that happen tonight; tomorrow was too important.

He finished his ale and ordered another round. As the barkeep set his drink on the counter, he asked, "Do you guys have any insight into the alchemist being executed this week?"

Axel rolled his eyes. There hadn't been an alchemist captured in over fifty years and it was all everyone had been talking about. He'd never understood what was so terrible about them. Being able to transmute worthless metal into gold seemed like a harmless, albeit marvelous ability. "We know little more than you. King Otto convicted him of practicing alchemy, and his public beheading will serve as a reminder that it's unlawful. No quarter is given to those pursuing it."

The barkeep nodded. "Do you know how they caught him?"

"They don't fill us in on the details, but they want to set a precedent, so it's another fifty years before we see another. We'll be there, like you, but at least we're getting paid." Axel smirked into his mug.

The barkeep shook his head, leaving them alone. Axel and Stefan drank in silence, like old friends could. It was one reason Axel liked him—no need for mindless chatter. Merely being in his presence brought companionship. After downing his second ale, he waved his empty tankard, ready for something stronger, and ordered a mead.

Stefan eyed him warily. "Be careful. You know where this can lead. I'll have one with you before I visit my wife.

The last thing I need is to be too drunk to perform my husbandly duties."

Axel shook his head. They rarely got nights away from Frostgarde so Stefan was eager to connect with his wife. "I'm amazed you found a woman who doesn't drive you to drink. You're one lucky bastard."

"Luck has nothing to do with it, Ax. I respect and love her the way she is. I don't try to change her."

"Perhaps you found the exception: a woman that doesn't need improvement. They start out nice and sweet to hook you, but once they sink their claws in, it's nothing but trouble. I can handle it at the beginning, but eventually, the weight of dealing with so many problems becomes exhausting."

Stefan rubbed his face in exasperation. "How often must we rehash this conversation? You're missing the point of being in a relationship."

"That's exactly why I take care of my needs at a brothel. Both of us know exactly what we're getting, and there're no strings attached." Axel thought of Mistila, who worked at Inga's brothel. They'd clicked after seeing each other a few times, and she understood him with no expectations.

The potent aroma of honey wafted from his mead. He put the tankard to his lips and let it settle on his tongue. The overwhelming sweetness threatened to make him gag, but the fruity aftertaste helped to balance out the intensity. The second draw was more palatable, and by the third, it went down effortlessly. Axel sighed and let the comfort of the mead wash his worries away.

He was barely half finished when Stefan slammed his empty tankard on the bar. "That's it for me. Take care of yourself, Ax, and try not to get into trouble." He patted Axel's back before leaving him alone with his thoughts. Now he could relax without fear of judgment. He ordered another mead and retreated to a private table in the corner near the hearth. The glow from the fire, combined with the effects of the alcohol, removed his lingering anxiety. Drinking in solitude put him in a better mood, and his head grew heavy, his mind roaming freely. The image of Stefan with his wife made him long for a woman who could empathize with him on a deeper level, yet all his relationships were riddled with complications. His thoughts drifted back to Mistila, to feeling the warmth of her body pressed against his. She wouldn't judge him. That was what he was paying for.

Axel finished his drink and stood, his unsteady balance making him realize how drunk he was. He was going to feel that second mead in the morning. His rational self was screaming at him to return to the barracks, but his overwhelming loneliness was impossible to ignore. He braced himself against the wall as he staggered for the exit, determining whether to visit Mistila. He'd confirm if she was free, and if not, he'd return to Frostgarde. What was wrong with enjoying a woman's comforts on a celebratory evening? He would deal with the fallout tomorrow. He always did.

As far as brothels in Koenigsberg went, Inga's was one of the cleanest in the city. Despite its lack of opulence, like those in the nobility district, a man could find an affordable, disease-free girl with which to share a bed. Its proximity to Frostgarde made it a favorite of the knights, as it was more reputable than those near the port.

Axel shuddered when he thought of the bordellos the sailors frequented. He typically avoided the harbor, but he'd found himself there at the end of one drunken evening. He was with another knight, who'd claimed he knew a place with attractive women. The promise sounded appealing, but it proved too good to be true. While the girls were moderately attractive, they were significantly overweight. Axel had been portly when he was young, so he didn't mind a woman with a few extra pounds, but these were much larger, and ever since being teased as a young bairn, he'd despised the sight of fatty flesh. No amount of alcohol would arouse his manhood enough to bed those women. He'd left and vowed never to be cheap at a brothel. You got what you paid for.

He arrived at Inga's and scanned the room. Three men chatted at the bar while another group flirted with a girl near the fireplace. He enjoyed watching the ladies interact with customers. They were instructed to act timid and naive, while persuading patrons to pay higher prices, and Inga's girls knew how to work the room. Axel searched fruitlessly for Mistila, so he waited at the bar. If he didn't find her soon, he would ask Inga, who was always around.

The gorgeous red-haired barkeep smiled at him. "Hey handsome, what can I get for you?" All the bartenders were women. They weren't courtesans, but they primed the patrons with steady drink and flirtatious compliments.

He ordered an ale as a stunning older woman approached him from the kitchen. Long blonde hair cascaded along her shoulders, framing an ample bosom that begged to be stared at. Her stylish yellow dress amplified her curvaceous figure in a most desirable way. Soft white lace hung from the sleeves, outlining her delicate feminine hands. Axel's nose tingled from the flowery fragrance emanating from her.

"Well, look what the wolf dragged in. If it isn't Axel Albrecht having quite the evening. What brings you out tonight? Drowning your sorrows over a broken heart? Or perhaps celebrating a big night at the gaming hall? Are you a merry drunk, or will I see you crying over a woman's bosom later?"

Axel winced. "Hello, Inga. I'm celebrating. It has been a long ten years, but I'm leaving the Curtain and moving to the keep."

Inga smiled while caressing his back. "Congratulations, you finally made it to BlackGuard after all these years. I knew you would get there. That drink's on the house, but it's your last, honey. I don't need you getting sloppy, and you shouldn't be showing up to work with a hangover."

As usual, she was right. He liked Inga and wanted to remain on her good side. She was sharp as a knife and could take a quip as well as she could give one. She took meticulous care of herself and her establishment. Axel longed to meet a woman who embodied her qualities. He gazed at her through glassy eyes. "I appreciate your concern, but I'm not here to cause trouble."

She cocked an eyebrow. "I hope you remember that, because I'm going to hold you to those words."

"Why do you say that?"

Inga shrugged. "Call it women's intuition. I'm fully aware of what's going on around me, and I'm sensing some odd feelings coming from you. Maybe it's the ale, but for someone celebrating, you sure seem on edge. Like a cat ready to pounce."

He considered her remarks. "I'm thrilled to have a position with more opportunity, but perhaps I'm anxious about starting something new. It should be better for me, but what if it isn't? I remember a similar excitement when I left the Boar's Gate. No more listening to arseholes lie or threaten me. I longed for peace and quiet on the Curtain. That feeling wore off after a few months, and I grew bored. Time dragged, and soon a twelve-hour shift felt like a week. I would daydream about going back to the Boar's Gate just to get some action."

Inga caressed his back and rubbed his shoulders. "I understand. You look to the future with anticipation, expecting it to be a marked improvement over the present. When it arrives, you continue looking ahead instead of enjoying the moment. You're constantly chasing something that doesn't exist, hoping to avoid the pain of your present situation."

He shrugged her off. "No need to get philosophical. I guess I'll see what happens over the next few months." She might be right but he was in no condition to process that now.

"Alright, Axel. I got a new girl that's exactly your type.

Beautiful brown hair, skin as white as porcelain, and a tiny waist with hips meant to hold on to. Not to mention an ample bosom that entices even me." She winked, flashing a seductive smile.

Axel chuckled. "I am more of an arse man, but picturing you with another woman is stirring a few ideas, among other things. But I'm a creature of habit, preferring the comforts of something familiar. Where's Mistila? I haven't seen her. I'm almost hoping she isn't here, as I can't bear the thought of seeing her with another man."

Inga giggled as she shifted her eyes toward the staircase. "What do you think happens when you're not here? The ladies patiently wait for their special man while turning down other suitors? I'd be out of business within a month."

"I know it's not realistic, but if I don't see it, then it didn't happen. That mentality has saved me a lot of headaches."

"By ignoring reality and assuming everyone exists to serve you? Anyway, Mistila is here, but indisposed, so if you want to continue living with your head in the sand, I suggest you leave now. I don't want to shatter your illusion."

Axel stretched his arms and yawned. "I suppose you're right. It's getting late, and I need to be ready for tomorrow. I drank more than I intended and feel a headache coming on. No need to make it worse."

"Now you're thinking," she said. "Let me know the next time you plan on visiting, and I'll be sure Mistila is ready for you. Now, please allow me to escort you out."

He emptied his tankard and nodded. There was no need to waste good ale. As they were leaving, he heard laughter coming from the stairwell. Inga locked his arm in hers and dragged him toward the door. "Come on, Axel, let's not delay. Your bed is waiting."

Axel, in his drunken stupor, thought the giggling sounded like Mistila. In the back of his mind, he knew he should leave now. Nothing positive would come from seeing who she was with. He couldn't afford to lose his cool.

Instead, he froze, focusing on the staircase, lingering to see who came down. In slow motion, two sets of legs descended step by step, one wearing a forest-green dress he was intimately familiar with. He had told Mistila it brought out the green in her eyes, making them sparkle like emeralds.

But he was more interested in the other set of legs. He saw high black boots, similar to his own, only more polished. Next came the bottom of a black surcoat with gold trim, draped over black mail. His stomach clenched and his head whirled with dizziness. It was a knight of the BlackGuard. Inga continued dragging him to the door, and his feet moved, but his eyes remained fixated on the stairs. When the two figures emerged, Axel gasped, his worst fears realized—Mistila was linked arm in arm with Basel. Anyone would be better than him. He despised Basel almost as much as he hated Gunter. The two of them had tortured Axel relentlessly when they were young. If it wasn't for his friendship with Stefan, he wouldn't have survived to manhood. He'd been mercilessly teased for being too fat, too slow, too gullible, too uptight, and too weak. It wasn't until Gunter and Basel joined the Knights of Frostgarde that he had gotten a temporary reprieve from their abuse; they were two years older and were too preoccupied at the Boar's Gate to worry about him. However, once Axel became a Gate-keeper, it had started again. He'd thought he would never make it through training. Once he had, the teasing subsided—but they'd devised new ways to get under his skin.

Axel's feet reflexively carried him toward the couple. Inga held onto his arm, trying to detain him, but he pushed her off. Mistila smiled. "Hello, Axel, it's good to see you. I'll be with you after I escort your friend out."

He ignored her and focused on Basel, who was smirking at him. "What's got you so hot and bothered? Get lost, you horse's arse."

Without breaking stride, Axel clenched his fist and swung a hard left hook, crushing his nose. Basel staggered backward, clutching his face as blood poured between his fingers, down his uniform, and onto the floor. Axel was stunned by his own actions, and Basel wasted no time throwing him onto an empty table, which collapsed beneath his weight. Stars floated around his head as it slammed against the floor.

Basel was clutching his nose, trying to contain the blood seeping from it. "You arsehole! I'm going to kill you for that, piggy."

Inga's guards rushed to break it up. Two men held

Basel while a third yanked Axel to his feet and pushed him to the far corner.

Inga rushed to Basel's side. "Someone grab a cloth. We need to stop the bleeding."

The barkeep came immediately with a stack of towels, and she sat Basel down and held one over his nose. "I think it's broken. Can anyone set it straight?"

A guard with a nose that looked like it'd been broken multiple times answered affirmatively. "Has your nose ever been broken?" he asked Basel, who shook his head in response. "This is going to be bloody painful. Ready?"

Basel nodded, and the guard cradled his face before snapping the cartilage in place. Blood poured from his nose until it set. "Get the towels back on."

"I'm so sorry, Basel," Inga said, quickly covered his nose. "Is there anything I can do? Get him a drink on the house."

He shook his head. "Thanks, Inga. It wasn't your fault. It was Axel Arsehole's. I'll deal with him at Frostgarde. His commander will be interested in hearing about this." He glared at Axel with a bloody smile.

Axel watched in horror, knowing he should have left when he'd had the chance. Stefan and Inga had tried to warn him, but his stubbornness wouldn't allow him. His head ached from a sharp pain on his forehead, and he felt a tender lump forming above his eyes. It would be obvious to everyone he had gotten in a fight.

Inga was incensed. "Mistila, get him out of here," she said, pointing at Axel.

Mistila ran to take him to her room. He braced himself against the banister as she guided him up the stairs. The sight of the other whores and their clients gawking at them horrified him upon reaching the upper landing. As they approached her room, she pushed Axel in and onto her bed. He rolled over to find Mistila standing over him. "You arsehole! You are incapable of controlling yourself."

Axel looked at her, dumbfounded. "I can't believe you're blaming me. He started it!"

"Without uttering a word, you went up to Basel and punched him in the nose."

"Exactly! I didn't say a damn thing, yet he called me a horse's arse and told me to get lost."

Mistila clutched her hair, frowning. "So whenever someone says something you don't like, you hit them? Maybe Basel was being an arse, but that doesn't give you the right to attack him, let alone cause a scene that damages my reputation."

He knew she was right. The alcohol had impaired his judgment, leading to a complete loss of control. He hadn't realized he was that far gone. "I'm sorry. I came here to celebrate with you. When Inga told me you were unavailable, imagining you with another man made my stomach turn. The sight of you with the person who made my life miserable was too much to handle."

"You idiot. Why don't you think before you act? You got it all wrong. I wasn't seeing Basel. We came downstairs at the same time. I'm not even his type. You're jumping to conclusions you assume are right."

Axel exhaled, relieved. "So you weren't seeing another man? That makes me feel better."

"You're doing it again. I never claimed I wasn't seeing another man. You are so judgmental. I said I wasn't seeing Basel. What do you think I'm doing here? I may act like you are the only man in my life, but that's my job. You can't be threatening my clients. I'm sorry, Axel, but I won't see you anymore. You're bad for business."

Axel's jaw dropped as panic set in. His terrible night was getting worse. "Please give me another chance. I know I behaved poorly, but I swear it won't happen again. Isn't there anything I can do?"

Mistila shook her head. "No, I'm done. This is my livelihood, and I need to keep it professional. I can't get wrapped up in my patrons' problems. I'm sure there will be plenty of other girls willing to take your coin."

Sheepishly, he glanced at her with a timid expression. "So I'm allowed to come here, but I can't see you?"

"You're still making assumptions. I don't know if Inga will allow you back. Discuss that with her. I know she takes pride in running a professional establishment and doesn't appreciate drama."

Axel smiled at her suggestively. "So how about one last time? We're already in your room."

She put a finger to her lips, contemplating. "Given your condition, it will probably be quick, but I'm still going to charge you the full price." He nodded eagerly. "Okay, one last time." She grabbed his chin and gently stroked his beard. "I can't turn away your handsome face, no matter how sorry it looks."

Axel savored his last moments, watching Mistila disrobe. The sight of her undressing stirred an intense desire to devour her. Her brown hair fell lightly along her back, exposing her sumptuous, naked body. He gently wrapped his hand around her waist and guided her to the bed. As he lay on her, he kissed her forehead, down her nose and cheeks, and made his way to her neck. She moaned softly as he continued to her breasts, caressing them with his mouth. With each flicker of his tongue, her nipples grew more erect, and her moaning increased in response. He continued down her chest to her soft belly, where a silver ring pierced her navel. Mistila grabbed his head, pushing him farther downward. He obliged her by positioning himself between her legs and caressing her inner thighs before moving his mouth to her sex. He began licking the outside before burying his tongue deep inside. Pressing harder, he flickered faster, causing her to gyrate until she shook in ecstasy on his greedy mouth.

Axel rose and pressed his body close to hers. He grabbed his semi-erect member and sought to enter her. Whether from alcohol or stress, he struggled to reach his full girth. Frustrated, he ultimately inserted himself before thrusting. He stared into Mistila's eyes, attempting to kiss her, but she turned aside. After a short time, he withdrew and let his seed dribble on her stomach. While it was not his best performance, he rolled next to her, satisfied.

Mistila caressed his arm. "I will miss that tongue of yours. It always satisfies me."

After his release, Axel was drained. The night was catching up to him. "Thank you. I better leave before I fall asleep. I'll be in enough trouble as it is." As he kissed her forehead, a soft smile adorned her face, and they got dressed.

When they were both clothed, they headed downstairs. The mess had already been cleared, and Basel was gone. Mistila escorted him to the door, saying, "I'll miss you, Axel. I hope you find peace." He smiled and kissed her cheek before hurrying home to Frostgarde. A sense of unease washed over him as he anticipated tomorrow. It was sure to be the ominous start he'd been hoping to avoid.

# Chapter 3

## *Reporting for Duty*

Axel awoke to the sounds of Watchmen leaving for their day, his mouth dry and his skull throbbing. This was not how he was supposed to start his new life. Still in uniform, he stood, bracing against the wall for balance. A wave of nausea hit, forcing him to sit back down and grip his head until the feeling passed. Upon seeing bloodstains on his tabard, he let out a groan. He must have drunk more than he remembered. He scratched his blond beard and rubbed the crust from his pale blue eyes. A sharp pain shot through the knot on his forehead as the events of the evening returned. It was going to be a long day.

He needed water to soothe his parched throat. He stumbled from the barracks, stopping to pee in a large wooden trough. Once relieved, he drew a bucket of well water and guzzled it, allowing the cool water to spill onto his chest. After drinking his fill, he washed his face and cleaned off the remnants of the previous night. He hoped the blood wouldn't be noticeable on his black tabard, but some of it had gotten onto the silver boar blazoned in the center. He tried removing the red stains, but the emblem was ruined. Fortunately, the BlackGuard would issue him a new uniform. Based on its condition, they would either salvage his old one or repurpose it. The king's concern about spies had led to a strict policy of one uniform at a time. Previous infiltration attempts at Frostgarde had prompted the Koenigs to be cautious.

Axel returned to the barracks and rummaged through his chest, ensuring he had all his belongings. He would move into the keep when he reported to Commander Jurgen. With a gleam in his eye and a radiant smile, Stefan strolled in. "Hey Ax, are you ready? Looks like you made it back in one piece." As he approached, he grimaced, shaking his head. "I guess I spoke too soon. I've taken shits more appealing than you. What the hell happened?"

Axel sighed. "I don't remember everything, but parts are coming back that I'd rather forget. I should have left with you."

Stefan stroked his chin with feigned concentration. "Let me guess. You were innocently minding your own business when someone made trouble for you. It wasn't your fault. You were only reacting."

"Well, it's true!" Axel said with a scowl. "I wasn't the one being an arse. Maybe I overreacted, but I won't stand idle while Basel insults me." He recounted his evening at the brothel. "Mistila won't see me anymore, and I doubt Inga will let me back because of that bloody arsehole!"

Stefan listened as he rifled through his own chest. "You know how Basel and Gunter are, yet you still let them bother you, like you did when we were bairns."

Axel grimaced in annoyance. "The last thing I need is a lecture. You were always bigger, so they left you alone. Anyway, I don't want to talk about it. Let's report and get this day over with."

They finished gathering their gear and headed for the keep. Activity in the inner bailey had already gotten lively. As they strolled past the training grounds, they witnessed the new recruits honing their skills to become Gatekeepers, the echoes of swords clashing in the background. They reached the imposing portcullis that shielded the entrance to Frostgarde Keep where two knights stood guard, watching those who passed through.

Stefan saluted. "We're here to report to Commander Jurgen."

The guards looked at Axel, snickering. "We've been expecting you. That's quite a bruise you've got there. If we're ever involved in a brawl at a brothel, your help will be most appreciated."

His face flushed bright red. He hadn't even started and was already being teased. He stood tall, struggling to control his rage. "I was strengthening my skull so I'll be as thickheaded as you idiots." The insult was weak, but still boosted his spirits.

One guard feigned offense. "It can be stressful here. In fact, I may need to relieve some tension tonight. I hear Mistila has more availability these days."

"You better not! Or I will—"

The guard stepped forward. "You'll listen as I describe it in meticulous detail."

"Come on, Ax," Stefan said, pulling him through the gate. "Looks like our new colleagues have heard of your escapades, so that means Jurgen has too."

Axel sighed with a sinking feeling that he would be back on the Curtain before the day was over. They passed through the great hall, which bustled with activity. The smell of freshly baked bread permeated the room. Kitchen servants scurried by with remnants of the morning's breakfast, and Axel's mouth watered as platters loaded with smoked fish, hard cheese, and fresh fruit passed through. "Looks like the servants here eat better than we do."

"That's the kitchen crew," Stefan replied. "I hear they make extra so they have leftovers for themselves. I'm sure Chancellor Heinz will say something if he finds out. As stingy as he is, it won't slip past him for long. One of these meals will be someone's last." Although the king ruled Vilsheim, the chancellor handled the day-to-day governance.

Axel watched them scuttle past with envy. "It doesn't help that I ate little yesterday. I'm starving."

They continued past the kitchen, turning down a narrow hallway leading to the eastern wing that housed the BlackGuard. Their quarters included their own small dining room, several bedrooms, and the armory. The common area was empty while the surrounding rooms were all dark, save one. Stefan pointed at the lit doorway. "I suppose we should start there."

Inside an older man sat at a desk, surrounded by stacks of paper. His skin was weathered, permanently darkened from too many days in the sun. The snow-white hair covering his head was a stark contrast to his leathery face, which had a hard expression, offset by a softness in his eyes. A warrior's braid hung down his back while a long silvery beard draped over the top of his protruding chest. Two lit sconces adorned the walls, and as their flames flickered, the men's shadows danced on the floor.

Stefan stepped into the room, saluting. "Commander Jurgen. We're here to report for our first day, sir."

The old man appraised them while stroking his beard. "Head bald, big like a bear. You must be Stefan." He turned to Axel, frowning. "A large welt on your head, hungover as a bairn after his first night drinking. Your reputation precedes you, Axel."

Sweat beaded on Axel's forehead, anxiety coursing through his body. He needed to pull it together. "Yes, sir, reporting for duty."

Jurgen examined him closely, casting him a doubtful glance. "You're not off to a good start. My sleep was interrupted by Basel's ranting—he claims you assaulted him. I don't appreciate being awoken for something so pointless."

"No, sir, I apologize. We were celebrating our last night on the Curtain, and I went a little overboard. I can't sit idle while someone insults me though. I had to defend my honor." Axel knew a little about Jurgen. Strength and honor were important to him, and he hoped to strike the right chord.

"I understand you attacked him over a whore."

"He insulted me while I was trying to strike up a conversation, so I hit him. I admit I should have been quicker with my wit than my fist, but my mind was still foggy."

Jurgen raised an eyebrow. "Let me set the record straight now. I don't like folk who can't handle their drink and loathe when my men fight with each other. Do I make myself clear?"

"As clear as a frozen lake. You won't have any problems with me, sir."

"Good, good," Jurgen said to himself while nodding his head. "You have an excellent record over many years. While I can't blame a man who stands up for his honor, there are better ways to handle it amongst ourselves. It's one thing when you are quarreling with outsiders, but we are on the same side here." He looked at the piles of paper on his desk. "I've got enough problems without dealing with drama. Let's get you outfitted with new uniforms and settled into your quarters. By the look of these tabards, they are going into the repurpose pile. Yours is a mess, and his is too damn big to fit anyone else." His face softened, and a brief smile appeared. "Grab your chests, and I'll take you to your room."

Jurgen led them out of his office. "This is the main room, where we have meetings, dine, and relax when off duty. That over there is the bathroom. All the holes lead to chutes that carry your waste to the basement, where it's disposed of by servants. The armory is behind the door next to my office. It stays locked, and I have the only key.

We keep tight records of our equipment." They approached a row of doors on the other side of the room. "These are the sleeping quarters. There are two in a room. They aren't much, but it beats sleeping in the barracks with a dozen others."

He opened a door. "You'll share this one. Your uniforms are on your bed. Get dressed, and bring your old ones to my office. Be quick about it." He left to resume his paperwork.

They entered a room not much larger than a dungeon cell. Their beds consisted of straw-filled mattresses atop stone blocks, with a designated spot for their trunks. Their uniforms were already laid out, and Axel pointed to one. "Judging by the size of that surcoat, I'm guessing that's yours." He put his chest near the other bed and took a seat. "These mattresses are much more comfortable, and we don't have to worry about sleeping on the wet ground when it rains."

Stefan burst into laughter. "Are you sure that wasn't your piss?"

Axel chuckled. He was in better spirits. His stomach had settled, and his nerves no longer tingled. Jurgen had given him a pass, and his new quarters were a much improved upgrade. Once they'd unpacked, they changed into their new uniforms. Axel removed the sleeveless black tabard and grey mail armor that he had worn for the past ten years. Its color made the Watchmen difficult to spot atop the Curtain, and its thick wool kept them warm in the chilly wind high atop the hill. The Koenig's silver boar sigil adorned the tabard, designating them as Kingsmen. He held it up, giving it a last look before putting that phase of his life behind him.

His new uniform was much more impressive. The dull grey mail was swapped for sleek jet-black armor, and the ebony surcoat with its intricate designs outshined his old tabard. The combination had prompted their designation as the BlackGuard. Its sleeves came as far down as the elbows, while its overall length extended past Axel's knees. It was made of wool and lined with a fur that he did not recognize. A silver boar graced the front.

Stefan smiled with palpable excitement. "These new uniforms are incredible."

Axel cracked a wide grin. "These are much better than our tabards. We will command respect wearing these."

Stefan belted a great laugh. "Indeed. It doesn't change who we are, but it will damn well change other people's opinions of us. We should get back to Jurgen."

Axel nodded as they took their old outfits to his office. Jurgen was engrossed in his paperwork, so he cleared his throat to get his attention. When Jurgen didn't budge, he tried louder, causing the commander to glower at him. "Yes, I heard you the first time. You need to work on patience. You'll need it here. I have a lot of work preparing for the alchemist's execution. We haven't had one in fifty years, so everything needs to be perfect. Now, where were we? I see you have your uniforms, so let's visit the armory. Follow me."

He led them to a thick wooden door he unlocked using a key hanging from his neck. The room was bigger than it first appeared and loaded with weapons. One wall was lined with swords of varying lengths and styles. On the other side were a variety of axes, including short throwing ones and a wicked two-handed great axe.

Jurgen assessed them. "You both have a long sword and a dirk. Axel, grab a halberd and a single-bladed axe. Stefan, you also get a halberd, but take the double-bladed axe. You are big enough to wield it. Always wear your sword. When you're guarding a location, bring your halberd. When protecting a person, use the axe. The halberds are imposing but cumbersome to carry. Only use them while you're stationary." He inspected them and nodded. "Now you look like the BlackGuard I was expecting. Dump your old uniforms in the corner. A servant will deal with them."

After leaving the armory, Jurgen stopped. "I need to get back to work. We have two important events, bringing a lot of visitors to Koenigsberg. The execution is later this week, and all knights will be on duty. The king intends to display his full power to discourage others from ever attempting to practice that dark magic." He paused and shuddered before continuing. "The following weekend is Queen Helena's fiftieth birthday ball. Visiting nobles will be among the guests, and you will be assigned one to guard. I'll fill you in more later. For now, I want you stationed at the portcullis. You may retire when the next shift relieves you. I expect both of you here tomorrow morning to receive your orders. Are we clear?"

"Yes, sir." They saluted.

"Excellent, dismissed," Jurgen replied as he went into his office.

They relieved the two guards without incident. Standing at his new post, Axel realized Jurgen was right about patience. It was a long, slow day that involved little activity, and he was fine with that for now. Thoughts swirled in his mind as he speculated what the lord or lady assigned to him would be like. He hoped it would be someone pleasant. A son or daughter of a minor lord would be fine with him. As long as it wasn't anyone from one of the barons' families. The last thing he needed was more scrutiny.

# Chapter 4

## *The Alchemist's Execution*

On the morning of the execution, Axel woke in a restless mood. They would behead the alchemist in front of all of Koenigsberg, while the entire garrison of knights at Frostgarde guarded their king. That meant seeing Basel and Gunter. His nerves tingled at the thought. He preferred to avoid confrontation, but most interactions with Gunter involved a conflict. He never failed to spoil any good thing that happened to Axel.

The two were opposites in every way. Gunter was lean, outgoing, athletic, skilled with a sword, and arrogant. He'd always believed in his own greatness and expected others to share that opinion. Axel had been a fat child, uncoordinated, slow to master a weapon, and reserved. He was nervous when meeting new people while Gunter relished it. Axel was a wallflower, while Gunter needed to be the center of attention. When they were kids, Gunter attacked his deepest insecurities, much like his father, and despite Axel's success as a knight, Gunter still loved to torment him.

He yawned and stretched before climbing out of bed. There was no use dwelling on it. It was time to face it head-on. Stefan stirred as he got dressed. "That time already?"

Axel nodded. "I'm afraid so, my friend. It should be an interesting day. I don't know what to expect. What do you think?"

Stefan shrugged. "I'm as much in the dark as you." He hesitated before adding, "Are you going to be alright with Gunter? You don't act like yourself around him. Remember, I'll be by your side, like I always am."

"Thanks, I trust you will. He infuriates me, but the sooner I face him, the sooner I will stop dwelling on it. I'm afraid breaking his friend's nose only made it worse." No doubt Gunter would have something disparaging to say.

Stefan rose to get dressed. "Maybe you won't see him. This is an important day, and Jurgen emphasized he has no tolerance for petty squabbles. He's aware of your history and intentionally placed us on the opposite side of the chamber."

"Yeah, it's the first thing I noticed. We'll have words at some point. It's only a matter of when. Let's go."

They entered the main hall, where the BlackGuard was gathering. Axel scoured the area but saw no signs of Gunter or Basel. Jurgen, looking every bit their leader, strolled to the center of the room, decorated in full ceremonial uniform.

He exuded confidence and poise as he urged the stragglers to hurry. "Today is not the day to dawdle. We have a tight schedule and don't need the king's attention on us."

The rest of the men left their rooms and surrounded him. Axel scowled as Gunter and Basel approached from the opposite corner. Gunter caught him staring and smirked before mockingly saluting and turning his attention to Jurgen. Axel forced himself to focus on his commander as his stomach twisted in knots.

"Today, the king is executing an alchemist. He is setting a precedent that alchemy is not tolerated in Vilsheim. He needs his full authority on display, so all knights not on guard duty are required to attend. The execution is scheduled for midday, so one hour prior we will meet in the bailey outside the portcullis. Once all regiments are gathered, the king's procession will march to Koenigsberg's town square. The Gatekeepers will lead the way, followed by the Watchmen, with the BlackGuard trailing. I will break us into two groups. Half will be in front of the king's entourage while the other half will guard the rear. King Otto will be accompanied by Queen Helena and the royal family, as well as Chancellor Heinz and any guests he has invited to sit with him. The IceGuard will protect his inner circle.

"The Gatekeepers and Watchmen will serve as crowd control while we defend the king from potential threats. Although we don't expect trouble, we will prepare for it. Are there questions?" Jurgen looked around the silent room before dividing them into two groups. Axel and Stefan were assigned to the squad leading the king, while

Gunter and Basel were allocated to the rear—the more important position.

After being dismissed, the knights went about their assigned duties. Axel and Stefan rushed to the kitchen for a quick breakfast before heading to the portcullis. The inner bailey was bustling with activity as the knights congregated. It was a rare occurrence for all four ranks to assemble in one location. The Koenig's boar standards could be seen scattered among a sea of blue, grey, and black uniforms clustered together. Combined, they were a formidable force and an intimidating display.

Jurgen arrived and rounded up his men. "The chancellor will be here soon, ensuring everyone is properly arranged for the king's arrival. Stand back by the portcullis, but don't block the entrance. Break into the groups that I assigned earlier, each flanking one side of the gate."

The men split up into two groups as Chancellor Heinz, accompanied by the IceGuard, entered. A tall, lean man, the chancellor had dark grey hair and a long pepper beard that glistened in the morning sun. He wore a black silk robe, trimmed with gold embellishments, and a silver coif over his head.

"Attention!" While typically soft-spoken, the chancellor could make his voice carry when needed. "King Otto will be here soon, so I want everyone positioned as your commanders directed. Do not upset him by being disorganized."

"Yes, sir," they replied as the chancellor strolled to the keep's entrance and watched. Axel and Stefan lined up behind their former comrades. It grew silent as they waited; nobody wanted to draw the chancellor's attention. Axel grew impatient. It was past midday, but the king still had not shown up. It was rude to make them wait in the scorching sun. If a knight had been this late, they would have been punished. The rules didn't treat everyone equally, and it wasn't fair. After what seemed like an eternity, the IceGuard began passing through the portcullis, preparing for the royal family. They were the highest ranking knights and most elite fighters in all of Vilsheim. Only the most adept members of the BlackGuard had a chance at joining them.

Axel knew he was not skilled enough to reach that level. This position was as high as he would ascend and where he would spend the remainder of his life. The best he could hope for was better assignments or special favors if he performed well. Gunter, however, would join the IceGuard as soon as he gained more experience. Axel didn't care—the quicker he got promoted, the less he'd have to see him. Unfortunately, everyone else knew this about Gunter, which only added to his arrogance. Other knights gravitated to him, eager to secure his favor. While the IceGuard was technically part of their garrison, they were kept isolated. Their station was buried deep within the keep, inaccessible to the rest of the knights. Their proximity made them privy to private conversations involving the security of the kingdom. Rumors among the staff said the king even allowed them time with his concubines when they pleased him.

Joining the IceGuard had its drawbacks; their tongues

were cut out after they swore an oath to safeguard the king until death. The Koenigs were adamant about keeping confidential information within the keep, and men without tongues could not reveal secrets. A small smirk escaped Axel's lips as he envisioned Gunter getting his tongue removed.

King Otto von Koenig emerged, accompanied by his wife, Queen Helena. Trailing them were several other well-dressed nobles Axel didn't recognize, most likely visiting from another city. The rest of the IceGuard followed, protecting their rear.

"Welcome, Your Majesty," the chancellor said with a bow. "We have everything in order and await your command to march into the city."

King Otto peered over his vast army before slowly nodding his endorsement. He was a large man, half as wide as he was tall. While his belly protruded from the black mantle draped over his body, his shoulders were broad and his chest as strong as one who'd spent years performing hard physical labor. Stretching across his breast was the Koenig family sigil: a black boar, outlined in gold. Atop his head, a golden crown encircled his brow. Another boar adorned its center, with fire-red rubies for eyes. Queen Helena stood poised in a golden robe, complementing her husband. She was a petite, bony woman with a stern visage. Her expression was reserved, yet she maintained an image of unfettered power. A majestic aura surrounded the royal couple, signifying the gravitas of the message being delivered.

"Excellent," the king replied in a baritone voice that

carried across the bailey. "Let us show the citizens of Vilsheim what happens to those that disobey the king's law. Knights, are you ready to convey the full might of your king?"

The knights responded in unison, "Yes, Your Majesty."

King Otto's laughter echoed throughout the air as his eyes gleamed with immense pride. He motioned for them to proceed.

"Gatekeepers! Commence your march into Koenigsberg," the chancellor said to the first group. At his command, they advanced down Frostgarde's hill. Axel waited patiently for the Watchmen to clear before the BlackGuard trailed behind. After passing through the upper gate, they began their descent to the Boar's Gate. The procession moved with a purposeful, orderly pace.

When they reached the bottom, the Gatekeepers opened the colossal gate necessary to let their large group pass. They stationed additional Gatekeepers outside, ensuring none of the crowd could get to the heart of the procession. Citizens lined the streets, hoping to catch a glimpse of the royal family as they proceeded to the center of the city. The crowd turned restless, jostling each other. Some onlookers were shoved into the street, only to be violently forced back by the knights.

When they reached the town square, they were greeted by a large crowd, eagerly awaiting the execution. A stage with a flight of stairs leading to the gallows had been erected for the event, a large stone block positioned in the center. An imposing figure, clad in black plate armor, reflecting the sun, stood alone on the platform. A boar-crested helm rested upon his head, and he carried a nasty bearded double-bladed headsman axe in his outstretched hands. Knights surrounded the entire structure.

Across from the stage stood another raised dais, where the royal family was taken, while several well-dressed citizens were already seated in a large grandstand nearby. These merchants were the backbone of the city's economy, their wealth and goods driving its prosperity. They wore formal attire as if attending a grand ball. Many had already begun the merrymaking, drinking from large goblets of wine. The streets were filled with peasants and tradespeople raising celebratory tankards of ale and crying for justice. The ambiance was jubilant and festive despite the somber reason for gathering. Axel's anxiety began to rise. Bloodlust and alcohol made for a deadly combination. It would only take a small spark to set the crowd into a full-blown riot. He was relieved they had their entire garrison present, should the situation get out of hand.

Once the royal family had settled with wine and appetizers, the chancellor advanced toward the main stage. The crowd cheered louder with each ascending step, their excitement turning feverish. From atop the gallows, he held his hands up to silence the crowd. "Fine citizens of Koenigsberg. I, Chancellor Heinz, humble servant of Vilsheim, am honored to present King Otto von Koenig, the thirty-third monarch of the Koenig dynasty, and his beautiful wife, Queen Helena." The royal couple stood as the audience continued applauding. "Along with today's execution, we are honoring the fiftieth year of our queen. Her birthday will be celebrated next weekend with an elegant royal ball, attended by citizens from all over the kingdom. Please join me in wishing her the happiest of days. May we be blessed with many more to come." The crowd roared in approval as the royal family sat down.

"King Otto, Queen Helena, members of the royal family, our fine nobility, and, of course, citizens of Vilsheim. It brings me no pleasure to say we are gathered here today for a most unfortunate reason. Among us is a man who violated one of our most sacred laws: practicing the dark art of alchemy. A practice so vile and disgusting that it threatens our very existence. Who knows what evil is let into our world when one attempts to alter physical reality. IceGuard, bring forth the prisoner!"

The doors of a nearby tavern swung open, revealing a man accompanied by four guards in bone-white uniforms. The man was wearing a long red robe embroidered with arcane symbols. Based on his greying beard and wrinkled forehead, Axel guessed he was about twenty years older than him. His drooping face and gaunt appearance suggested he had been deprived of nourishment. Although his arms were bound behind him, he held his head high as he stared into the crowd. His grim expression contrasted with eyes that still sparkled with life. The crowd booed as they pushed forward, eager to get a better view. The knights forced them back, clearing a path to the stage. A few brave audience members threw rotten fruit as they advanced through the crowd. The alchemist ignored them, but the IceGuard accompanying him grew agitated, and the BlackGuard quickly found the culprits and violently subdued them. Axel moved his attention to the king. A mischievous smile had appeared on his face as he witnessed the events unfold; he enjoyed using violence to force compliance. The king gave a slight nod for the chancellor to continue.

"Citizens! Citizens! I appreciate your indignation at the wickedness of this man, but refrain from throwing objects. I assure you, this man will get his just due. Those who ignore this guidance will spend an unpleasant night in the royal dungeon."

The pushing and shoving continued as the prisoner was driven through the crowd. Upon reaching the stage, the alchemist was ushered to the waiting chancellor. They positioned him so he faced the king, and the alchemist held his head high as he stared into his eyes. The king glared back, his smile turning to a scowl. His face grew flushed and his eyes blazed in fury.

The chancellor positioned himself in front of the alchemist. "Lucian, you stand accused of violating the king's law for practicing alchemy. By engaging in this heretical act of black magic, you not only disrespect the king, you endanger the entire population of Vilsheim. Who knows what demonic actions you have set in motion. What doorways have you opened that may threaten us? This sinister practice has been outlawed for this very reason. You tempt not only your fate, but ours as well. You are a pariah to society, and your death serves as a warning to others thinking of undertaking this blasphemous act."

As the chancellor droned on, Axel's attention wandered. How did another person practicing alchemy affect him? What was so dangerous about transmuting metal? He imagined how much better his life would be if he could create gold. He would have the freedom to leave Frostgarde and explore the kingdom while living life on his own terms. Perhaps he might own a farm where he could grow his food and not depend on others. He would offer to help others who did things the right way. Above all, he would garner respect. Gold meant power, and power meant respect. He understood why someone would risk it; the allure of the reward was hard to resist.

The chancellor's loud cry drew Axel's attention back to the event. "Lucian, do you have any final words before we put you to death?"

The alchemist gazed stoically upon the gathered crowd. His eyes met Axel's, and the corner of his mouth turned upward in a knowing smile. Axel furrowed his brow. Why had the alchemist looked at him? "Alchemy is the process of transformation," he said, lowering his head in submission but showing no signs of fear in his final moments. He was impressed the man could remain so calm in the face of death. Did he really have the ability to transmute gold?

The chancellor awaited the king's signal to proceed. Otto stared at the alchemist, eyes blazing with hatred. He stood up and boomed, "Behead this man," while making a slicing gesture across his throat. He let out a maniacal laugh, then shouted, his voice echoing, "Let this be a warning to you all. Anyone engaging in alchemy will suffer a similar fate. A public execution in front of your friends and family, so the shame you bring upon them will be visible to all."

The knights grabbed the alchemist and forced him to his knees before the headsman's block. He struggled, but was overpowered. The executioner approached as they tied him to the block until he could not move. The crowd grew silent in anticipation. It was so quiet Axel could hear the man beside him panting. With two hands, the executioner lifted the axe high above his head, the sunlight reflecting off its blade. With a dramatic outcry, he slammed the axe upon the alchemist's neck. Blood splattered across the executioner, leaving red streaks on his black armor. The severed head fell into the waiting basket while the rest of the body held firm against the block. The executioner lifted his axe in triumph, to the crowd's roaring approval. One knight retrieved the head and forced it atop a spike protruding from the stage. In the days to come, it would serve as a reminder of the seriousness of the offense. The king glowered over his audience and nodded in affirmation, accepting the applause.

With the execution complete, the knights gathered into formation and began their ascent back to Frostgarde. Gatekeepers cleared the area around the royal family, some heading toward the Boar's Gate. The bulk of the Gatekeepers would remain behind to maintain order while the rest would continue up the hill. When they reached the bailey, the Watchmen withdrew to man the

Queen's Curtain and observe the crowd for areas of rioting. Axel and the rest of the BlackGuard remained outside the keep until the IceGuard had escorted the royal family through the portcullis.

Jurgen assembled his men. "Excellent job today. Everything went as smoothly as expected. I will pass along any news I receive from the chancellor. All of you are ordered to report to me at some point today. We have the queen's birthday to prepare for, and we will guard the nobility visiting for it. I will give you your assignments then. Until then, you're dismissed."

Axel felt somber as he left the bailey. Despite the remarkable spectacle he'd witnessed, an unsettling feeling lingered. The way the alchemist had looked so defiantly at the king made him curious if there was more to the story. How did alchemy really work, and why was the king so afraid of it?

# Chapter 5

## *Old Friends*

Axel and Stefan made their way to the grand hall, where the king was hosting a lavish feast to commemorate the day. Axel's eyes lingered on the enticing fare, hoping for a chance to pick at any leftovers, yet he couldn't stop thinking about the execution. "I prepared for the worst, but everything turned out better than I expected."

Stefan chuckled, shaking his head. "You're always looking for trouble that rarely occurs. What did you think would happen?"

"It could have been anything. Imagine if the crowd refused to stop throwing food, and the scene escalated into a riot. Or if the alchemist complained about injustice to cast doubts on his guilt."

"No significant issues arose, so what does it matter at this point?"

But Axel's curiosity had already been kindled. "Maybe he knew something important. What makes the transmutation of gold so terrifying that it requires him to be safeguarded by hundreds of men?"

Stefan scowled in annoyance. "There you go with your conspiracy theories, always assuming something sinister is unfolding behind the scenes. I know you—you seek problems where there aren't any. Sometimes you need to accept a situation for what it is."

"I suppose so, but I can't shake this nagging sensation that there was something else going on." When Axel became preoccupied with something, he struggled to think of anything else. "The prospect of creating gold is tempting. Can you blame a man who risks his life to make it better? What would you do if you had that power?"

Stefan halted mid-stride, his brow furrowing. "Listen, I don't enjoy talking about a subject that led to a man's death. You need to be careful about bringing it up. That was the point of a public execution. You're looking for trouble. Who knows what doors are opened when it's practiced. Perhaps gold is the treasure used to entice an alchemist to allow evil spirits into our world. It's been outlawed a long time, and smarter men than us have put these rules in place for a reason. I don't want to discuss this any further, and I advise you not to bring it up with anyone else."

Axel pursed his lips. He loved Stefan like a brother, but he wasn't one for deep conversations. There was nothing mysterious about him; what you saw was what you got. He envied that in some ways. Stefan enjoyed the simpler things in life and avoided the philosophical topics that Axel preferred. He was only introspective when they discussed their feelings, while emotions were the one subject Axel avoided. "I thought alchemy would be an interesting discussion while it's fresh in our minds, but I guess this topic is too deep for you. If you prefer, we can discuss what's for dinner. You don't find it fascinating that there is a mysterious power we don't understand?"

Stefan grimaced while rubbing his forehead. "I saw a man executed for a crime that's punished more severely than murder. I don't think it's wise to question it a few hours later. It's this attitude that keeps me out of trouble when you're always in the middle of it. I'm maintaining a low profile, obeying orders, and enjoying my new role. Why are you so damn interested in alchemy, Axel?"

"Yes, why are you so interested in alchemy, Axel?"

He turned to find Gunter approaching, with Basel trailing. Gunter smirked mischievously behind his pointy black beard. "You didn't think you could make it through the day without seeing me, did you? Since you're new here, I need to make sure you understand the rules in the keep. Things here work differently than on the Curtain. Considering the broken nose you gave Basel, I thought you needed a lesson. Since he was too spineless to deal with you himself, I guess it falls on me." He rested his hand on the pommel of his sword.

Axel glanced at Basel, who shrunk behind Gunter, scowling. His nose was straight, but still swollen. Axel cringed and rubbed the bruise on his own head. "He gave as good as he got. My head is still throbbing from being thrown through a table. I say we're even."

Basel stepped forward with a puffed chest. "You

sucker punched me! You assumed I was fucking your whore and lost control because you can't handle your drink. I would have beaten your drunk arse if Inga hadn't stepped in."

Gunter rolled his eyes, and Axel frowned while clawing his beard. "That's not what I recall. I admit I was woozy, but I remember you insulted me first. Maybe I overreacted, but if you weren't an arsehole, neither of us would be injured. You assumed you could do as you wished without consequence."

Gunter stepped closer, pointing at Axel. "Oh, that's droll coming from you. I haven't forgotten that you undermined me when I was your commander on the Curtain. You stabbed me in the back, and now you're picking fights. Despite all that, you were still promoted to the BlackGuard. Did Jurgen even punish you?"

"He clarified that I acted inappropriately and fighting amongst ourselves will not be tolerated."

"Well, get this through your thick skull, then. I'm keeping my eye on you. Fuck up again and you're done. If you even think about starting shit, I'll be on your arse. Jurgen's going to hear about it anytime you're late or disobey orders. You've been a thorn in my side far too long. I'm a more respected knight and a better swordsman. I can't figure out how you've made it this far, but it ends now."

Axel's chest tightened as he glowered at Gunter. "You were a bully as a bairn, you were a bully on the Curtain, and you're still a bully now. No one respects you; you're only tolerated because the king wants you for the

IceGuard. You're just an arsehole who knows how to use a sword."

Gunter's face flushed crimson as he started drawing his blade, Basel behind him, cheering him on. "That's it. I'm going to teach you a lesson, you cocksucker. I'll show you who's a bully."

Axel felt a wave of anxiety flood through him as his muscles tensed. He had no intention of getting into a duel with Gunter. That would not end well, and he couldn't afford any more trouble. Fortunately, Stefan stepped in. "Let's not get ahead of ourselves. You two need to calm down or it will end badly for both of you. Do you believe eliminating Axel will quicken your path to the IceGuard? You're smarter than that, Gunter."

Gunter bristled, but after a few deep breaths, he grinned, removing his hand from his sword. "I was kidding, of course, but I want to make sure he knows who's in charge here. He's lucky to have a friend like you. It must be exhausting having to rescue him from his constant blabbering. My apologies." He feigned a sarcastic bow. "You were about to tell us why you find alchemy so interesting, Axel."

Axel's stomach leaped into his throat. He didn't need Gunter presuming he was interested in alchemy—the sight of Axel's head on the executioner's block would surely please him. He laughed nervously. "I'm not interested in alchemy. I was simply discussing the day's events. It's rare we see someone beheaded."

"It sure sounded like more than that. Remember, I'll be watching you. If I hear of any involvement with you and alchemy, it will not end well for you." He slid his finger over his throat, much like the king's gesture during the execution. "Let's go, Basel. I've had enough of this arsehole," Gunter said as they walked away.

Axel breathed a sigh of relief, but he couldn't let Gunter think he was scared. Against his better judgment, he blurted, "Hey Gunter, let me know if there is anything I can do to expedite your promotion to the IceGuard. The sooner you're there, the less I'll have to hear from you!" He stuck out his tongue and snickered.

Gunter made a rude gesture and continued walking.

Stefan shook his head, pleading with Axel. "Blood and ashes, can you stay out of your own way? Are you looking to get yourself thrown out of Frostgarde?"

With a tinge of shame, Axel met his gaze. They'd had this conversation multiple times throughout the years. He knew Stefan was right, but there were some things that he couldn't understand. Stefan hadn't been bullied and tormented when they were young. Nor had he been raised by a father who was ashamed of him. He'd been supported by parents who respected and encouraged him, and his natural strength and sheer size discouraged others from teasing him. Axel had been slow and fat, making him a prime target for the other children. If he didn't fight back, the bullying only got worse. "You've never had to worry about being humiliated by others. I have to earn respect while your presence demands it. You will never understand."

"It's you who doesn't understand that it's not only physical size, but how you carry yourself. Despite being smarter than me, you over analyze everything and focus on the wrong things. You find problems that never cross my mind. But enough of that. Let's get to our post before we are late."

They reached their post as the feast was winding down. The rest of the afternoon was uneventful. The few guests that remained finished their meals and carried on with their day. Axel's mind drifted to Jurgen's meeting that evening, when he would get his first substantial assignment. The BlackGuard were assigned to members outside of the immediate royal family and families of visiting barons. Protecting nobles was a great honor. Once again, he hoped he wouldn't find himself entangled with someone too significant. He yearned to gain a deeper understanding of the events unfolding in the kingdom— not be directly involved in them.

There were four barons in Vilsheim, but only two held substantial power. The Verone barony was east of Koenigsberg and further inland. It was ruled by Baron Kaiser Helmuth, who had no patience for insubordination or dereliction of duty. He was not a man to anger and was known for making his subject's lives miserable. Verone was the home to the University of Verone, the most prominent gathering of academia within the realm. It was the pride of the barony, and Baron Helmuth was meticulous about keeping its excellent reputation.

The other prominent barony, Wismar, was located north along the same coastline as Koenigsberg. It was ruled by Baron Diedrich Vogel, who was known for having two homely daughters. Marrying either of them would bring tremendous honor and elevate the status of any family—though they would have to endure a lifetime with a woman who lacked physical appeal, all while facing the watchful gaze of Baron Vogel. His daughters were his pride and joy. He had no tolerance for infidelity and expected the same from his constituents. There would be no marrying one and adopting a paramour on the side. The baron was a patient man as long as you respected his family.

After their shift ended, Axel and Stefan had a quick meal in the kitchen before returning to their quarters. It was late, and the moon had already risen. They were supposed to meet with Jurgen, but as his office door was closed, they decided to wait until morning. Once they were settled, a loud pounding shook the door. Without warning, Jurgen pushed it open and strolled in. "There you are. I thought I told you to come see me when your shift was done."

Stefan quickly sat up. "Our apologies, sir. We just arrived and your door was closed. We assumed you were done for the night."

"When I tell you to do something, I expect you to do it. If the door is closed, then knock."

"Sorry, sir," Axel replied. "We didn't want to bother you. It won't happen again."

"Good, good. I have enough to worry about. There is so much to do for the queen's party. I wish they hadn't scheduled it so close to the execution. There isn't time to plan this much activity in such a short period. Once I provide your assignments, I can cross another item off my list. Baron Vogel requested that new recruits guard his daughters during his visit. Axel, you are assigned to Annaliese, and Stefan will have Amelia."

Axel's face tightened, concealing his disappointment. This was the exact scenario he was hoping to avoid. Jurgen paced the floor, his hands clasped behind his back. "The baron is very protective of them. He wants them treated with the utmost respect, and your job is to ensure that. What I am about to tell you should not go beyond these walls. To put it delicately, his daughters are rather plain. He hopes to find a match for them at the ball. This is not the first time he has come seeking suitors. During his last visit, their assigned guards made unsavory comments behind their backs, and unfortunately, word spread throughout the BlackGuard before finding its way to the girls. They were devastated and hurried to tell their father. Those men are no longer at Frostgarde."

Jurgen's eyebrows furrowed. "The baron wanted a fresh start and asked for guards who had no knowledge of the previous visit. I want you on your best behavior. Not only do I want you to keep your mouths closed, but shut any others that insult them as well. The king has made it clear that his brother-in-law's visit will be pleasant. This is an excellent opportunity to lay the foundation for your future success—or ruin it once and for all."

The knot in Axel's stomach tightened. He could not afford to mess this up. While it sounded simple, that only meant more opportunities for unforeseen problems. He needed to get in the right frame of mind. "Yes, sir. You can count on us."

"Axel, this is your chance to set yourself on the right path. If you make it through without incident, I'll forget all about your previous transgression. I'll even make sure Gunter leaves you alone. I'm aware of your history."

Axel smiled, relieved. "Thank you, sir, I appreciate it." Now that he had a chance to rectify his mistake, he would not ruin it.

Jurgen muttered something about getting back to work as he shut the door behind him.

Stefan lay back on the bed, resting his hands behind his head. "Sounds like they got their eye on you, Ax. I hope you're ready."

Axel got under his blanket and rolled on his side. "Yeah, I'll be focused. What do you know about these ladies?"

"Not much more than Jurgen told us. I know they're unattractive, and one might be overweight. I think Annaliese, but I'm not sure. Their names sound so similar, I get them confused."

"Amelia is the fat one, and Annaliese is the uglier one. I have heard her referred to as horseface on account of her long, homely face and big buck teeth. She sure sounds like one ugly woman. I feel sorry for the poor bastard that betroths her." A mischievous giggle escaped Axel's lips, betraying his inner amusement.

Stefan sat up and glared at him. "Don't you dare talk about them like that. That's what Jurgen just cautioned us about. Do you want to get released like their last two guards? I'll not have you put my job at risk." He rolled over, facing the other way.

Axel frowned. "What's your problem? You asked what I knew. Why are you being so negative?"

"Because it sounds like you're enjoying it. Enough blathering. It's been a long day and I'm beat."

Axel turned on his back and rested his hands behind his head. Stefan was right. He was on thin ice and the last thing he needed was more attention on him. He should be more cautious and avoid expressing his thoughts. He couldn't afford to screw this up.

# Chapter 6

## *A Noble Welcome*

Axel waited outside the keep, along with Stefan, Jurgen, and Chancellor Heinz, to welcome Baron Vogel to Frostgarde. The king's reception would come later this evening at a feast in the baron's honor. A messenger from the Boar's Gate brought news of the family's approach. They were arriving earlier than expected, resulting in an impromptu welcome party.

The chancellor was irritated, scowling as he barked orders at the servants. Meticulous about planning, he was annoyed by the unexpected change in schedule. "Clear everyone from the walkway to the keep. I don't want peasants impeding his path. It's crucial we maintain a natural, organized appearance." He wrinkled his nose and waved his hand to clear the air. "Get those horses out of here. I don't want the baron's first impression to be tainted by the smell of shit. Jurgen, get over here."

Jurgen stepped forward. "I'm right here, sir."

"Are your men ready? It is imperative we avoid any mistakes during his visit."

"They are ready, chancellor," Jurgen responded. "Both are new to the BlackGuard, with no preconceived knowledge of the prior incident. They understand the seriousness of this assignment." He motioned to Axel, stating, "This is Axel Albrecht, charged with guarding Annaliese, and the big man, Stefan Oxtail, is assigned to Amelia."

The chancellor appraised the men with a wary eye. "Axel and Stefan, I'll remember your names. I don't want trouble from either of you. Do whatever they say, no matter how strange it sounds. If you're ordered to brush their hair and dress it with bows, you obey."

"Yes, sir," they replied as the gate at the Queen's Curtain creaked open.

The chancellor positioned himself at the head of the welcome party as servants holding flower baskets and refreshments stood nearby. Jurgen stood a few paces behind with his knights flanking him.

Axel watched the baron's entourage enter the inner bailey. Baron Vogel was a simple, purposeful man when compared to others of his status. He did not waste his time on frivolity, so his entourage was small; only a few servants and a handful of guards accompanied the carriage that carried the family.

They stopped a few yards in front of the chancellor before his guard opened the door to assist them as they exited. Baron Vogel was the first to emerge. He had a thin build and a long, somber face that hadn't smiled in years.

What little hair remained was slicked back, emphasizing his broad forehead. Bushy sideburns dangled past his jawline, accompanied by a large pepper-grey mustache. His attire consisted of a red surcoat with black trim, adorned with the family's eagle sigil.

Baroness Gisele Vogel followed her husband. A short, rotund woman, she wore a black dress with red embellishments, contrasting the baron's outfit. Her belly protruded, extending past her breasts, with wide hips that matched her height. Fat rolls cascaded from beneath her chin, descending over her voluptuous bosom. The guard was careful she didn't stumble and humiliate herself.

The baroness was followed by a taller and thinner young woman. Blonde hair tumbled down her shoulders, framing her breasts and drawing attention to her ample cleavage. Full hips flanked her narrow waist, and her red dress tightly hugged her body, accentuating her curves. But her smile revealed two large buck teeth, resembling a rabbit. Her long, drawn face was like her father's, its thinness highlighting her prodigious nose. Even her eyes were mismatched, with one brown and one green. This was an ugly woman, no matter how flattering her figure. Axel assumed she was Annaliese—she couldn't be more horselike.

The other daughter, Amelia, was shaped like the baroness, shorter and broader than her sister. While she was not as fat as her mother, she would be if she continued eating like her. Instead of fat rolls, her smooth face blended into her thick neck. Axel struggled to see any semblance of a chin. It was not surprising they struggled to find husbands, considering they took after their parents. It would be easier if the baron wasn't so stubborn about fidelity. Having one as a man's only option for the rest of his life was daunting.

Chancellor Heinz strode forward to greet them. "Baron Vogel, it is wonderful to see you. King Otto and Queen Helena welcome you to Frostgarde. We prepared refreshments after your arduous journey, along with flower arrangements for your lovely ladies."

The baroness and her obese daughter eyed the sweets as the baron scowled at them. "Thank you, chancellor. Your preparedness for our unexpected arrival is much appreciated. Unloading the ship was quicker than expected. Give my wife and daughters the flowers, but hold the refreshments for now," he ordered his staff.

The baroness frowned, but gracefully accepted the flowers. The baron presented his family before asking, "I was hoping my sister would be here to greet us. Are we not worthy of her time?"

The chancellor lowered his head, feigning sympathy. "Of course you are. Unfortunately, the royal family's busy schedule made it impossible to accommodate your early arrival. You will see them at tonight's feast, which is being held in your honor. The queen is grateful you're here to celebrate her birthday."

The baron stared at them with eyes like daggers. "I see." He turned to Jurgen and his men. "Were you able to find suitable men to protect my daughters?"

"Indeed. We have two exceptional knights who've defended Frostgarde for twenty years and were promoted to the BlackGuard last week. Commander Jurgen, present your men."

Jurgen stepped forward and bowed. "Greetings, Your Grace. I am Commander Jurgen of the BlackGuard. Stefan will be assigned to Amelia, and Axel will be assigned to Annaliese. Knights, introduce yourselves."

Stefan and Axel bowed before approaching their respective charges. "Greetings, my lady," Axel said to Annaliese. "I'm Axel, and I'm honored to be of service during your stay. If there is anything you need, please let me know."

She stared at him with a suggestive gaze, assessing him from head to toe as she smiled alluringly. "Pleased to meet you. I'm sure I will find something useful for you." She offered her hand, staring into his eyes. He hesitated before taking her hand to kiss it. "Ooh, such a gentleman too," she said, fanning herself.

He blushed as the baron flashed a disapproving glance. "Just doing my duty, my lady."

After the introductions were complete, the chancellor said, "Well, you must all be tired after your journey. We've prepared a wonderful suite for you. Let's get you settled in so you can relax before tonight's festivities." He ordered a servant to guide them to their quarters, with Axel and Stefan following.

Upon their arrival, the servant bowed and gestured for them to enter the suite. Axel and Stefan remained outside, guarding the entrance. After they'd gotten situated, Baron Vogel left to meet with the other nobles who'd traveled for the queen's celebration. The baroness accompanied him, hoping to find a snack before the evening meal. That left their two daughters alone for the afternoon. Axel and Stefan stood outside the door, ensuring they were not disturbed.

"So, what do you think of the ladies?" Axel asked. "The rumors were surprisingly accurate. I see why it's been difficult finding them matches. If the baron allowed their husbands to take a woman on the side, it would be more tolerable. The power and prestige garnered might be worth the sacrifice. If Annaliese bore a son, they would have an heir to take over the family. Personally, I couldn't fathom the idea of her being the sole woman I lie with for the rest of my life. Some things aren't worth the price."

Stefan grimaced and motioned for him to be quiet. "I'm glad I'm happily married and don't need to worry about those things. Be silent. Someone is coming."

Axel heard the shuffling of feet as a dark shadow appeared around the corner of the hallway. A large man approached with a smaller figure at his side. As they drew closer, he could see it was a knight in the milk-colored uniform of the IceGuard, and the smaller figure beside him was Princess Ilona, the king's only daughter. She had gorgeous blonde hair pinned under a silver tiara trimmed with rubies. In its center was the boar sigil, symbolizing her royal status. Her light blue dress hugged her curvy figure, accentuating all the places Axel appreciated in a woman. The dress highlighted her deep blue eyes, which sparkled with youthful enthusiasm. Her red lips turned into a beaming smile as she approached them. The baron's daughters lacked everything that this girl possessed. She had a magnetism that drew attention to her. She was the kind of woman that men fantasized about.

Axel and Stefan immediately stood at attention. "Good afternoon, Your Highness," Stefan said, offering a deep bow.

The princess acknowledged them with a brief nod. "Good afternoon, gentlemen. I heard the baron's family arrived, and I would like to visit with my cousins. Would you let them know I am here?"

"Of course, Your Highness," Stefan replied. He went through the door, leaving it open so the others could hear. "Good afternoon, ladies. Princess Ilona is here to greet you. Shall I let her in?"

"Of course," Annaliese replied. "Please invite her in. We would love to visit with our cousin."

Stefan reappeared to escort the princess into the room, with her guard trailing behind. Axel's stomach twisted with uncertainty as he contemplated whether to allow the man inside. The princess didn't seem surprised, so he thought it best to remain quiet outside. They would let him know if he was needed.

Stefan eyed the guard as he left the room. Behind him, Axel heard the vibrant squeal of young girls excited to see each other. "Good heavens," Ilona said. "You two are here by yourselves and left your guards outside? What's the point of requesting special protection if you won't use them?"

Annaliese blushed. "We thought it was improper to be alone in our chambers with the men, princess."

"None of this princess stuff. We are cousins, and I insist you call me Ilona. You can save the decorum for formal events, but not when we're alone. These are not ordinary men; they are your guards. I understand them remaining outside when your family is here, but not when you are alone. One can never be too careful. My Baldor goes everywhere with me." She gripped the knight by the forearm.

Annaliese turned bright red. "I assumed all men have the same thoughts and desires. I don't want to put us in a compromising situation."

Ilona covered her mouth, smirking. "It's true that all men share similar thoughts, and I have no doubt that these men are no exception. But what do you think would happen if they tried anything? My father would start with castration, and things would only escalate from there. You couldn't be more safe." She ordered them to enter.

Axel winced at the thought as he entered the room. He'd been unaware of the consequences of getting too friendly. Talk of castration added another level of stress to his already frayed nerves. Not that he had any intention of seducing either of them.

Laughter erupted from Ilona as she pointed at him. "See how uncomfortable he is at the mere mention of it." His face flushed, sweat forming on his forehead. "But as a gentleman, you would never engage in any inappropriate behavior, right?"

He sputtered, "Of course not! I mean, of course I am. I never even considered it."

Annaliese hung her head, dejected. "It didn't cross

your mind? I wouldn't want you to act on it, but it's nice to dream about a man desiring me like that. How am I ever going to find a husband if a simple guard doesn't want me?"

Axel wiped the perspiration from his forehead. "No, my lady, that isn't what I meant. I take my duty seriously, and honor will not allow me to consider such things." How had he gotten into this mess? He'd only made things worse trying to act polite. He noticed Baldor struggling to contain his amusement. "Please forgive me if I offended you. I mean no ill will." He writhed at Stefan, who shrugged helplessly.

The princess covered her mouth as she giggled. "Now you have him all out of sorts, Annaliese. Of course you meant no harm. Be a dear and wait with the other guards while I speak to the ladies. We want you in the room, but don't need you engaging in our conversation."

Axel sighed with relief as he settled next to the other men. Baldor winked at him while still trying to stifle his laughter.

Ilona situated herself as Annaliese brought out the refreshments they'd received earlier, and Axel's mouth watered at the tempting snacks. Maybe they would share. Amelia grabbed a small frosted cake along with a cranberry tart, while Annaliese poured tea for each of them before settling in next to her sister.

Ilona selected an apricot slice and blew on her tea to cool it. "Now that we are situated, we can discuss the reason you're here. It's your best chance to find a husband, and I'm here to help."

Annaliese looked into her teacup. "Thank you, Ilona. We could use any help you can suggest. The thought of never finding someone worries me, and I believe my father feels the same way. He is so frustrated with us. He has gone to great lengths to find sufficient matches, but none have fared well. Men will marry us, but not out of genuine attraction or desire. It's the opportunity to become a baron they're after. I want someone who loves me, with no expectations or ulterior motives. Is that too much to ask?"

"Of course not," Ilona replied as she rubbed her arm. "I feel the same way. Imagine a man that wants to marry into the royal family. Of course, my brother will be king, but any child I bear will be in line for the throne. I won't settle for just any man."

Amelia shifted in her seat, and Annaliese flashed a nervous smile. "What?" Ilona asked, confused.

"I don't wish to offend you, but I would hardly say we are in similar positions," Annaliese replied. "While I understand you may have men that want you for your power, there is a rather sizable difference between the two of us and you."

Illona furrowed her brow, confused. "And that is?"

Axel listened, fascinated by the conversation. Could Ilona be this dense? The princess's stunning looks made her desirable to any man, regardless of status. With her alluring figure and mesmerizing eyes, it was easy for anyone to become entranced. Unlike the sisters, her status was just frosting on the cake. Amelia could be passable if she lost some weight, but the way she was focusing on food, he did not think that was likely. She was destined to become obese like her mother.

Annaliese hesitated before saying, "You're beautiful, Ilona. How many suitors professing undying love have you turned away? Men must be lining up to shower you with attention, while I have had more than one man tell me how much I look like his horse. A horse that he doesn't want to ride." Tears welled in her eyes, and she turned her head in shame.

"You poor girls! While I take your point, have you considered that men treat you as unworthy because you think of yourselves that way? Believe in yourselves. I've been taught that beauty is in the eye of the beholder. Think of yourselves as more attractive and you'll feel that way."

"I don't know how," Annaliese replied. "I've been told I was ugly my whole life. When I look in a mirror, I only see a horse. Even Father told me that if I wasn't so ugly, he could have found me a husband years ago. He says if we find a husband first, the love will come. But I've seen how men look at me. There is no love in their eyes. Only pity for themselves at the sacrifice they're making. I'd rather be alone than have a man that way. Father says my chances are dwindling as I get older and this may be my last opportunity. I'm worried he's going to send me away to be a priestess, so he won't have to face the shame."

"He tells me I need to lose weight," Amelia added. "Don't eat those cakes. Haven't had enough for dinner yet? Do you want to end up looking like your mother? He was furious with the chancellor for bringing snacks, as if it were a cruel joke on me and Mother."

Ilona gasped. "He did no such thing! Offering refreshments to guests is proper manners. My parents know the primary reason for your visit and have gone to great lengths gathering a few potential candidates. We have the best intentions."

"We know he meant no ill will," Annaliese said. "It's a touchy subject for Father. We appreciate the gift. The cake was delicious."

Amelia agreed around a mouth full of frosting. "These are wonderful. I sampled a couple earlier when he wasn't looking. The more I'm insulted for being fat, the stronger my desire to eat becomes. It's a never-ending cycle. Eat, get teased, feel sorry for myself, and eat more." She brushed the crumbs from her dress.

Axel felt sorry for the girls. Their father sounded like an arsehole. He knew what that was like. He wondered if the king had ordered the chancellor to provide sweets to annoy the baron. He'd heard the king enjoyed playing mind games. It would not matter that it was his wife's brother. He shuddered at the thought of the suitors they'd selected, hoping it wasn't another cruel joke at the girls' expense.

Princess Ilona was startled by her cousin's comments, but remained positive. "I have the finest courtiers in Vilsheim and will have them attend you while preparing for the ball. They are excellent at accentuating the most flattering features while drawing attention away from the less desirable ones. Annaliese, you have a fantastic figure.

You should show it off more. I know many young girls that would love to have your structure. And Amelia, you have a lovely complexion and gorgeous hair. They should be able to find something that cinches you in and draws more attention to your face. Come to my quarters on the day of the ball, and we'll prepare together. We shall find you both husbands before this visit is over."

"That would be wonderful," Amelia replied. She was so enthused she even put down her tart. "Thank you so much."

Axel flinched as Annaliese grinned in agreement. Her smile only showed how large her teeth were. It sounded like the plan was to focus on Annaliese's body while ignoring her face and to work the same magic in reverse for Amelia. He eagerly awaited the outcome.

Ilona rose from her chair. "I'm glad that's settled, but I must be going. I only had time for a brief visit. Tonight's feast will start soon, and I must prepare. Please let me know if you need anything. You'll have a wonderful time here."

The three women said their farewells before Baldor escorted Ilona out.

Axel and Stefan followed until Ilona halted them. "You two remain inside when the ladies are left alone. You shall only go outside when the family is here. Is that understood?" The two men nodded in agreement as the princess made her way to her chambers.

# Chapter 7

## *The Mud Pit*

Later that night, Axel stood alone outside the baron's chamber. When the family retired for the evening, only one man was required to stand guard, and he'd agreed to take the first watch. It was nice to have quiet time to himself, but he was struggling to slow his mind down. The girls' conversation from earlier that afternoon had stuck in his mind, much of what he'd overheard from Amelia reminding him of his relationship with his own father, stirring unresolved feelings.

As a young boy, Axel was big for his age. Compared to Stefan, who was tall with muscle already filling his clothes, he was short and stocky. He was always hungry and felt as though he never got enough to eat. His mother was lenient with snacks and often snuck him extra portions during mealtime, but his father treated Axel's weight as a source of shame, perceiving him as lazy and worthless. While other children enjoyed playing outside,

Axel preferred staying indoors to read. He loved books and would devour any he could get his hands on. His mother had taught him to read at a young age, sparking a lifelong interest. He was a fast learner, prompting her to devise creative solutions to challenge him with bigger words and more complicated subjects. The family's supply of books was limited, so she traded with other families to continue his studies.

Axel enjoyed reading books on a wide range of subjects. He researched how the original Koenigs had conquered Vilsheim and begun their five-hundred-year dynasty. He learned how the barons had come to power and continued to have a tenuous relationship with the royal family to this day; the Koenigs had faced the challenge of extinguishing multiple rebellions, as certain defiant barons sought in vain to assert their independence. Frostgarde held a special place for Axel, fascinating him like nothing else. Perched atop the highest hill in Koenigsberg, it provided an unparalleled vantage point from which to command the sprawling city, and with only one route to reach its summit, the castle was impossible to siege. Hidden beneath the keep, a network of tunnels was constructed, allowing for the covert transport of food and offering an escape route for the family. It was a primary reason the Koenigs had remained in power for so many years.

Despite his mother's encouragement, his father regarded his studies as a waste of time, and Axel witnessed his parents quarreling about it numerous times.

The worst argument occurred when his dad tore up his books and forced him to take part in the annual tug-o'-war competition.

"Why is he wasting his time reading, Osanna?" His father, Axos, stood amidst the clutter of ripped pages, seething with anger. "He needs to be outside helping me with the chores. I can't afford to hire extra help. He should be contributing to our family by now, not be an additional burden."

His mother clutched the only remaining book tightly to her chest, preventing her husband from destroying it. "Why can't you be more patient with him? I understand he struggles with physical tasks, but he is trying his best to please you. When you criticize him for his mistakes, it only erodes his confidence, making him more tentative. Don't you understand?"

"I understand he is a lazy piece of shit who can't stop stuffing his face. If he wasn't so fat, things wouldn't be so difficult for him. Sneaking him small portions of your food under the table is only worsening the situation. Now you're getting too skinny. Why are you both against me? He is too fat and you're too thin. You know I like more meat on you."

Axel watched from the table at the far side of the room. He loathed hearing his parents fight, especially about him. His father's stern words toward his mother only intensified his guilt. He felt the urge to cry, but knew if he did, it would only make his father more upset.

Axos glared at his wife. "I don't want you giving him any extra food. He gets too much already." He shot a menacing glance in Axel's direction. "You need to get out of the house more often. I don't want you inside during the day. I added your name to the participants' list for the bairns' tug-o'-war event taking place this week. This year, a merchant is donating one of his retired oxen to the winning team. With six boys to a team, that's seven stones worth of meat for each person. You will contribute to this family, and it starts by using that fat arse of yours to win that competition."

Axel couldn't hold back the tears any longer and shielded his face. "No, I can't be in that. I'm not good enough, and the other boys will tease me. Don't make me do it, Da, please. I'll do more around the house, but I beg you, don't make me do that." He struggled to control his emotions as he pleaded with his father.

Axos poked him in the stomach. "You sniveling bastard. What did I do to deserve a son like you? You're going to take part and use all that blubber to win the tournament. Finally, an opportunity where your weight can be put to good use." He flashed a sinister smile, making Axel's stomach churn.

Consumed by a deep loathing, he yearned to vent his rage on his father, but fear crippled him. Instead, he nodded his understanding.

"Good, now get to bed!"

Axel glanced at his mother, who smiled before urging

him to go. He wiped the fallen tears from his face and fled to his bed in the cellar.

The weather was bleak and cloudy on the day of the tug-o'-war. Rain had fallen steadily for two days prior, but stopped well before dawn. Axel had hoped the event would be postponed or canceled, but luck was not on his side. The muddy conditions only added to the challenge, promising more entertainment for those in attendance. His fortune took a turn for the worse when the teams were drawn. He was ecstatic to hear Stefan was on his team, but grew ill when Gunter and Basel's names were called.

Gunter grimaced when he saw Axel was on his team. "Why are we stuck with the piggy?" He got in Axel's face, jabbing his forefinger into his chest. "You better not cost us this tourney, piggy. Your fat arse better prove useful or you'll be sorry. I have a lot riding on this."

Basel giggled. "With all that extra weight, he can be our anchor."

Gunter rolled his eyes. "Don't be stupid, Basel. Stefan has the size and strength to be the anchor. Piggy is too weak. We'll bury him in the middle and hope all that extra fat makes it harder for the other teams to pull us. I'll be in front, and you'll be behind me. Piggy will be next, with the other two following in front of Stefan. That's our best chance with this team."

Basel's face flushed red as Stefan agreed it was an excellent strategy. The merchant supplying their prize was given the honor of judging the event. He gathered the boys around a large mudhole in the middle of the field to explain the rules. It was a winner-takes-all, sixteen-team, single-elimination contest with four wins needed for victory. To win, a team must pull all of their opponents into the mudhole. Anyone who let go of the rope was disqualified for the rest of that match. The boys divided into their respective teams, and the contest began.

Their first match unfolded as well as Axel could have hoped for. Applying his weight as leverage, he leaned back, pressing his heels into the soft ground, and tugged with all his strength. His team easily dragged their opponents into the muddied water. With a victorious smile, Axel looked at his father, who shook his head and held up three fingers. During the next two matches, they worked cohesively and dominated the other teams. However, it was taking its toll on Axel. He was panting after the second match and gasping for breath after the third. Blisters formed on his hands, causing pain when he gripped the rope. The thought of having to go through one more match weighed on him, but he was determined to push through. If they won, he would not only earn his father's praise, but might even gain Gunter's respect.

The two remaining teams gathered for the final match. With urgency, Gunter shouted at his team that if they didn't win this one, everything they'd accomplished thus far would be meaningless. Axel grabbed the rope and assumed his familiar position. The field had transformed into a muddy mess after the previous matches, making it difficult to establish solid footing. When the judge ordered them to begin, he gritted his teeth and tugged as hard as he could. Pain shot through his hands as his blisters tore on the rough rope. In an attempt to reposition them, he found himself slipping and lost his balance on the slick terrain. As he tumbled, he lost his grip and his feet slammed into Basel, directly in front of him. Basel's cries echoed through the air as he plummeted and his grip on the rope slipped away. With two boys downed, the other team easily pulled the other four into the mudhole.

Axel's eyes filled with shame as he glanced at his father, who was shouting curses at the top of his lungs. Gunter, covered in mud, sprang up and clenched his fist. "You fucking idiot, Basel. We just lost the contest because of your incompetence. I'm going to teach you a lesson."

Basel backed away, terrified. "I didn't do it. Axel lost his balance and crashed into me. It was his fault, I swear!"

Gunter turned to Axel with fire in his eyes. "I should have known it was you, piggy. I knew you would screw this up for me, and now you're going to pay."

He ran at Axel, tackling and pinning him to the ground, then sat on his chest and rained blows upon his face. Axel covered his head, trying to defend himself. His mother screamed, and Gunter was dragged off him. "Let go of me, dammit, I'm going to kill that pig!"

"No, you're not," Stefan said as he held Gunter in a tight bear hug. "Losing doesn't give you the right to attack us."

The judge and a few parents rushed over to separate the boys. Gunter was drawn away and given to his father, who stared at him with disgust. He grabbed his son's arm and yanked him away as Gunter screamed, "It wasn't my fault. I did everything I could to win. Please don't hurt me! It was piggy that made us lose."

Axel looked up to see his own father glowering at him. "Look at this mess you caused. Do you realize how much you've humiliated me? You had a chance to do some good for our family and you blew it. I'm ashamed to call you my son. We're leaving before I have to hear anything."

Axel jumped to his feet and looked to his mother, who wrapped her arms around him. Axos scowled. "Don't you dare coddle him, or I'll be handling both of you when we get home."

Axel was overwhelmed, physically drained, struggling to catch his breath. His hands ached, and pain emanated from his face. Blood trickled from his swollen mouth, while bruises adorned his cheeks. The embarrassment and humiliation were unbearable, and tears welled up in his eyes until his father's stern gaze silenced him. His mother attempted to comfort him by placing her arm around his shoulder, but he resisted and trailed behind his father, heading home.

Axel breathed a heavy sigh as he recalled his childhood. His father had been a real arse. If there was anyone who could empathize with the sisters, it was him. He loathed being called piggy, and it bothered him they still referred to him that way. Annaliese must harbor the same resentment for horseface—no one wanted to be compared to an animal. And he knew how much he'd felt like a prisoner trapped in his own fat body. Axel lowered his head and groaned. How could he have been such an arse? Rather than mocking and ridiculing the girls, he should be defending them. As a knight and, more importantly, a decent human being, he vowed to be more chivalrous.

# Chapter 8

## *The Queen's Ball*

"We need to hurry. We can't keep the princess waiting. She told us to be there at midday. We have a lot of preparation to do before tonight's ball," Annaliese said to her sister. "I'm so excited. With Ilona's assistance, this will be the night we find a husband." This was the happiest Axel had seen her since their arrival.

Amelia sighed as she picked at her gown. "I wish I shared your enthusiasm. I'm worried I won't fit into my dress. How could I have gotten fatter since we left Wismar? I swear it fit better at home."

Annaliese furrowed her brow as she threw her hands in the air. "It couldn't possibly be all those pastries you've been sneaking. You need to learn to control yourself, sister, if you don't want to end up like Mother."

Amelia's eyes grew wide in horror. "Of course I don't, but why does everything taste so delicious here? Back home, it's much easier. Being in unfamiliar places makes me uneasy, and when I'm anxious, I crave food."

"Don't think about that now. I'm confident that Ilona's handmaidens will figure out how to squeeze you into your gown. Stay positive and trust that things will turn out for the best."

"That's easy for you to say. You resemble Father with your tall, slender figure. Why did I have to take after our mother? I look like a cow. It's not fair." Amelia buried her head in her hands and sobbed.

With a gentle touch, Annaliese raised Amelia's chin and gazed into her eyes. "How many times do we need to have this conversation? Underneath that chubby face, you are very attractive. At least you can lose weight. I look like a horse, and nothing will change that." She embraced her sister. "Now is not the time to argue. We need our inner beauty to shine, and it won't happen by worrying all afternoon. Let's be on our way. Do you have everything?" Amelia nodded as Annaliese ordered Axel to gather their belongings.

"Yes, my lady," he replied, grabbing her trunk. It had all the essentials she needed to prepare, including the dress she would wear.

Stefan grabbed Amelia's trunk, and they left to meet the princess. The royal chambers were in the back of the keep, isolated from the common areas. It contained several suites and a private great room, where the family dined and held confidential meetings with other high-ranking officials. It could also be sealed off from the rest of the keep, maximizing the safety of the royal family if Frostgarde were to be attacked.

Two IceGuard sentries were stationed in front of

massive double doors, etched with black boars. "Well met, fellow knights," Stefan said. "We are escorting the queen's nieces, Lady Annaliese and Lady Amelia, for a visit with Princess Ilona. She offered the use of her handmaidens as they prepare for the ball. May they enter?"

The stockier guard eyed them suspiciously, making no sign of letting them pass. Finally, he slowly opened one door and gestured for them to go in. The two ladies entered while Axel and Stefan stayed behind.

"Aren't you coming?" Amelia asked them.

"No, my lady," Axel replied. "We are not of sufficient rank to enter the royal suite. However, the finest guards in the kingdom will be here protecting you. We will be here to escort you when you leave. One of these guards will see you to the princess's room."

The taller guard smirked and shook his head. He tapped his nose mockingly at Axel, silently chortling. The stocky guard shut the door while waving them off dismissively. They walked away to enjoy an afternoon to themselves.

Axel scratched his beard, confused. "What was that about?"

Stefan burst out laughing. "You're always making friends. It meant you're an arse kisser and have shite on your nose!" Axel's face turned bright red. "Don't let it bother you. Since they can't speak, they need to find other ways to amuse themselves. I'm sure they were flattered. Let's find something to eat. I'm starving." They headed to the kitchen to see what they could scavenge.

They returned to the royal suite later that afternoon to wait for the ladies. When the door opened, Axel's jaw dropped at the sight of the baron's daughters. Were these the same two homely ladies they'd accompanied? Annaliese's red and gold dress sparkled as it clung to her body, accentuating her svelte figure. Her hair was swept up, with two long strands flowing down to frame her face. Makeup softened the size of her nose and accentuated her porcelain-white skin. Her full lips, painted red, drew attention away from her buck teeth. Excitement shone from her eyes, lighting up her face in anticipation of tonight's gala.

Amelia looked equally stunning, cinched into her black and red gown, which slimmed her wide body and emphasized her ample bosom. Her generous backside had been lifted, creating a curvaceous and robust appearance, with no signs of sagging. In contrast to her sister, Amelia's hair had been left down to elongate her face. A thick, bejeweled choker encircled her neck, obscuring the waddles below her chin. He noted the marked improvement. "Lady Amelia, you are stunning, and Lady Annaliese, that dress complements your exquisite figure perfectly." Stefan nodded in agreement.

Amelia blushed. "Thank you, Axel. I'm flattered. I don't recall anyone calling me stunning before. Do you really think so?" She batted her eyes at him.

His jaw dropped in disbelief, and he fought to suppress the grimace that threatened to contort his face. What had he gotten himself into? There was no way to backtrack without being rude. He blurted out the first thing that came to mind. "Of course you do. Any man will be lucky to dance with you tonight."

"Thank you," Annaliese replied. "You are too kind. We must hurry back. We need to find our parents and proceed to the ball."

The knights remained outside the guest suite until the baron and his wife emerged with their daughters in tow. He was dressed in his formal military uniform while she wore a dark red gown embroidered with gold trim along the collar and sleeves. Axel noted the stark difference between Baronesse Gisele and Amelia. While her daughter had everything tucked and tightened, Gisele's appearance was much sloppier, her fat bouncing with every step. The sight made Axel shudder as it brought back vivid memories of his own jiggling belly in his younger days.

They led the family to Frostgarde's great hall, where the ball was already underway. Guests socialized with drinks in hand, and Axel noticed Chancellor Heinz was engrossed in a lively discussion with an opulently dressed merchant, his cerulean tunic buckled loosely with a bright gold belt. He appeared as if he was already well into his cups. A small orchestra to the right of the throne played soft, ambient music, greeting guests as they arrived. He had never seen the room more festive. The king's banners cascaded from the ceiling while the walls showcased sigils from Vilsheim's noble houses. The tables were beautifully decorated with Koenig silver and black, and hand-carved wooden animal centerpieces added a touch of charm.

Baron Vogel's family would dine with the queen, so

they were escorted to the main table before Axel and Stefan took their customary positions along the wall. Knights were not expected to stand with their charges at formal events, allowing guests to enjoy the evening unimpeded while still being safeguarded. They would always have someone accompanying them whenever they left the ball, though.

As the chamber filled and the guests took their seats, Chancellor Heinz rose to address the room. "May I have your attention! Lords, ladies, fine citizens, I know many of you have traveled countless leagues to celebrate our beloved queen's birthday. Today is a day to not only honor her, but all of Vilsheim. Let us put aside any petty differences and acknowledge all that we have accomplished together. It is time to enjoy ourselves." The audience roared and pounded their tables.

"Let us now welcome the royal family." The king, accompanied by his wife and children, entered from a door beside the throne. "I present to you Princess Ilona, Crown Prince Fridolf, King Otto, and tonight's guest of honor, Queen Helena von Koenig!" The audience rose from their seats with thunderous applause, along with spats of whistling and shouts. "Please join me in wishing her a joyous fiftieth birthday."

The orchestra played the traditional birthday song while the crowd sang along. Amidst the cheering, Chancellor Heinz sat with the royal children, while King Otto remained standing next to the queen. He gestured for silence before beginning. "Greetings, loyal subjects. It is wonderful you are here to celebrate my dear wife on her special day. I want to express my gratitude to everyone who made the effort to come in person. First, Baron Vogel of Wismar, brother of my lovely wife, please rise." Diedrich stood awkwardly and bowed before the king and the audience. "Baron Friedrich of Ravenna, who traveled all the way from our northern border." Baron Friedrich, seated on the other side of the king, rose and bowed as well. "Finally, Baron Bjorn of Grimmdorf. You traveled the farthest, and I will not forget the honor your family has exhibited. Now let the feast begin!"

Axel listened to the introductions as he leaned against the wall with folded arms. Baron Helmuth's notable absence was a sign of disrespect. Vilsheim consisted of four baronies, making the barons that governed them the most powerful men outside of the royal family. They believed the king wielded too much power and the taxes levied against them were too steep. To appease them, it had become a tradition for the crown prince to wed a baron's daughter, making her the future queen. When it was time for King Otto's father to select his son's bride, it had come down to Wismar and Verone. None of the past five queens had been from Verone, and Baron Helmuth thought it was their time to rule. He offered his younger sister, Lady Irmina, for Otto's consideration. However, the prior reign had not been a prosperous one, and the king hoped to rectify that. Wismar, being on the coast, generated the most revenue of any barony. To strengthen that relationship, the king chose Lady Helena of Wismar over Lady Irmina.

Baron Helmuth had taken the rejection of his sister as

a major slight, resulting in bad blood between him and the crown to this day. Rumor was he was ill and unfit to travel, but many believed he didn't want to attend the celebration of the woman chosen over his sister. To make matters worse, he hadn't even shown the courtesy of sending his son, the future baron, in his stead. Rather, he'd sent his daughter, which was sure to further widen the rift between the two families. King Otto was not the type to let insults go unpunished, and Axel expected more problems from Verone in the future.

Once the feast was finished, Axel circled the room, looking for suspicious activity. The music grew louder as minstrels performed, to the raucous delight of the crowd. He focused on locating the baron's daughters. Annaliese was still seated at the main table, talking with a young man, engrossed in their conversation. He watched as Amelia approached them from the dance floor, panting with each step, beads of sweat dripping down her reddening face. She tried to talk to her sister, who was clearly trying to brush her off. Annaliese made a histrionic gesture, which caused Amelia to storm off. She made for the wine table and quickly gulped a cup down.

As Amelia's situation was deteriorating, he set out to find Stefan; he should monitor her in case she wanted to leave the ball. He found him across the room, talking with Jurgen. Stefan gestured for him to come over.

"What's going on, Stefan? Is everything alright?"

"Everything fine here, Ax. My wife sent word that our roof is collapsing—she's panicking. I need to check on the damage and make sure she is alright. I need you to keep an eye on Amelia for me."

"Is this allowed? What if the girls need to leave?"

"I need you to watch them both for now," Jurgen said, nodding. "If they leave together, then you'll accompany them. If only one wants to leave, let me know and I'll monitor the other until Stefan returns."

"Yes, sir. Amelia seems upset and may want to leave soon. I'll let you know if she does, so you can stay vigilant with Annaliese."

"Perfect," Stefan said. "You know, Ax, perhaps you can relate to her, considering that two of you have something in common. Maybe she needs someone to talk to that understands her situation." With a suggestive glance, he stroked his stomach.

Axel winced at the idea. He despised discussing his past because it stirred up feelings of his own inadequacy. He shrugged before adding, "I better get back to them. Please don't be long." He resumed his spot against the wall, feeling a sense of foreboding as he kept an eye on the two ladies. Annaliese was now dancing with the man. At least she was enjoying herself.

His heart skipped a beat when he couldn't find Amelia. He casually strolled around the room, but his stomach was in knots. It was unfair to be stuck watching both girls. His worries faded when he found her at the dessert table, filling her plate with frosted yellow cakes topped with plump blueberries. He maintained his distance as she sat at an empty table near the wine bar. As the servants poured, he longingly wished for a cup to steady his fragile nerves. He debated sneaking a drink, but knew he was already in enough trouble with Jurgen.

The wine was flowing freely, and many guests were taking full advantage. He overheard two men attempting to speak in whispered tones, but they were so drunk they didn't realize how loud they were. He recognized one as the merchant he'd seen socializing with the chancellor when he first arrived. Envy welled inside as he yearned to be drunk and carefree like them.

"I'm telling you, Rudolph," the merchant slurred. "I think there are others practicing alchemy in Vilsheim. My business requires me to travel extensively in the western region, and I've picked up rumors it's practiced in Ravenna. My guess is the small town of Coburg, near our northern border."

The mention of alchemy caught Axel's attention. He'd been curious what others were saying about the subject since the execution. He moved a little closer and turned his head so he would be better positioned to hear them.

Rudolph scowled. "I'm not stupid, Kasper. I know where Coburg is. What makes you think an alchemist is there? Has the town grown suddenly rich? I know I'd have a hard time hiding it if I could create gold."

Kasper took a long draw from his goblet. "No, no, an alchemist wouldn't want to draw attention. That's foolish. If it were me, I'd hide it from others. Maybe travel and say I earned it overseas."

Rudolph glared at him through glassy eyes. "It sounds

like you've given this a lot of thought. Do you want to learn alchemy? I'd be careful if I was you."

Kasper choked on his wine, spilling it on his jacket. "Egads, no, man," he said as he fumbled at his lapel. "I was only thinking how easy my life would be if I could make gold instead of working so hard for it. Besides, perhaps there's a reward for turning in an alchemist. So many possibilities."

Rudolph raised an eyebrow. "Then why do you believe there's one in Coburg?"

"I never said that!" Kasper's breathing became labored as he tried to gather himself. "I only said I heard rumors near Ravenna. The alchemists were rumored to have fled north when they left Verone. Wouldn't Coburg make sense? There're plenty of places to hide in those mountains."

"So your only clue is a rumor they vanished north when it was outlawed?" Rudolph chuckled, struggling to maintain his balance. "You're ridiculous and even more drunk than I thought."

Kasper fell silent, his eyes nervously darting around the room, sweat beading on his forehead. His curiosity got the better of him and Axel inched closer, checking on Amelia as she worked on her dessert platter. He couldn't resist eavesdropping, despite his better judgment, and he looked down as he tried to concentrate on the pair's words.

"I have come across a very interesting piece of information," Kasper said with a whisper. "Apparently, when the alchemists fled, they created a creed that would help others find them. I came across a verse that goes:

> *To the north where winter blows*
> *Gold is found where knowledge flows*
> *Within the lotus field found*
> *An open mind no longer bound*

They adopted the lotus as their symbol because of its instrumental role in alchemy."

Rudolf rested his arm on Kasper's shoulder as he erupted in laughter. "That's your clue? A poem about a lotus? There's no mention of Coburg. You should really drink less, my friend, unless you want to find yourself on the headsman block someday."

Kasper appeared agitated but laughed it off. "Of course you're right. I was only telling you of the rumors I've come across while traveling. Never mind, I shouldn't have brought it up. Now, if you'll please excuse me, I hear someone calling my name." He scurried away, leaving Rudolf alone at the bar.

Axel found the entire conversation fascinating. Despite Rudolf's efforts to minimize the situation, he was suspicious of Kasper's excessive nervousness and dismissive behavior. How often did Axel let go of a subject when he was inebriated? He often became more argumentative, trying to prove his point. There had to be a hidden story here.

He remained deep in thought until a voice startled him. "Well, Axel, did you hear anything interesting?" He turned to find Gunter staring at him with an impish smile.

His stomach queasy, Axel tried to steady his voice before responding. "What are you talking about?"

"Don't play coy with me. I watched you eavesdropping on that conversation, even heard a piece myself. Still curious about alchemy? Perhaps you want to be an alchemist yourself?" Gunter raised an eyebrow suggestively.

Axel tried to remain cool while panicking inside. "I have no idea what you're referring to. I was watching Lady Amelia." He pointed to where Amelia was seated, but found her chair empty instead. He only then noticed she was walking back to the table where Annaliese and her suitor were chatting.

"It looks to me like you weren't paying attention to her at all. You seem quite distracted."

"Damn you, Gunter! Stop bothering me. You're the one disrupting my concentration. Don't you have something better to do? I need to check on her."

Gunter was still talking as Axel walked away. "It's unfortunate she's too good for you. You would make a fine pair of piggies. Despite how you look now, we both know you're still that intimidated little fat boy."

Axel rushed back to the wall with a clear view of the main table. Of all people to witness him eavesdropping, why did it have to be Gunter? There wasn't a worse person to suspect him of alchemy. The comment about being fat struck a deeper nerve. He knew there was some truth to it. The voice in his head was notorious for bringing it up at the worst times, and his current lean, powerful physique did not diminish it. Ysabelle used to tell him how handsome he was and enjoyed running her hands over his muscles. Even Mistila had complimented him on his body. But somehow, his thoughts were always louder.

He took a couple of deep breaths and refocused on the girls. They were having another spirited conversation. Annaliese was attempting to step away and persuade Amelia to follow. They were probably going someplace private to argue. He sighed as he went after them, hoping there wouldn't be a problem.

# Chapter 9

## *No Good Deed*

Annaliese excused herself to her admirer and gestured for her sister to follow her. They headed toward the entrance of the hall, away from the loud music and dancing guests. Axel trailed from a close distance, hoping to overhear their conversation despite the surrounding noise. The hairs on the back of his neck stood up, and a chill ran down his spine, as if his body could sense trouble on the horizon.

Annaliese spoke in an exasperated, harsh tone. "What's your problem? I finally have a man giving me his earnest attention, and you're ruining it."

The heaviness of her sister's gaze caused Amelia to avert her eyes. "Did you hear what they said when they approached us? Your suitor told his friend he could have the fat one. They were trying to be quiet, but they were already judging us." She wiped away the sweat still dripping from her forehead.

"Yes, I heard him. I admit it was in poor taste, but you

did nothing to help the situation. Your bitchy, sarcastic demeanor emerged the moment they arrived. How do you expect to attract anyone acting like that?"

Amelia's finger jabbed toward her sister, punctuating her frustration. "You should have had my back. Instead, you laughed at their stupid jokes and told them I had too much to drink. You used me to earn their favor. I thought we were in this together." Axel hesitated, curious if he should step in. This was turning ugly. The last thing he needed was them fighting with each other.

Annaliese's face bore a guilty expression. "You don't understand. You're the younger daughter and still have a chance to find someone. I'm running out of time, and I need to make concessions if I want to get married. Father said this is my best chance. If I fail here, he doesn't know what to do. He told me he was sorry I inherited his ugly face and wished I looked more like Mother. How do you think I feel when he calls me ugly? Underneath your layers of fat is a beautiful woman. I don't understand why you can't control yourself when it makes you miserable."

"You're calling me fat now?" Amelia clenched her fists. "Your incessant pursuit of a man demonstrates your selfishness knows no bounds. Even degrading your own sister. How dare you!"

Annaliese gasped as she clutched her chest. "How can you think that of me after all we've been through? I have nothing but love for you!"

Amelia's cheeks burned with a deep shade of red as her body quivered and she fought to remain upright. "I need more wine." Axel's eyes grew wide. If she collapsed, he would need to carry her to the room. Stefan should be the one doing that and was better suited for it. He rubbed his temples and sighed. Why did he have to leave him alone with these two?

"You're drunk and don't need any more wine. Come sit with me for a moment." She grabbed Amelia's arm, but her sister pulled away. Annaliese took a seat and motioned for her to sit. "Take a moment to sit with me and breathe."

Amelia remained hesitant, but sat next to her. Axel breathed a sigh of relief that things were calming down.

"I'm sorry he called you fat. I didn't like it either, but I was afraid to say anything that might scare him off. When I see him, I will mention it. We're in this together, right?"

Amelia stared into her empty cup and nodded. "What if things go well with him? I will be all alone. You'll have a family, and I'll be the overweight spinster everyone pities."

Annaliese caressed her sister's back, pulling her close. "I think your judgment is being influenced by the wine. It's best that you go back to our room and get some sleep. Things will be better in the morning."

Amelia stared through glassy eyes, drool forming on the corner of her mouth.

"Well, perhaps not tomorrow, but things will appear better when your mind clears. I need to get back to the table and make the most of this opportunity. You understand, right?"

Amelia nodded, and the sisters hugged. Axel took it as a sign the conversation was over and Amelia was ready to leave. Not wanting to intrude, he approached with caution. "Pardon me, ladies. I've been watching from afar and want to ensure everything is alright. Is there anything I can do?"

Annaliese stood and faced him. "Hello, Axel. Where's Stefan? Amelia needs to go to the room."

"Stefan had an urgent family matter. My assignment was to keep a close eye on both of you and accompany you when you leave. We can go now if you're ready."

"My sister is ready, but I'm not. Can you take her to our room? I'll be staying until late into the evening. I hope Stefan will be back by then."

Axel was reluctant, but he had to obey his orders and separate the girls. "Don't worry, my lady. Commander Jurgen will be here in the event Stefan is delayed." He scanned the room and found him near the king's table. "You remember Jurgen from your first day. He is near the head table. He will see to your needs until Stefan returns."

Annaliese rubbed her sister's shoulder. "Axel will take you to the room and stand watch until we return, okay?" Amelia nodded. "She's all yours. I'll make sure Jurgen and my parents know that you're bringing her back to our room. Keep a close eye on her. She's in a fragile state and needs compassion and rest."

"She is in excellent hands. I will ensure she remains safely in her room." He bowed to Annaliese before offering his hand to Amelia. "Shall we go, my lady?"

She took his hand as he helped her to her feet. She stumbled, but Axel caught her before she fell. He winced at the burden, causing Annaliese to frown. "It's alright, I got you. Here, allow me to assist," he said as he offered his arm.

He didn't realize how drunk Amelia was until they were walking to the room. The stench of alcohol emanated from her pores as they meandered through the keep. She leaned on him, attracting curious glances from the passing servants. Axel did his best to keep her upright, but it was getting more difficult with each passing step. They'd barely passed the kitchen when Amelia collapsed against him, throwing him off-balance. Bracing himself, he kept her steady, preventing them from tumbling to the ground. She needed to get off her feet, and he wanted a break. In the hopes of encouraging her to make it back on her own feet, he suggested they rest for a moment.

In an alcove off the main hallway, he spotted a bench that provided a stunning city view, making it the perfect spot to relax and show her the sights. "Let's sit and take a moment to admire the beauty of Koenigsberg at night." Weariness overcame her, and her head drooped, but Axel's swift tap on her face snapped her back into focus. "You don't want to fall asleep here, so keep your head up and look outside. Trust me, this is a sight you don't want to miss. Look out the window and tell me what you see." As he gazed out the window, he was treated to a magnificent display of the city in full swing. Lights sparkled with life, dancing like fireflies in the night. The window let in a gentle breeze, tinged with the briny smell of the sea below. Having seen it countless times as a Watchman, Axel was bored with the view, but the sight might catch Amelia's attention and redirect her focus.

"Beauty," Amelia said, to his surprise. "I see beauty everywhere. The lights of the city are stunning from this vantage. The silver glow of the moon along the ocean waves is sublime. Even you are beautiful. Your eyes are as blue as the water, and your face is as chiseled as the walls of the castle. I find beauty in all things, except in my own reflection. When I look in the mirror, I see a girl gradually morphing into a massive leviathan." She blinked her tears away before leaning her head against the wall.

Axel was torn. He felt sorry for the girl. What Gunter had said about understanding her situation was true. He knew the embarrassment of being fat, the shame it brought to your family. The hopeless feeling of being trapped in a living prison. His memories of strangers judging him while making snide comments made it a struggle to get through each day. However, his father had taught him to hate self-pity. When he'd sought sympathy, he was met with anger, making him more miserable. From a young age, he'd learned that self-loathing should remain inside where others couldn't see or use it against you. Everyone disliked something about themselves, but the clever ones knew how to conceal it. "Don't say that, my lady. If beauty's in the eye of the beholder, then believing everything is beautiful except yourself is a personal issue. Maybe others perceive you differently than you see yourself."

Amelia scowled. "Who are you to say such things? Are you a knight or a philosopher? It's easy for you to say how I should think of myself. You don't have to live in this disgusting body. I can't even look at my mother anymore, as all I see is myself in a few years. At least she married before she grew fat. I'm twice the size she was at my age." A sigh escaped her lips, the aroma of sour wine lingering in the air.

Axel winced as he pictured her in a few years. He hadn't intended to offend her and was stunned how she'd used his words against him. He tried to remain positive. "If your mother was thin, then there is a thin body within you as well. You just need to find it." He smiled as if he had imparted some profound wisdom.

Amelia snorted at him. "You're an arse. Please stop trying to cheer me up. I would rather dwell in my misery than have a knight lecture me. Men have it so much easier than women. They can be fat and ugly and no one holds it against them. So spare me your pity and keep your opinions to yourself." She stood up, appearing much steadier. "I'm ready to go back to the room now. I need to be by myself."

Axel was bewildered. Despite his efforts, he consistently found himself saying the wrong thing. He debated sharing his childhood struggles, but frustration held him back. He was only trying to help, so she had no right to treat him like that. He stood and offered his arm. "I apologize, my lady. I will escort you to your room now." If she wanted him to stay quiet, that just made his job easier.

Amelia narrowed her eyes but still took his arm, and they continued on their way.

Axel brooded over their interaction. She knew

nothing about him or his struggles. She couldn't understand the hard work and determination needed to become a knight. The abuse he'd suffered from his training officer was harsher than any spoiled noblewoman's experience. She was oblivious to the bullying he'd endured as he struggled to complete his drills. On the flip side, could he grasp the inner turmoil of a young lady struggling to fulfill the responsibilities imposed by her noble family? He decided he was better off keeping his mouth shut. It wasn't his responsibility to comfort her.

Their conversation had sobered Amelia enough that she could walk without leaning on him, and they made it back to the guest suite with no further interruption. Axel opened the door and surveyed the suite before allowing her to enter. The rest of the family was still at the ball, but he waited outside until she gave him permission to enter.

He hesitated. "Are you sure it's appropriate for the two of us to be in here alone? I wouldn't want anyone getting the wrong idea."

Amelia rolled her eyes as she waved him in. "Stop being ridiculous. Ilona said that the guards need to be in the room unless my family is here. What would happen if someone were to sneak in when I was alone? You need to check the other rooms to ensure there are no intruders."

She made a good point. He confirmed the two bedrooms were clear and let Amelia know she could proceed. "Is there anything else you need? I'll stay in the common room and wait for Stefan or your family to arrive."

"No, that's all. Thank you for walking me back. I'm

afraid I wasn't very ladylike in my actions or my words. I've had too much to drink and let my emotions get the better of me. Please accept my apologies." She smiled, but tears had returned to her eyes.

"I have already forgotten it. I'm sure things will look brighter in the morning."

She shrugged and turned to enter her bedroom. She seemed so sad that before he could think about what he was doing, he blurted, "I understand, Amelia."

She paused before facing him. "What do you mean? What do you understand?"

"When we were resting, you told me I don't know what it's like to be bullied for being fat. But I know exactly what it's like."

With a furrowed brow, Amelia leaned forward, engrossed in his words. She crossed her arms, guarded. "Oh yeah? How would you know?"

"Despite my current appearance, I was an overweight bairn. I wasn't into the same activities as other boys my age. Rather than playing with swords or fishing, I read. I loved reading. The stories provided an escape from my miserable life and let me imagine myself as a knight on a quest to save the princess or find buried treasure. My mother encouraged me to read, but my father despised it. When I read, I ate, even when I wasn't hungry. It kept me occupied while reading. The more I read, the bigger I grew. And the fatter I was, the harsher my father's criticism. He called me an embarrassment and cursed fate for having a useless son, so I buried my shame by eating more. That was at home, but it didn't stop there. I was teased and called piggy by the other children. To this day, I work with them and still hear about it. Despite not being that overweight bairn anymore, I sometimes still feel that way."

Amelia's expression softened as she listened, her anger fading away. "I never would have believed that by looking at you. You embody the image of the valiant knights I imagined while reading similar tales, rescuing the princess from the clutches of a wicked dragon."

Axel blushed. "That is kind of you. Sometimes I still have that lingering sense of being fat, and it emerges during the most inconvenient moments."

She nodded, letting her arms fall to her side. "I appreciate you telling me this. Perhaps you do understand. It's true you can't judge a person by appearance alone. How did you overcome it?" She was now alert, looking at Axel with hope in her eyes. She sat on the edge of the sofa nearest to him. "I would love to lose weight, but it's impossible living in a castle with an abundance of food at my disposal. I would appreciate any guidance."

Her request made his stomach twist with apprehension. His intention was to be relatable, not to provide advice. "In Koenigsberg, when a boy turns sixteen, he can join the Knights of Frostgarde. It's considered a great honor to serve the royal family. Families that don't have the coin to support their children often enlist their boys. Once they make it through the initial training, they are admitted as Gatekeepers. The training requires a high level of rigor and demands focus and discipline to succeed. Boys lacking the fortitude are rooted out and sent back to their families, bringing them additional shame. My father was already humiliated and couldn't wait to be rid of me on my sixteenth birthday. When he left me at the Boar's Gate, I decided I would never return home. I used my hate to push me through. By the end of each day, I was physically and mentally exhausted, but that resentment drove me."

As Amelia listened, she became lost in her own thoughts, her gaze drifting off into the distance. "I don't blame my father for his feelings. It's his duty to keep the family name alive by finding a suitable heir. I'm ashamed of my lack of self-control. How did you control yourself during your training?"

He laughed, finding the conversation more comfortable. "I had no choice. We were active all day, either training or performing drills. Food was rationed, and I could only eat at mealtime. It was impossible to get through the training without losing weight. Hunger consumed me as I struggled to complete the drills without collapsing. The other boys mocked me because I always finished last. I endured their accusations and beatings when our entire unit was punished for my delays. It hardened me and made me into the man you see today. I'm indebted to the opportunity it afforded me, but would not wish it on anyone."

Amelia sighed and hung her head, looking agitated again. "I guess there's no hope for me. There is nothing like that for girls, let alone a baron's daughter. You were fortunate to have an opportunity like that to inspire you. Despite the efforts of my family to limit my eating, there are always servants willing to sneak me food to maintain my favor. I am going to become a fat, lonely old maid!" She covered her face and wept.

Frustration welled up inside Axel—he'd just exacerbated the problem. He was attempting to relate, and she was using it as another opportunity to whine. "Amelia, I'm telling you that you need to find something that drives you. Where losing weight becomes more important than eating. No one else can do this for you. Just like my father couldn't make me lose weight—I had to do it myself."

She stared at him through glossy eyes, seething. "Yourself? You had an entire army helping you. Your story made me believe that there was someone who actually understood. You may know the struggles of being overweight, but you can't appreciate the hopelessness of being unable to change. I thought you were being kind, but you're just like everyone else, making me feel bad about myself. Why would you do that to me?"

Axel's frustration turned to anger, and he tried to stay composed. The way she'd turned the situation back on him was dumbfounding. He spoke louder and faster as he stumbled over his words. "Why, I—I did no such thing. I was trying to encourage you. You can change if you put your mind to it. Quit whining about your life and find something that motivates you to change it. Speaking from experience, self-pity will get you nowhere."

Amelia stood up, flailing her arms as tears ran down her cheeks. "Thank you for your generosity. I'm thinking of using my anger at you as a source of inspiration. I bet I can lose weight without an entire army supporting me. What do you think of that, pretty boy?"

"I'm glad I could be of service," he said in a monotone voice.

She raised her hands, screaming at him. "Get out of here! I don't care what Ilona said. Wait outside where I won't be anywhere near you. I don't want you around anymore. Leave." She pointed to the exit before walking to her bedroom and slamming the door.

How had the evening fallen apart on him? Maybe Amelia was still drunk and wouldn't remember the conversation. He didn't need Jurgen hearing about this. Besides, she wasn't his responsibility. He was only guarding her as a favor, so they'd better not blame him for her condition. Why would they take the word of a spoiled drunk girl over his? She took no responsibility for her actions. She was at fault for being fat, just like he was. It was wrong for her to criticize him for making the most of his opportunity. Her reaction proved she wasn't strong enough to do what he'd done. Some people lacked accountability for their own choices.

Axel waited outside until Stefan arrived to relieve him about an hour later. He apologized for the delay and told Axel he was free to get some rest. Axel briefed him on his encounter with Amelia as Stefan listened with a horrified expression. He promised to take responsibility for the evening, but Axel stormed off, angry at him and Jurgen for putting him in this position. If Stefan had stuck with Amelia as he was supposed to, none of this would have happened.

# Chapter 10

## *A New Assignment*

"We have a couple of issues that I need your help with," Jurgen said to Axel, who was rubbing the remnants of sleep from his eyes. He'd woken early this morning to harsh pounding on his door—the commander wanted to see him immediately. Jurgen, still dressed in his uniform from the previous night, peered through blood-shot eyes as he recounted the events that had unfolded after Axel's departure from the ball.

The man pursuing Annaliese had had too much to drink and became excessively handsy with her. He'd gotten her alone and used the opportunity to pressure her into putting her mouth on him. Annaliese had firmly expressed her disapproval, stating that she had no interest in engaging in that type of behavior with a man she hardly knew. The young lord became angry, claiming that she should consider herself fortunate for receiving any attention, preying on her vulnerability and exploiting it to fulfill his own desires. She screamed when he tried taking what he wanted by force, and Jurgen had swiftly intervened to ensure nothing inappropriate occurred. The assailant had been taken to the dungeon, where he was awaiting punishment.

Baron Vogel was irate when he heard the news. Upon learning that Axel had been taken from Annaliese to attend to Amelia, he confronted the king, claiming their security was supposed to be assured. Otto was furious, demanding to know why Annaliese's guard had been removed. Jurgen appeared before the king and the chancellor to clarify the situation: he'd taken responsibility for watching Annaliese when Axel left the ball. He also suggested that the family should bear some blame for their daughter's intoxication. As for Annaliese, Jurgen had broken up the encounter before anything but insulting words were exchanged, and Chancellor Heinz believed they could find a solution with the baron.

"This was all before Baron Vogel found out about you and Amelia," Jurgen said. "Did you really tell her to stop whining and eat less so she wouldn't look like such a pig?" He rubbed his temples as he released a heavy sigh.

Axel gasped in horror, his eyes bulging from his skull. He was wide awake now. "She said what? I did no such thing! I tried to sympathize with her, told her I was an overweight bairn." He thought back. Had he said something insulting, or had she misunderstood his meaning? He remembered telling her to stop whining and discover something that would motivate her to lose weight. But he would be the last person to refer to her as a pig, knowing all too well the hurtful impact of that label. She was misrepresenting their encounter.

Jurgen clasped his hands behind his back. "She mentioned you were put in a position to lose weight and then flaunted it in her face. Do you know what she is referring to?"

"I told her how my father forced me to join the Knights of Frostgarde and described the struggles I faced during training. The continuous drilling left me exhausted, and my rationed meals prevented me from overeating. She's correct that I didn't make a conscious choice to lose weight. What I did was much harder. I had to drag my fat arse out of bed each morning and fight the urge to quit. My choice was simple: make it through training or be sent home humiliated. I told her she needs to find something that motivates her."

Jurgen frowned. "I see. Why did you bring up your situation? Our role is to observe in silence and take action when necessary. You're not her advisor." His voice rose as he continued. "From now on, keep your mouth shut and follow my orders exactly as I tell you. If they want to talk, be polite but keep it brief. Are we clear?"

Axel nodded as he breathed a sigh of relief. "Does this mean I am not dismissed?"

Jurgen folded his arms across his chest and glared. "No, but we have another situation to deal with, so don't think you're getting out of this unscathed. Your lack of self-restraint in sharing your opinions has once again led to negative repercussions. When the baron heard Amelia's story, he was incensed. Chancellor Heinz attempted to soothe him, but he has reached his limit with Frostgarde. His family is leaving tomorrow, and he wants you nowhere near them for the remainder of their visit. The chancellor assured him you've been pulled from the assignment, but the king hearing your name twice on such an important evening has caused a major problem for me. The chancellor wanted you out of the castle right away, but I think I found a solution that will smooth things over. I have an idea that will give you time away from Frostgarde to repair your reputation."

Axel was nervous but intrigued. Most of all, he was frustrated. Why had he gone against his instincts and opened up to Amelia? Fat lot of good that had done. And why was he in trouble when Stefan, Jurgen, and Amelia had caused the entire situation? The chancellor's eagerness to dismiss him was also unsettling. Perhaps time away from Frostgarde was precisely what he needed. Not having left the city since childhood, he found the idea of traveling tempting. He stood up straight and asked, "What are my orders, sir?"

"It's fortuitous you mentioned your training experience. We're discharging a recruit who isn't meeting expectations. As you're aware, not every trainee is fit to join our ranks. However, this is Lady Irmina's son, Dirk, the nephew of Baron Helmuth. Relations between the king and the baron have grown worse over the years. You may recall Irmina was the original choice to marry the king before his father changed his mind and chose Queen Helena instead. Baron Helmuth continues to harbor a grudge. Dirk is a spoiled brat with an enormous sense of entitlement. His family has grown tired of his arrogance and incessant whining. His mother believed that formal discipline could shape his negative attitude and begged her brother to sponsor him as a knight. Because of the tense relation between Verone and the crown, King Otto agreed."

He confirmed Axel was following before continuing. "Dirk doesn't meet our standards. Training is tough for everyone, but even tougher for those who aren't naturally suited to the field. They must persevere when their body wants to quit, much like yourself. Despite all the chances we've given him, he continues to show little effort, always finding more things to complain about. As the baron's nephew, he has received more chances than most recruits get. But we have a duty to safeguard the king, and the boy is just not Frostgarde material. We must send him home despite the increased tension it will cause."

Sympathy stirred within Axel. He understood being resentful that life wasn't fair. "What do you need from me? Am I expected to accompany him back to Verone?"

Jurgen nodded as he paced the floor. "Our goal is to prevent him from leaving with Baron Helmuth's daughter. We don't want Dirk complaining to her about his experience here the entire trip home. We want you to escort him. Just the two of you. It will be quicker, and we can avoid gossip reaching the baron before you arrive. The king will send a message that he has been relieved of his duties. This should be a family issue that need not involve the entire kingdom."

Axel stroked his beard. Although he was thrilled to

leave Koenigsberg, he dreaded spending time with an obnoxious child who would undoubtedly irritate him. "This will improve my situation? Will I be trusted to look after another member of a baron's family?"

Jurgen stopped in front of him, looking directly in his eyes. "Leave that to me. The chancellor won't care who I select as long as I put my arse on the line to vouch for him. This should give folks here time to forget about the whole incident with Baron Vogel's daughters. I need your word that you'll take care of this without any mistakes. Show understanding and support to the lad, but be careful not to cross the line. If you're successful, your position will be secure upon your return. This is your last chance."

Glad to have another opportunity, Axel assured Jurgen that he could handle it without incident.

A sigh of relief escaped Jurgen's lips as he relaxed. "Excellent. You should be on your way no later than midday. Begin packing, and I will meet you at the inner bailey in two hours. Fresh horses and rations will be provided for your journey. You're dismissed."

Axel saluted and left to pack. In his travel sack, he put a change of clothes, flint, his dagger, and extra bandages. He fastened his bedding, which included a head roll and a wool blanket, on the outside before taking a final glance around his room with bittersweet resignation. Just when he thought he had found a place to call home, he was forced to leave because of factors beyond his control. Amelia's deliberate twisting of his words compounded his frustration. When things didn't go their way, nobles could often become petulant. What if Dirk would offer more of the same? Jurgen had admitted he was a spoiled brat. Axel's new role fell short of his expectations, leaving him disheartened. Did he still want to be a knight?

The question stuck in his mind. What did he really want at this point in his life? A promotion to the IceGuard was out of the question, so he would remain in his current role until death. He buried his head in his hands as he reflected on the repetitive patterns in his life. It never failed: whenever things were going his way, something came along to ruin it. He calmed himself, wiping the tears from his face. Crying was cathartic, allowing him to release his pent-up frustration.

His thoughts drifted to the alchemist. He couldn't get the king's anger at the man out of his head. It had to mean something. Was the transformation of lead into gold possible? How different would life be with that kind of power? Axel dreamed of owning property, free from the control of others. Wealth would allow him to live life on his own terms for the first time. He felt a spark of excitement stirring inside. Was alchemy worth the risk if it could offer him that? He was willing to do whatever it took to determine his own destiny, even if it meant facing death. He stood up and began pacing the floor, a semblance of a plan coming to mind. He would give his all to this assignment, but if it didn't succeed, his focus would shift to locating the alchemist. If he failed this job, there would be nothing but pain awaiting him here.

Where could he expand his knowledge of alchemy? The lines on his forehead deepened as he focused on the question. His only lead was the Alchemist Creed, which might take him to Coburg. Axel threw up his hands and groaned. That wasn't much information to work with. He decided to think about it more on his trip. Thinking of Verone reminded him of the university located there. Alchemy had been studied at the University of Verone when it was still legal. A huge smile spread across his face. There had to be something he could learn there. At last, circumstances were working out in his favor.

He was ready to leave when Stefan burst through the door. "I'm glad you're still here. I just received the news and wanted to apologize before you left. The whole evening was a waste of my time, and look at the mess it caused. I'm so frustrated with my wife for overreacting."

Axel put a hand on his shoulder. "It's okay, I understand. If I was more attentive to a woman's needs, maybe I wouldn't be in this predicament. I need to go on this adventure. It will be good for me to get away from Frostgarde and clear my mind. As long as I can keep the little shit from getting on my nerves, that is." A nervous chuckle escaped him.

"May your journey be smooth and peaceful and your return home safe. I hope the time away is beneficial. I was able to sneak away for a moment, but need to be getting back." Stefan embraced him in a big bear hug before returning to his post.

Tears welled as Axel watched him leave, wondering if he would see his friend again.

He left the keep, looking for Jurgen, taking his time and enjoying his last moments in Frostgarde. He'd dedicated twenty years to the castle and might never see it again. Axel felt more alive than he had in years. Having a purpose outside of his job was invigorating after spending so long serving others. He found Jurgen outside the stables, directing the stable master as he prepared their horses. A large black destrier was selected for Axel while a chestnut palfrey, five hands smaller, was chosen for Dirk. He handed the tack to Axel and told him to prepare his horse, while doing the same for the palfrey.

Jurgen watched as Axel saddled his horse. "The success of your trip is crucial for both of us. I'm counting on you to be on your best behavior. Here come the kitchen servants with the rations I requested. A few bread loaves, a round of cheese, salted meat, and some fresh fruit. I'm also providing a little wine to make the journey more pleasurable. Please use it with care."

Axel blushed as he took the fare. He packed the food, ensuring the wine was in his saddlebag. He might need it while riding, should the lad prove troublesome. "When is the kid arriving? I thought we were in a hurry."

Jurgen shrugged. "Commander Bremer wanted to see him off personally. You know how he acts when dismissing trainees. He is convinced he could have done more to ensure they succeeded. We know that's silly; you're proof of that. It boils down to the lads themselves, and they're all unique. Here they come now."

Axel saw his former commander heading their way, leaning on a walking stick as he crossed the courtyard, a blond boy in tow. Bremer was getting old. His hair had transformed from the grey Axel remembered to a frosty white. A silver beard hung to his chest, tied with the same gold beads he had worn for years. Sun exposure had etched deep lines on his reddish face, and his sunken eyes considered them as he waved. Axel studied the boy, curious about who he'd be traveling with. Dressed in such elegant attire, he seemed more prepared for a lavish banquet than a demanding journey. He had an annoyed expression on his scrunched face, and his eyes darted around, as if he expected some kind of threat. Axel hoped it was jitters, or this was going to be a long trip.

Bremer lifted his hand to greet them before embracing Jurgen. "It's good to see you. I apologize for being late. My men attempted to bring him here without my knowledge, and I had to halt their efforts. Hello, Axel. It's been a while. I hope you're staying out of trouble." He laughed as he slapped Axel's back. "I'm only kidding. Congratulations on your promotion to the BlackGuard. I always knew that you would turn into a fine knight one day. I still use your story to inspire the new lads." He grabbed Dirk's shoulder. "Unfortunately, it didn't work on him. Dirk, this is Axel, the man I have told you stories about. He'll be taking you home. Perhaps you can even learn a thing or two from him on your way." He winked at Axel.

Dirk scowled at him with intense loathing. "I have heard plenty about you. Commander Bremer always shared stories of your accomplishments whenever I faced a challenge. My life is complete now that I've met the famous Axel," he said with scorn.

Axel was shocked. It was unfair of Dirk to judge him

when they'd never even met. What had Bremer said that made the boy despise him? He gave a half-hearted smile. "Bremer likes to embellish my old stories to inspire the recruits, but I assure you, it was a matter of which fear ran deeper: being ridiculed by my peers or having to face my father in shame. I guess I was lucky to have a bigger bastard for a father as motivation." The three knights laughed together.

Dirk puffed his chest, his face contorted with anger. "Are you calling my father a bastard? I am the nephew of Baron Helmuth Kaiser, and you should show me more respect. I will not tolerate your insults."

Axel's eyes rolled in exasperation. "Calm down, Dirk. I'm just having fun. We have a long road ahead of us that's going to feel even longer if you don't lighten up."

Bremer patted Dirk's back as he exhaled in frustration. "His sensitive nature, coupled with that huge chip on his shoulder, is why I had to discharge him. I tried my hardest to make him stop, but he's as stubborn as a mule and couldn't get out of his own way. Listen, lad, you're going home, where you'll be safe. There's no point in wondering what could have been. Use the time to consider what you want out of life. If you keep fighting with it, you'll get crushed under the weight. Nobody is trying to make you miserable, despite what you may think."

Tears formed in the corner of Dirk's eyes. The awkward exchange made them all realize it was time to go. Bremer helped Dirk mount his horse while Axel finished packing. Jurgen approached as he mounted and whispered, "Try your best not to get under each other's skin. The less interaction between you two, the better. Make haste and you can have him there within a fortnight. Spend a little time in the city if you like. Take your time coming back. In a month from now, I bet this will all be behind us. Do nothing to draw more attention to yourself. Understood?" Axel nodded and shook his hand. "One more thing," Jurgen added while handing him a sealed scroll. "This letter states you are on official king's business. If you run into any trouble while you're in Verone, hand them this and they'll be compelled to help. It's been signed by King Otto, so take good care of it."

Axel rode to where Bremer and Dirk were saying goodbye. "That's everything. Farewell, Jurgen. Farewell, Bremer. Time to get this lad home." They rode down the hill toward the Boar's Gate.

# Chapter 11

## *The Pig Sty*

A xel and Dirk had been traveling for a week and were almost halfway to Verone. Their brisk pace allowed for little conversation, and Axel used the quiet time to contemplate his future. Standing watch had given him plenty of time for reflection, but staying active helped him maintain his concentration.

It had been a pleasant ride through the crisp, clean country air. After passing the farmsteads surrounding Koenigsberg, they encountered few travelers. Friendly farmers waved to them as they passed through the countryside. A young lady offered them fresh apples, which Axel readily accepted. Fruit picked from the branch was a rare treat. Most of his allotment came from the bottom of oak barrels, often bruised and browning.

They had spent the last two days traveling through the forest on a well-maintained road, under the shelter of a leafy canopy that allowed ample sunlight to illuminate their path, listening to the sweet melodies of chirping turtledoves that fluttered among the trees. Axel hoped to be out of the forest by the time they made camp this evening. The mountains separating the coast from the inner plains of Vilsheim would be the most difficult leg of their journey, so he wanted a good night's rest before proceeding.

He weighed his options after he returned Dirk safely home. He planned on visiting the university, but was unsure how to gain access. He needed to devise something more clever than asking for a book on alchemy. The Alchemist Creed and the verse about the lotus field came to mind; it might be better for him to start his search there rather than on alchemy itself. At least it would garner less scrutiny.

Despite his intention to use this time for planning, traveling with a young recruit kept bringing back memories of Axel's own training. It had been the worst experience of his life. When his father had abandoned him at the Boar's Gate on his sixteenth birthday, he'd howled for his mother to save him as his father pulled her away, his escalating shouts making it difficult for Axel to gather the courage to leave her. Only after she was able to speak to him in private could she calm him down. She convinced him to stay strong and do his best, and he squeezed her and promised he would.

A xel's heart sank as he watched his father walk away after dumping him at the Boar's Gate. The last thing he said to him was: "You sniveling shit. You're no son of mine. Perhaps if you succeed here, I may welcome you back to the family, but until then, you are dead to me."

He clutched his bag, which contained his only belongings, including his favorite book that his mother had slipped in. It was the story of the rise of the first Koenig king, who convinced the other barons that a single ruler would bring more prosperity than a bickering council. Axel was led into the gatehouse, where he waited as the guard conversed with someone. Peering through a narrow window, he observed the crowd outside the gate, eagerly advocating for an audience with the king. Curses echoed into the chamber as the sweaty masses pushed and jostled for position near the front of the line. The scorching sun amplified the rank smell of the huddled mob who fought to gain entry.

Axel was brought to an older man with salt-and-pepper hair who studied him, examining him from head to toe as if determining his worthiness. "Well, boy, you want to join the Knights of Frostgarde, do you? I'm Commander Bremer, in charge of the Gatekeepers and new recruits. Before we begin, let me make one thing clear. Because of our strict standards, only the most disciplined and resilient trainees complete our program. Those who persevere become knights who are entrusted to safeguard Frostgarde and ensure the royal family is protected behind these walls. This castle has stood over four centuries—it has never been breached, and I aim to keep it that way. Every knight is a critical part of our defense. We are only as strong as our weakest soldier."

He stood and gripped Axel's shoulder. "You're about to experience the most demanding trial of your young life. If you fail, you will be dismissed and sent home in disgrace. But if you succeed, you will be stronger and more capable than you've ever imagined. Do you think you have what it takes? Speak now, as it's the last chance to leave with your dignity." He kept his eyes locked on Axel, awaiting a response.

Axel shifted his gaze, fixating on the floor. He yearned to tell Bremer he didn't have the required skills and should be sent home. Home to his comfortable bed and the solace of his favorite books. However, the dread of facing his father and the shame it would bring prevented him. Despite his fears, this was his only opportunity to prove himself. He forced himself to peer into Bremer's eyes and said, "I can do it, sir. I'll do my best to make you proud." He mustered a half-hearted smile.

Bremer's face softened, and he spoke in a somber tone. "I know you will, boy. I see it in your eyes. The guard told me your father was an arsehole, abandoning you here. I bet you hate him. Let me give you a little secret. Channel that anger and frustration into overcoming the challenges that await you. It's the only way you'll survive. Let's get you started."

Bremer brought him to the Gatekeepers' training arena. More than a hundred men of varying ages had been divided into groups and were sparring with each other. In an isolated quadrant, a large man was working with five boys around Axel's age. As they approached, he recognized Stefan, his towering figure distinguishing him from the other trainees. Handing Axel a practice sword, Bremer urged him to enter the fray. He leaped into action, swinging with reckless abandon at Stefan, who evaded the misguided attack before landing a powerful strike to his ribs. Axel crumbled to the ground, contorting in pain.

Bremer roared with laughter as Stefan extended a hand to Axel. "That's the spirit! I admire your enthusiasm to jump right in, but you need to learn to control yourself." He focused on Stefan. "This is Axel. His dad deserted him at my gate. He'll be with the novice unit, so I'll leave him with you to teach him the basics."

Stefan's face lit up with a wide grin. "Yes, sir. I know Axel, so I'll watch out for him and guide him through the process."

"Don't take it too easy on him. I'm holding you responsible if he isn't ready." Stefan nodded, and Bremer told them he would come back later to check on them.

Stefan took Axel into their circle and introduced him to the other boys, and he realized he was not that much different from them. Other than Stefan, who already commanded a great deal of respect, the rest were skittish and apprehensive. They welcomed him before Stefan instructed them on basic sword forms. Axel labored while performing the drills, but managed to finish them. Panting hard and drenched in sweat, he struggled to keep up as Stefan led them on a run around the field. He lagged behind the other boys, who had to wait for him before moving to the next exercise. When he finished, he fell onto his back, gasping for air. Perspiration poured from his head and into his eyes, stinging them. "Water, please," he said to anyone who would listen.

Stefan stood over him and kicked his side, pointing to a barrel on the other side of the arena. "Water is over there. Get it yourself. We spent the last ten minutes waiting for you. You need to keep moving."

Axel groaned. He wanted nothing more than to curl up with a good book. It had only been a few hours, and the urge to quit was already crushing. Since that wasn't an option, he forced himself to his feet and headed toward the water barrel. The cool water refreshed his dry mouth and scratchy throat as he gulped it down. But the moment he was satisfied, his stomach convulsed, and he regurgitated most of the water back into the barrel. Cries of shock and disgust echoed behind him.

Through bloodshot eyes, Axel noticed a nearby Gatekeeper regarding him. "You're the first recruit in two moons to do that. I thought we had a new record. Boy, don't expect others to clean up your mess. Grab the bucket and take it to the well on the other side of the arena."

Axel spent ten minutes trying to empty the barrel. It was still halfway full, and it was too heavy to tip over. He eventually upended it by bracing his back against it and pushing with his feet as hard as he could. He lost count of the trips needed to refill it with the bucket, but his muscles were sore and his joints ached by the time he was finished. He rejoined Stefan, whose cohort was practicing a new form. Axel grabbed his practice sword and attempted to follow along.

The drilling continued throughout the afternoon, though luckily they took several breaks. Bremer checked on them and told Axel he looked like shit. He called an end to the day, and they were given time to clean up before the evening meal. During dinner, Axel noticed Gunter and Basel seated at another table. They were older and had already been promoted to Gatekeepers. Gunter caught him staring and pointed toward his own eyes and then at Axel before resuming his meal. Axel lost his appetite, terror gripping him. He longed for a place to hide. Things would be hard enough without Gunter bullying him.

Stefan noticed he wasn't eating and slapped his back. "You need to eat to keep your strength up, Ax. You've got a long way to go."

Axel stared at his food and forced himself to finish every bite. He couldn't remember the last time he hadn't felt like eating.

When it was time to retire, Stefan escorted him to the barracks near the training field. The Gatekeepers were housed in three buildings, and he was taken to the smallest bunkhouse, used for trainees and those recently promoted. The barrack was nothing more than rows of straw-stuffed pallets. Most already had bags lying on them, while a few had locked chests at their feet. He counted six vacant pallets and assumed those were his options.

Stefan watched him scan the room. "We aim to keep recruits divided by skill, but we may need to shuffle people, depending on the size of the group. The older boys take the spots against the wall. As we're trainees, we're in the middle of the room. It's uncomfortable, but you get used to it." He pointed to a group of eight that were in the center. "Ours are all occupied, so you'll have to find a different one." He pointed to one against the wall with a chest. "That's Gunter's, and Basel's is beside it. You probably want to stay away from those."

Nausea engulfed Axel as he began hyperventilating, and concern filled Stefan's eyes. "Easy. Don't start stressing about Gunter. No matter how much trouble he causes, he can only push the boundaries so far. Commander Bremer knows he likes to haze the new guys, but doesn't let it get out of control. He says it helps reinforce the camaraderie among our squad. Remember, their aim is to mold us into knights, not shatter our resolve."

Axel was dizzy and needed a place to sit down, so he chose a bed on the opposite side of the hall from Gunter's. He inhaled a few deep breaths as he muttered to himself over and over, "I can do this."

Soon after, the other trainees arrived, ready to go to bed. It was half full by the time Axel stretched out on his straw mattress. Though it wasn't as comfortable as his bed at home, lying down to rest felt wonderful. Exhaustion set in, his body aching from his shoulders to the soles of his feet. He knew it would be worse tomorrow when his muscles stiffened. Sleep came fast, and it wasn't long before he was snoring.

"Axel, time to rise and shine." In his half-awake state, he thought he could make out the distant murmur of voices. "It's time to get up now." He kept his eyes shut, refusing to open them. He was comfortable and not ready to start the day. With the blanket wrapped around him, he rolled onto his side. With a jerk, he was flipped onto his back and slapped in the face, jolting him awake. Four blackened shapes stood over him, staring down. Axel tried sitting up, but multiple sets of hands held him down. Another hand covered his mouth, and he was staring face-to-face at Gunter. He could feel his warm breath tickling his nose.

Gunter's mouth twisted into a maniacal grin, his eyes gleaming with mischief. He put a finger to his mouth, motioning for Axel to stay quiet. "You little shit. Do you think a fat pig like you could ever become a knight? You are a coward, too soft and weak to even handle your own fights. How can you protect anyone else? I'm going to make you so miserable that you'll beg Commander Bremer to send you bawling to your father."

Were they going to kill him? A waft of a foul fecal odor permeated the air, and his terror increased as he worried about further humiliation. He tried to cover his nose, but Gunter's hand was in the way. He realized what Axel was doing and laughed. "I see you noticed the smell. I bet you thought you shit your pants. The good news is you didn't. The bad news is you are going to wish you did. We wanted to make sure the piggy felt at home, so we brought you a gift. We are giving you your own sty."

Laughter erupted from the other boys, echoing through the room. Axel saw a bucket dripping with brown muck hovering over his stomach. He thrashed from side to side, trying to get up, but remained pinned to his bed.

The noise piqued the curiosity of the other recruits, who eagerly craned their necks to see what was happening. Gunter looked around the room and shrieked, "Everyone, mind their own damn business. This doesn't concern you. Anyone who interferes will get the same." The boys nearby lay back down, pretending to ignore what was happening while trying to catch a glimpse. Gunter reached for the bucket. "Give me that thing and hold him tight. On the count of three, I'm dumping the shit on him. Be ready to move your hands if you don't want to get hit."

He counted to three and, with a swift motion, flipped the bucket, unleashing mounds of feces, covering Axel from chest to thighs and speckling his face with the foul substance. "Now piggy is at home in his sty. Welcome to Frostgarde, Axel. I hope your stay is pleasant." He stood, laughing like a lunatic.

As the other boys joined in, Axel couldn't help but notice their uneasiness around Gunter. Everyone knew he was deranged. The boys returned to their beds, leaving Axel covered in pig shit. He was too shocked to move and lay there until nausea hit him. Feeling disgusted with himself, he stood up as clumps of feces dropped on his filthy bed. The putrid odor was overpowering. The other boys stared—even Stefan seemed shocked. He made a sympathetic face before rolling over in the opposite direction.

Axel went outside to the nearby well to clean himself, dumping buckets of water over his head while shivering in the chilly air. In the shroud of night, his emotions became too much to bear, and he bawled, wondering how he would ever make it through training.

$A$s they continued on the road to Verone, Axel tried to look at Dirk with a sympathetic eye. While he empathized with his struggle, he couldn't understand why these privileged children couldn't muster the mettle to persevere through their obstacles. They only whined about their circumstances. He wanted to relate, but the boy's lack of fortitude gnawed at his insides. Axel's resentment of his father and his promise to his mother had given him the stamina to fight through each day. Every night, he'd cried himself to sleep, emotionally drained and physically exhausted. He was the weakest trainee, always finishing last in their drills, but against all odds, he'd completed his training. It was astonishing how easily the nobles could break, as if made of glass.

Being welcomed by the Gatekeepers as one of their own had been one of the most satisfying moments in Axel's life. He couldn't wait to tell his parents so that they could finally be proud of him. Tragically, his parents were killed by raiders while he was training at Frostgarde, and he never saw them again. He remained haunted by heartrending memories of his mother, while anger toward his father still simmered in the pit of his stomach. Despite Axel's success, including a promotion to one of the most prestigious posts in the kingdom, that cruel, merciless voice continued to taunt him, branding him a failure.

# Chapter 12

## *An Act of Chivalry*

A xel paused to comprehend the enormity of the expansive plain before them. The gentle rays of the sun filtered through the clouds, casting a warm glow on the open grassland, where trees stood like sentinels in the distance. The air felt crisp and invigorating after consecutive days of rainfall. A hawk caught his eye as it soared high above, its wings spread wide as it hunted for its next prey. They'd spent the last few days on a crooked trail leading into the Verone valley. The mountains had proved to be more challenging than he anticipated. The path was narrow, forcing them to dismount and tread carefully over the rocky terrain. Heavy rainfall made their passage even more arduous, as they had to navigate slippery rocks and wade through muddy ground.

Dirk's constant grumbling had only made the already unpleasant trek worse. He remained silent at first, but once the journey became challenging, he more than made up for it. Axel tried to tell him that complaining wouldn't make things any easier, but the stubborn boy ignored his advice. The situation took a turn for the worse when Dirk slipped on the treacherous trail and fell into a gulch, forcing Axel to come to his rescue. Rather than thanking him, Dirk blamed him for not preventing his fall. Upon reflection, Axel realized his reaction had been a little delayed, as he couldn't help but enjoy watching Dirk slide down the ravine. His laughter echoed as he pulled Dirk out, which only fueled the boy's anger and put him in an even worse mood.

During their first few nights on the mountain, they were able to find refuge from the rain, taking shelter under ledges that protruded from the cliffside. When he asked Dirk to build a fire, the boy admitted he didn't know how. He tried to teach him, but Dirk showed little interest. Despite Axel's attempts to convince him, his arguments about the importance of basic survival skills fell on deaf ears, and he openly condemned Dirk for his incompetence, his voice filled with frustration and disappointment. He explained it was this behavior that had caused Bremer to dismiss him from Frostgarde. This further aggravated the boy, and they didn't speak for the remainder of the evening. Last night, they hadn't been able to find a place to take shelter, so they'd slept in the rain and woke up drenched and covered in mud.

But now that they were out of the mountains, Axel's mood brightened. "The sun feels great, and there's nothing but clear skies ahead. I think the worst of the rain is behind us. It should be smooth traveling the rest of the way." A broad grin appeared on his face as he gave a friendly wink.

Dirk groaned. "Smooth travels? I'm soaked and caked with mud. This is not how a lord should be treated. How many more days until we reach Verone?"

Axel rolled his eyes. "You would know that better than me. We're closer to Verone than Koenigsberg. If we keep a steady pace, it should only be a few more days. The sun will dry us, and we can clean ourselves when we reach the river. At least we are out of those accursed mountains."

"I've had enough of sleeping on the ground. It's uncomfortable and my back is aching. We need to find an inn where we can get a proper bath and a hot meal. It would enhance my recap of our trip to my mother."

Dirk's mischievous grin sent a shiver down Axel's spine. However, the thought of an inn was alluring. A few mugs of ale would give him a temporary reprieve from this unpleasant experience. Jurgen had given him spending coin and two months' pay, so he could afford it. Nonetheless, he didn't like being threatened. "An inn sounds like an excellent idea. I wouldn't mind a good meal, along with a song or two. If you can cease complaining, we'll seek refuge at the first inn we encounter."

Dirk nodded, and Axel let out a sigh of relief. A pleasant ride in the sunshine and the prospect of a delightful evening indoors made him smile. He urged his horse into a canter as they set off through the meadows that lay ahead.

After hours under the warm sun, their clothes had

dried out, although they were now covered in hardened mud. Despite feeling uncomfortable, Axel much preferred it to being drenched. They were making substantial progress, and as midday approached, he spotted the river in the distance. This seemed like the perfect opportunity to take a break and stretch their legs. The road narrowed, leading to a charming stone bridge that arched across the flowing river.

"Let's cross the bridge and rest on the other side," he said. "We can wash our clothes, and hopefully there will be enough sun to dry us out again. Either way, it will feel good to get rid of this muck."

Dirk nodded, his eyes tired.

While crossing the bridge, Axel spotted a man mending a wagon wheel on the opposite side of the river. Beside him, a young boy was lying on his back with his leg propped up on a sack. The man noticed them and frantically waved his arms to draw their attention.

Axel raised his hand in acknowledgment. "Ho there. What seems to be the problem?"

The man was filthy, covered in oil and what appeared to be splotches of blood. Relief was evident in his face, but Axel detected caution in his expression. "Hello, sir knight. Thank goodness you came by. I could sure use your help. We were ambushed by bandits who robbed us and broke the wheel of my cart. I was able to remove and repair it, but I'm struggling to reattach it. My poor son's foot was crushed during the attack, and he cannot help. I'm not sure that he could even if he wasn't crippled— this cart is heavy."

Dirk pulled alongside Axel and said in a hushed voice, "I hope you aren't thinking of helping. I'm exhausted and want to get to the inn you promised. We don't have time to waste on these peasants. Who knows how long it will take."

Axel didn't want to stop either but knew he couldn't leave them stranded. He grabbed the reins on Dirk's horse and yanked him closer. Through clenched teeth he replied, "What kind of arsehole are you? The boy has a broken foot and needs our aid. Imagine it was you in his predicament. We're in your uncle's jurisdiction, and it's his responsibility to take care of his citizens. They pay taxes too. I don't need your help, so I'll lend them a hand while you wash in the river. We're stopping to rest anyway."

Dirk spat in disgust. "Fine. Just make sure this doesn't hinder us from finding a comfortable place to stay tonight; otherwise, I will mention it to Mother."

Axel buried his forehead in his hand. "You're going to report me for helping a farmer? I have no doubt she'll be deeply distressed." He continued across the bridge, disgusted with the boy. When he reached the embankment, he introduced himself.

"It's a pleasure to meet you, Sir Axel. It's rare to see a knight all the way from Frostgarde. How fortunate to have a king's man appear at the perfect time. I'm Braun, and this is my son Bane. We need to hurry home so my wife can tend to his wounded foot."

Axel dismounted to inspect the scene while Dirk headed to the river to wash his clothes. There was no way to reattach the wheel without lifting the cart. The job required at least two men. "I'll lift the cart while you slide the wheel back on," he told the farmer.

Because of the muddy conditions, it was hard to find stable footing. Every time Axel attempted to lift the cart, his foot slid deeper into the mud, causing him to lose his grip. He cursed as he dropped the wagon a third time. "Oak and ashes! They picked a fine place to ambush you. This is going to be harder than I expected."

Braun stepped back to reassess the situation. "You won't be able to lift it with your feet in the mud. Let's gather some larger rocks and make a place for you to stand. Once you're on steady ground, it should be easier to maintain your footing."

Axel acknowledged it was a good plan as they collected rocks along the riverbank. "Look for flatter ones that aren't wet. A slippery stone is no better than standing in mud."

They gathered a sufficient number to construct a makeshift platform and tried again. After several failed attempts, Axel finally managed enough stability for Braun to reattach the wheel. Once it was secured, they harnessed the mule back to the cart.

Axel collapsed against the wagon, exhausted. Sweat poured down his face, and he discovered fresh mud on his uniform. With impeccable timing, Dirk approached and said he was ready to leave. Axel scowled. "I still need to wash my clothes and rest a bit. That was our purpose for stopping."

Dirk pouted like a petulant child. "Yes, and I am now

clean and refreshed. It's not my fault you chose to spend your time playing in the mud. I want to go to the inn now."

Axel was so angry he forgot his weariness. With a burst of energy, he rose to his feet and seized Dirk's shoulders, shaking him. "You spoiled piece of shit. If I weren't so tired right now, I would teach you some respect. I'm going to——"

"Easy, Sir Axel," Braun interjected. "I understand how you feel, but it's obvious you're both road weary and in need of a break. It will be at least another day's ride before you find an inn on this road. We would be honored to have you as our guests on our farm. It's only a few hours ahead. I can't promise a bed, but I can offer shelter in my barn. You'll have that warm bath, and my wife bakes the best kidney pie you've ever eaten. We are indebted to you and would like to repay the favor by extending our hospitality."

Axel released the boy as relief flooded through him. "That sounds wonderful. Do you have any objections, Dirk? It's the best offer we'll get today."

He continued to sulk, but conceded. "Fine, but this was not our agreement. You still owe me a night at an inn. When I asked for a comfortable evening, I didn't envision a peasant's farm."

Rolling his eyes, Axel looked at Braun, embarrassed. "Thank you. We accept your offer." His expression, however, conveyed a different sentiment, apologizing for his companion's attitude.

Braun grinned and jumped on the cart. "Excellent,

Martene will be so happy. We hardly ever get visitors. If you can wait to wash yourself, I can promise a more pleasant bath than what you will find here."

Axel nodded and prepared to leave. Braun assumed the lead as Bane sat in the back of the wagon, his injured leg stretched out in front of him.

They rode along the smooth road for the next few hours. At a clearing near a clustered rock formation, Braun steered them onto a smaller path that led to a group of fields bordering the nearby forest. Axel tallied four little cottages and inferred that it was a small agricultural community where residents shared the responsibility of farming and crop upkeep. They approached a cottage surrounded by a garden of blooming flowers. Smoke billowed from the chimney, signaling that dinner was already in progress. Through an open window, Axel saw a heavyset woman with her hair in a bun, wearing an apron and sweating over a simmering stove. He could already smell the delicious scent of garlic and onion, causing his stomach to growl.

They paused in front, and Braun directed them to take the horses to the barn while he went inside. Axel and Dirk dismounted and escorted their animals to a dilapidated building near the field. It was old and weathered, but the roof was still intact. They fastened the horses outside near a trough and allowed them to drink. They were so exhausted they didn't notice the piles of mule dung scattered nearby, and both stepped in it. Axel sighed and calmly scraped it off while Dirk cried, "Ew, disgusting! This day keeps getting worse and it's all your fault. We shouldn't be here."

Axel told him to just be thankful they had a comfortable place to rest for the night. Dirk was too preoccupied cleaning his boots and cursing to listen, shooting an angry glance at Axel. They headed back to the cottage.

Martene bolted from the door and ran to the wagon, where Bane still lay. "My poor baby, are you okay?" Bane blushed as his mother showered him with kisses. She beamed at Axel in appreciation. "Thank you so much, sir knight. Welcome to our home. It may not be much, but you are welcome to whatever we have."

A warm smile radiated across Axel's face. It was gratifying to help a family in need and be acknowledged for it. He wished more people were like them. "Just being helpful, ma'am. I'm sure anyone passing by would have done the same. I could use a place to wash up before we eat, though."

"Of course," Braun interjected. "Martene, please draw our guest a warm bath. By the time he's done, the pie should be ready. The scent is already making my mouth water."

She gestured for Axel to follow her. "You don't need to be humble, sir. Most people would have ignored them. The city folk from Verone turn up their noses at the thought of helping us. People in this area take care of each other because we know it's all we have. Now, let's get you that bath."

Axel gave Dirk a dirty look and followed Martene

behind the cottage. She drew water from a nearby well and brought it inside to heat on the stove. As he waited, he couldn't help but admire the stunning flowers that enveloped the cottage. Near the garden's edge, a log bench was positioned near a small pond. He took a seat and inhaled a deep breath of crisp country air, gazing upon the water. He marveled at the large white flowers floating on the surface of the pond. There was nothing like that in Koenigsberg.

Martene returned, telling him his bath was ready, then took a seat beside him. "It's beautiful, isn't it? This is the place where I can be at peace. The flowers are flourishing this time of year."

A gentle breeze blew past, causing the blossoms on the water to sway. "It's breathtaking. The wind must blow them there from your garden."

She stared at him with a raised eyebrow. "Have you never seen a lotus?"

Axel's ears perked up. "That's a lotus? No, I've never seen one. How do they survive in the water?"

"They grow in the soil like any other plant, except they live underwater. When in bloom, their flower rises beneath the water and floats on the surface. They take in the light and warmth of the sun, only to return to the ground when night falls."

He was intrigued and eager to connect it to the Alchemist Creed. "Do they only grow in water? Have you ever heard of a lotus field?"

She erupted in a fit of laughter. "A field of lotus?

That's absurd. Yes, they only grow underwater. Where did you hear of something so silly?"

Axel's chest tightened. What if he'd risked exposing his interest in alchemy? "I've never heard of flowers that grow in water like this. How often do they bloom?"

"From my understanding, they thrive in warmer weather. They bloom in the summer before it gets too hot and go dormant in the winter chill." She stood and headed for the house. "Let's get you to the bath before the water gets cold."

He followed, lost in thought. The Alchemist Creed referenced winter and a lotus field.

> *To the north where winter blows*
> *Gold is found where knowledge flows*
> *Within the lotus field found*
> *An open mind no longer bound*

Everything Martene explained contradicted this verse. Perhaps alchemy was more than just transmuting base metal to gold. If an alchemist could do something that complicated, then growing a summer flower in cold weather shouldn't be difficult.

Axel disrobed and got in the bath. Before clearing away the mud, he took a moment to unwind and savor the calming warmth of the water, his muscles loosening as his body gradually released tension. After his bath, he washed his clothes and left them to dry on a large rock. He dressed in his spare clothes and joined the others for supper.

Braun and the two boys were already seated as Martene finished her final preparations. The delicious aroma wafting from the pie engulfed the room. Braun motioned for him to sit beside him. "Perfect timing. Now we can eat."

Martene wrapped the dish in a large towel and brought it to the table, before slicing it into eight triangular wedges. "We don't have enough for all of you to have two slices, but I know someone who is getting a second." She selected two thick slices and placed them on Axel's plate. The rest began with one.

Dirk and Axel were ravenous and tore into their meal. The room was silent as they all focused on eating. Dirk was the first one done and received a fresh slice from Martene. When Braun finished his portion, he wiped his mouth and asked Axel, "So, what brings a couple of knights all the way from Frostgarde into Baron Helmuth's territory?"

Axel swallowed a mouthful as he dug into his second slice. "I'm accompanying our recruit to Verone, where he has important family matters to attend to. I'll stay there for a few days before returning home." Dirk looked at him cockeyed while Axel rubbed his shoulder.

"We don't see many knights from Frostgarde or Verone much these days. The former baron used to have soldiers stationed along these roads, ensuring safe passage for travelers. However, Baron Helmuth believes that there is no need to patrol such a large area and opts to keep them closer to home." Braun scoffed as he spoke, disgust evident in his voice. "Rumors of tension with the crown are rampant, and the baron maintains a standing army in the city. With no one safeguarding the roads, raiders have become more commonplace, and us simple folk are left to fend for ourselves. Did you encounter any bandits on your journey?"

Axel shook his head. "No, we haven't. I guess we were lucky."

Braun chuckled. "Or they were smart enough to stay out of the way of two knights. Do you ever get a chance to speak with the king? Perhaps you could let him know what's going on and make sure he knows that Baron Helmuth is neglecting his responsibility to protect his people. Isn't that his primary obligation? Each baron is accountable for the governance and protection of the individuals within their district. Baron Helmuth keeps raising our taxes without providing protection or support. Maybe having the crown's attention will change his attitude."

Axel almost choked on his food when he noticed Dirk's face turning crimson while shooting daggers at Braun. Banc, who'd remained silent for most of their visit, chose the most inopportune time to speak up. "If the baron can't protect his subjects, the king should find a new baron that does, right, Dad?" As he looked at his father, his eyes lit up with pride and a smile adorned his face.

Dirk's anger had reached its boiling point as he leaped from his chair, his eyes locked onto the family with a menacing glare. "You wretched peasants, living in squalor amidst piles of shit! The baron's responsibilities are far greater than you can imagine. His concerns extend well beyond your meaningless farm. Compared to the city, this place is a sanctuary. If you experienced the threat of the real world, then you could understand." His eyes were bloodshot, and passionate spittle escaped from his mouth as he spoke. "Consider yourselves lucky that he allows you to keep any of your crops, instead of donating them to someone more deserving."

Without consideration, Axel backhanded him, knocking him into his chair. "Calm yourself, boy!" He sneered, his tone becoming threatening. "You are a guest in their home and will treat them with respect. You are oblivious of what the average person goes through, living a life of privilege while demanding others be more grateful. Have some humility, you arse."

Braun's family looked at each other, bewildered by the situation unfolding before them. Dirk glowered at Axel with seething hatred. "How dare you lay a hand on me. You know who I am. I told you not to stop for these peasants, but you ignored me. You neglected your duty and stayed silent as they insulted my uncle—and then have the audacity to attack me after I did your job! My mother is going to hear how you were plotting against Verone."

Axel was furious. This little shit was nothing but a thorn in his side. He was a useless, petulant child that had been coddled for far too long. "What makes you think I'll take you home with that attitude? I should leave you here and return to Koenigsberg. If you want me to finish this assignment, then get out of my sight and stop bothering these poor people."

Dirk threw his remaining pie on the floor and stormed out of the cottage, slamming the door. Axel tried to get his temper under control as he sat back down with the family. "I'm sorry about that. You deserve better. It's never acceptable to speak to someone that way, regardless of who they are." He took another bite of pie, but his appetite was gone.

Braun cleared his throat as he gathered his composure. "Think nothing of it. Obviously, we didn't know who he was or we wouldn't have said anything. It's been tough on us, but we need to be more careful in airing our grievances. You've been so kind to us, and we don't want to get you in trouble."

Axel laughed at the irony. "I can find trouble all on my own with no assistance. This assignment is a direct consequence of an earlier blunder. I have managed to anger two barons now. I hope my commander thinks twice about giving me any more responsibilities involving the nobility." He pushed his plate of unfinished pie away. "Nothing against your cooking, Martene, but I've lost my appetite. It's been a tiring day, and I'm ready to retire and get some much-needed rest. Don't worry about us. We will be on our way by first light."

Braun tried to convince Axel to reconsider, but his mind was made up. He said his goodbyes and went to the barn. He searched for Dirk and saw a bundle of clothes pressed against the far wall, curled on a bed of straw. Axel chose a spot near the door, maximizing the distance between the two of them. As he stretched out and stared at the crumbling beams of the barn's roof, his anxiety grew at the prospect of reaching Verone. He never should have struck the boy. He'd let his temper get the better of him. This was not the way he wanted this assignment to end. If this was his opportunity to demonstrate his worth to Jurgen, he was clearly squandering it. Searching for the alchemist was looking more and more appealing.

# Chapter 13

## *Verone*

Verone's skyline appeared on the horizon as they neared the end of their trip. Like distant trees, towers jutted from the landscape, adding a sense of grandeur to the scenery. A sigh of relief escaped Axel's lips as he recognized his time with Dirk was coming to an end. The days were blurring together, but almost a week had passed since they'd left Braun's farm.

On the morning of their departure, they'd gotten into a heated argument before finding common ground. Axel believed all people, regardless of status, should be treated with respect until their actions proved otherwise. Dirk argued he had no grasp of the intricacies of ruling a barony. If they treated their subjects as equals, it would lead to greater input on how they were governed, but the people's selfishness and lack of education prevented them from acting in the best interest of the community. The baron's duty was to foster a sense of equality among the citizens, while also emphasizing their subordinate status.

Otherwise, the barony would devolve into a state of mob rule. Axel didn't agree with that sentiment. He believed each person had a right to pursue their own happiness. If individuals took responsibility for their own needs, they would be less reliant on help from others.

Axel now understood why Braun's conversation had provoked Dirk, triggering his outburst—it challenged his core belief. He could sympathize with Dirk's volatility and inclination to overreact. His father would disown him for his failure at Frostgarde. Their journey must have felt like an inevitable fate that grew heavier with each step. As they drew closer to their destination, Dirk grew increasingly irritable and demanding.

Verone was situated on the same river that flowed into Koenigsberg's harbor. Boat travel would have been significantly faster, but they were never afforded that option. Perhaps Dirk was trying to prolong the inevitable for as long as possible. Axel found the inland port to be much smaller than what he was accustomed to, with simple fishing boats and merchant barges docked along its waterway. There was no room for the giant vessels that crowded the seaside ports.

Verone was one of the smallest cities in the Vilsheim, with only Grimmdorf, isolated to the east, being less populated. Despite being on the river, it was surprisingly clean and devoid of the filth that often plagued the waterfront. That was probably why it didn't carry the typical foul odor that Axel was familiar with on sweltering days. Once he explained he was escorting the baron's nephew home, the guards ushered them in. The sheer number of guards on patrol took him by surprise. Apart from the visible guard stations, squads of soldiers actively marched through the city.

Dirk noticed him studying the patrols. "This is the primary reason my uncle cannot spare men for garrisons outside the city. He is a stickler for cleanliness and demands that Verone maintain its reputation as the safest city in the kingdom. The university attracts students from all over Vilsheim and beyond, and they need to be protected."

Axel understood the need to prioritize the students' safety. "Where is the university? I have heard it's what Verone is famous for."

"On the other side of town," Dirk replied, pointing down the main street. "You can see the library tower in the distance. It's my uncle's pride and joy. If the entire town went up in flames, his only concern would be that school." He was no longer irritable and appeared resigned to his fate.

"It's on my list to visit while I'm here. I was given a few days of leave, and wanted to use the time to explore the sights."

"Only students and teachers are allowed on campus. You might be allowed to visit the library if you have a compelling reason." Dirk took a deep breath and released a heavy sigh. "My home is down this way. Let's get this over with." He started hesitantly down the road, dragging his feet along the way.

Axel nodded as he contemplated how to gain entry to the library. Jurgen's letter, along with his uniform, was proof he served the king. Considering the consequences he would likely face for this assignment, what other repercussions might he suffer for continued deception?

A large gatehouse loomed ahead, and the guard stationed there watched them approach, suspicion evident in his eyes. As they drew near, he recognized the boy and saluted. "Welcome home, Lord Dirk. They didn't inform me you were returning today." It was obvious he was struggling to make sense of the situation.

Dirk scratched his head uncomfortably. "My father doesn't know I've come back. He will be as surprised as you. Do you know where I can find him?"

The guard shrugged as he opened the gate. "Try his study. It's where he spends most of his time these days."

Servants whispered in hushed tones as they made their way through the courtyard and into the main house. Dirk received greetings from a few of them, but the majority ignored him, clearly wary. They rushed past him, limiting contact while peeking around the corner and gossiping to each other. The house steward appeared, offering a chilling welcome that made Axel's skin crawl and said he would accompany them. They strolled around the expansive manor and were guided to a spacious room on the third floor that had a spectacular view of the city. "Pardon me, Lord Holzer. Your son, Lord Dirk, is here, accompanied by a knight from Frostgarde," the steward announced before swiftly departing and closing the door.

Lord Derek Holzer rose behind his desk, his sunken eyes considering them as he assessed the situation. His military uniform hung gracefully on his lean, well-proportioned frame. Axel perceived a man whose piercing gaze mirrored his heartless demeanor, leaving little room for compassion. "Welcome home, son," he said with an icy tone. "I wasn't expecting you so soon. Your commander neglected to notify me you were coming to Verone. Am I to assume your training did not go well?"

Dirk stared, petrified, his hands trembling. In a jittery voice, he replied, "Yes, Father. They dismissed me. Although I did my best, I was treated unfairly because of who I am. They were worried I was a spy for Uncle Kaiser."

"I'm sure they had good reason for discharging you. As we discussed, this wasn't a suitable position for you. I expected failure, but assumed you would endure longer than this. I hoped to have a few months to decide what comes next. Once again, you fell short of my already low expectations and left me with another mess. Do you recall what I told you would happen should you fail?" Dirk nodded as tears welled in his eyes.

Axel was taken aback at how callous the man was, prompting flashbacks of his own father. His stomach clenched into a knot when Lord Holzer sneered and turned his attention toward him. "Who might you be, and why are you here? I find it hard to believe a personal escort was needed for someone so incompetent."

Axel kept it simple, hoping to make a quick exit. "Axel Albrecht with the BlackGuard, sir. I have other business in the city, and because Lord Dirk is the nephew of Baron

Helmuth, my commander thought a personal escort was appropriate."

Lord Holzer clasped his hands behind his back and stepped forward. "You're a knight. Why don't you give me your assessment of Dirk's performance."

"I never worked with Dirk. I'm stationed inside the keep while new trainees are kept near the Boar's Gate at the entrance to Frostgarde. The only time I spent with him was during our travels, and I can assure you he caused me no trouble." He nodded to Dirk, offering a comforting smile.

Dirk appeared surprised at his brief account of the situation, but then his expression shifted to one of malice. With a wicked grin, he said, "Don't be afraid to tell him what you really think of me. I believe you referred to me as a spoiled child after punching me in the face." He looked at his father with pleading eyes. "After we crossed the river, he insisted we stop to help a peasant with his broken wagon. To express his gratitude, the peasant invited us to his house, where he advised Axel to speak to the king about the lack of security outside of Verone. Of course, I reassured them that Uncle is doing everything in his power to protect them, and it's the king who is negligent."

Lord Holzer turned to Axel, his eyes gleaming with intrigue, hungry for every detail. "Is this true? Did you favor a lowly peasant over my son and then strike him?"

Perspiration beaded on Axel's brow. This was not how he'd envisioned the conversation going. He was getting what he deserved for trying to bolster Dirk. "It was more of a slap. It was the least I could do, considering how he treated them. In Koenigsberg, we are taught to be respectful in another's home. Having just been robbed, the farmer expressed his rising concern about raiders and asked me to inform the king. Of course I would do no such thing, as it is not my place. It would have been better if your son had brought that information for you to discuss with Baron Helmuth, who could have handled it within his jurisdiction. Dirk's petulant attitude is precisely what kept him from succeeding at Frostgarde, and I assume it's the reason he was there in the first place."

Dirk tried responding before his father cut him off, causing the boy to cower. "You took the side of a peasant and assaulted a lord. A loyal knight would have demanded an apology and punished their disrespect. This was an act of treason, punishable by death. You should have executed them in the king's name."

This family was disgusting. Axel found the idea of mistreating kindhearted people utterly revolting. It was clear why the farmers had such intense hostility toward the baron. "Those were not my observations, sir. Despite their misfortune, these were charitable people, attempting to aid two weary travelers."

Lord Holzer shook his head. "Your opinion is irrelevant. Your admission of violence against my son is what concerns me. It appears I am dealing with the incompetence of not one, but two failures. Thank you for bringing this to my attention, son. I will ensure the baron understands the severity of the conditions outside the city. However, do not assume you can speak for him. You gathered valuable information, but as usual, you bungled it. As for you, Axel Albrecht, I will make a full report of this to Frostgarde. I'm sure the king will be interested to learn how his knights treat nobility when away from the castle. They can deal with you. You are dismissed."

He summoned the steward, who arrived so fast he must have been eavesdropping at the door. "Please escort this alleged knight from my home immediately."

The steward led him out via the servant's door on the side of the manor. After his tense exchange with Lord Holzer, Axel had almost forgotten his primary reason for coming to Verone. Before the door closed, he asked, "Could you direct me toward the university? I have business to attend there."

The steward gestured toward the same tower as Dirk before slamming the door. Axel winced, then shook his head. Relieved that he was done with this obnoxious family, he headed for the university. He was more determined than ever to learn about alchemy after that exchange.

He used the tower to guide him, but still found himself getting lost. He tried venturing down multiple alleys, but all led to dead ends. When he tried to ask for directions, he was met with hushed murmurs and stony stares. The townspeople were clearly uncomfortable with his BlackGuard uniform and kept their distance. It was easy to find the city center, but navigating through the maze of alleys was frustrating. After finding himself circling back to the same place for the third time, and spotting a boy begging for coin near a large fountain, he decided a child might be more open to helping him. He came forward and deposited two copper pieces into his clay bowl. "You can earn these by providing directions to the university library. I'll give you another silver if you take me there yourself."

The boy's eyes lit up when he heard silver. After studying Axel, he replied, "Sure, I'll take you. I bet you had a tough time finding anyone willing to talk to you in that uniform. Folks aren't too fond of the king around here. I'd be sure to watch my back if I was you."

Axel nodded, confirming he was right. They walked along the main road before ducking into an alley that he hadn't noticed earlier. He recalled watching a dispute between a carriage driver and merchant here earlier— they must have been blocking the entrance. As they drew closer to the university, he could see more of the tower, including its enormous base. Two soldiers in bright silver plate mail guarded the gates of the campus.

The boy stopped at the entrance. "Inform the guards you want to go to the library and they should allow you to pass. It's the only part of the university open to the public. Once you're past the gate, take a left and follow the path, which will take you directly there." Axel thanked the boy and gave him the silver piece he'd promised.

As he approached the guards, they exchanged skeptical glances before questioning him about his business at the school. He explained he was on official king's business, which involved conducting research at the library. The guards whispered to each other before allowing him entry. They informed him that weapons were prohibited on campus and instructed him to leave his at the gate. He hesitated before handing over his sword, along with the axe that hung from his belt. When asked if he had more, he reassured them that was everything. But he withheld his dagger, concealed along his upper arm, as he felt vulnerable with no form of protection.

The closer he got, the more he marveled at the library's awe-inspiring beauty, its elaborate architecture tempting him to delve into the secrets it held. It was unlike anything he had ever seen before. Massive stone steps led up to the main entrance, flanked by two statues representing the Koenig and Helmuth families: a boar and a falcon. Axel took a deep breath before opening the door and beginning his personal adventure into the mysterious field of alchemy.

He was greeted by a lengthy entryway, illuminated by a row of sconces and a huge, opulent chandelier. A large desk, flanked by two spiral staircases, stood in front of another doorway at the far end. Seated behind the desk was a young lady with spectacles perched upon her nose, her hair gathered in a bun atop her head. She was so engrossed in her book she didn't notice Axel approaching. He glanced at her cluttered desk and, buried between two stacks of books, he discovered a nameplate that read Greta - Front Desk.

He waited to be acknowledged. But when she continued to ignore him, Axel grew impatient and cleared his throat. When that failed, he said, "Excuse me, Greta. I am interested in visiting the library. Is there any further information required for me to enter?"

Without glancing up, she replied, "What business does a king's knight have in the library?"

Axel already had his story prepared. "I am in Verone on official business, acting on behalf of the king. Ever since I was a child, I've loved reading, and I couldn't pass on the opportunity to peruse the largest collection of books in Vilsheim. The amount of knowledge contained in a single location is remarkable."

Greta put her quill down and folded her arms. "I didn't think it was necessary for knights to read. I thought they valued physical strength more than intellectual ability."

His jaw dropped in complete astonishment at her lack of respect. Other than the boy who'd guided him here, everyone in the city had been cold and unwelcoming. Already on edge, the last thing he needed was attitude from a girl working the front desk. "I thought it was open to the public. Please, just allow me in and I'll be out of your way."

She sneered as she pushed her glasses up. "You are mistaken. The university is owned and operated by the taxpayers of Verone. Therefore, the library is open to all the city's residents. It's closed to outsiders without authorization. If you don't have any actual business other than your boyish curiosity, please leave."

He was appalled at her rudeness and couldn't help raising his voice. "In case you hadn't heard, the crown executed an alchemist last month. As a result, the public's interest in alchemy has grown. I was tasked with investigating any books on alchemy that are still housed here."

But Greta just shook her head, pursing her lips. "So your official business is at the library, and you're here to learn about alchemy?" She chuckled to herself. "Why would the king choose a knight rather than a scholar to handle such matters? I find your story dubious. I can't quite put my finger on it, but there's something suspicious about you."

Axel was having a hard time keeping his temper in check. "Now you're accusing me of being a liar? Should I read you something out loud to prove that I'm not an ignorant buffoon?" He was ready to insult her own intelligence when he remembered the note from Jurgen. Instead of arguing, he reached into his pocket and handed her the document. "Here's your proof."

She snatched the letter from his hand, casting a skeptical glance. She noted the king's seal before reading aloud: "'The bearer of this letter is on official king's business. Please give them your full cooperation. Failure to do so violates the king's order and will be met with harsh punishment. King Otto von Koenig.'" Next to his name was another seal, further validating its authenticity. "I'm familiar with official documentation, and this appears authentic. However, it still doesn't explain why you are here."

He grabbed the note and stuffed it back in his cloak. "It isn't supposed to give details. Not everyone is privy to the king's affairs. You need only know I'm here on his behalf and that you're to assist me as I require. Now, please direct me to where I can find the books on alchemy."

Greta grunted before saying, "Through the door, up eight flights to the top floor. You'll find a section on magic, mythology, and other fairy tales. Any books left on alchemy will be there. I must warn you that our information on the subject is limited, as most of it was destroyed when the practice was outlawed. You're welcome to look through our selection, but don't remove any books. They are university property and may not leave the library."

After confirming his understanding, she motioned for him to enter. He brushed past her, taking one last look before going up the stairs. Greta's head was already buried in her book again, as if the interaction had never taken place. Now that he had used the king's authorization, there was no turning back. If word got back to Frostgarde that a knight had inquired about alchemy at the university, he would surely be discovered. He would need to remain vigilant from now on, watch for anything suspicious.

# Chapter 14

## *The Great Library*

As Axel ascended the staircase, he couldn't help but marvel at the grandeur of the architecture. The size of each floor was comparable to the plaza where he'd encountered his guide. He was excited to explore the library and pour over the wealth of knowledge contained within its walls and found it difficult to stay focused as he encountered a plethora of intriguing subjects that piqued his interest. Despite the temptation, he ignored thousands of books on history, science, and literature that he was eager to delve into.

The top floor felt claustrophobic in comparison, accompanied by a lingering musty scent. The low ceiling forced him to hunch over, while the dim lighting made it difficult to see. The room felt more like a storage area, filled with less prominent books. With no signs to direct him, he wandered up and down the aisles, scanning the shelves for a title to catch his eye. Greta had said it was in the magic and mythology section, so that was what he sought. Frustrated from browsing with no success, he sat at a table littered with stacks of books to consider other options. His primary goal was finding any alchemy-related texts, while books about the lotus were secondary. If he could find nothing on alchemy, he would head to the botany section to learn more about the flower.

Once he sat down, exhaustion overcame him. It had been an emotional day, and he decided to rest a moment to regain his focus. He pushed some books aside to lay his head down. His eyes grew heavy, and he dozed off until he was jolted awake by the loud crash of a book hitting the floor. He must have knocked one off the table while he was asleep. Once he regained his bearings, he rose and paced to energize himself, perusing nearby shelves. A book titled The Mythological History of Vilsheim caught his attention. He pulled the book out and scanned the table of contents. His interest piqued when he saw a chapter titled The Abolition of Alchemy and settled in to read it.

One hundred and fifty years ago, Vilsheim had been hit with a disease that ravaged the seasonal harvest, affecting the individuals who relied on those crops as their winter food source and the livestock raised for meat and dairy production. Underfed animals were prematurely butchered, producing smaller quantities of meat than normal. The peasants were starving and demanded relief from their king. King Ferdinand von Koenig was desperate to help his citizens and was forced to request aid from foreigners overseas. Knowing that Vilsheim was in dire straits, the other kingdom increased their prices to take full advantage of Ferdinand's tenuous position. To generate additional revenue, the king was forced to raise taxes, further incensing his already angry constituents, who were on the verge of revolting.

Ferdinand looked for alternative means to fund his endeavor, including magic. While his advisors discouraged this idea, they acknowledged the desperate times required extreme measures. A group of alchemists at the University of Verone were experimenting with chemistry and believed they had found the secret to transmuting lead and tin into gold. Ferdinand ordered an alchemist to come to Frostgarde and show him in person. The master alchemist in charge of the project, Starholf, traveled to Koenigsberg and attempted to transform a block of lead ore into gold.

He failed to produce the gold but assured the king that he was close. He requested a laboratory where he could continue refining the process until he achieved success. Ferdinand agreed and spared no expense in obtaining the finest equipment available for the alchemist to conduct his experiments. With the crown's backing, Starholf worked day and night trying to transmute the lead but failed over and over. After a few months, with nothing to show for his efforts, Ferdinand demanded that the alchemist produce gold or suffer severe punishment.

Starholf received one last opportunity to perform his experiment in front of the king. But his final attempt ended in disaster as he set off a massive explosion, destroying his lab and inflicting severe burns on Ferdinand. The enraged king accused him of being a fraud and ordered that he be publicly executed for dishonoring the crown. Furthermore, alchemy was designated as dark sorcery and banned across the realm. He terminated the university's alchemy program and had all relevant materials on the subject destroyed. The king decreed that from that day forward practicing alchemy was punishable by death.

Axel considered how this information could aid in his investigation. He was already aware that the original alchemist had been executed for failing at gold transmutation, but he couldn't understand why there wasn't more information on his methods. Had he ever explained his process, or had everything been destroyed in the explosion? Maybe the entire story was a lie. If the alchemist had failed, why did he need to die? Yes, the Koenigs were merciless and wouldn't hesitate to dispose of someone who displeased them. But then why outlaw it after this incident? What if the alchemist had actually succeeded, and the king wanted to prevent others from benefiting? Axel tugged his hair in frustration. Instead of finding answers, he had even more questions.

After returning the book to the shelf, he scanned the adjacent ones, discovering additional volumes on mythology, along with a few that were just fairy tales, but nothing more about alchemy. Faced with a dead end, he decided to expand his knowledge on the lotus. He moved to the science department on the third floor and located the botany section. There was an extensive selection of books on specific plants, including roses, tulips, and dahlias, but nothing about the lotus. He stumbled upon a book about aquatic plants and sat beneath a brightly lit sconce to flip through its pages until he discovered a chapter on water lilies and lotuses.

While similar, they were two distinct plants that grew beneath the water in their own unique way. Water lilies flowered on the surface and remained that way until they went dormant. Lotuses, however, grew underwater and flowered on the surface each day. At night, the lotus blossom would close and retreat to the bottom before rising again the next day. Its flower colors varied from red, yellow, blue, purple, and white, the white being the most prevalent. The lotus was also regarded as a symbol of enlightenment in certain regions outside of Vilsheim. None of this applied to Axel's quest and the flower's potential use in alchemy. Perhaps the pigment in a yellow lotus was a fundamental ingredient in the transmutation process.

He validated Martene's comment that they only grew in warm water, proving that a lotus field was not possible, while confirming they blossomed during the summer. He recalled the Alchemist Creed:

> *To the north where winter blows*
> *Gold is found where knowledge flows*
> *Within the lotus field found*
> *An open mind no longer bound*

Everything he'd learned thus far contradicted this passage. He sought a lotus field in a frigid environment. Axel slammed the book shut in frustration. Another dead end. He chose to keep the book on aquatic plants and revisit the section on alchemy. This time, he would focus on what the lotus represented in mythology.

Axel returned to the top floor and pulled out The Mythological History of Vilsheim once again. He reread the chapter on alchemy, looking for clues he might have overlooked, but found nothing new. He groaned in frustration. The library contained too much knowledge to not have more information on the subject. He poured through the mythology section, as well as the surrounding bookcases, hoping something had been misplaced. He was so engrossed in his search that he hardly registered a voice from behind, inquiring if he needed help. Startled, he turned to find himself face-to-face with an old man dressed in a plain red robe. The few strands of hair that clung to his head were swept back, creating a halo-like effect around his balding head and emphasizing his long snow-white beard.

The man extended a warm smile. "I'm Gottfried, one of the librarians. At least for now." He chuckled to himself. "Despite being told I'm too old and should retire, I continue showing up. I've been here so long, it's all I know. They think I'm a senile old fool and keep me on the top floor to stay out of their way—few folks come up here. I've forgotten more books than most have read, so if you're looking for something specific, I can probably find it."

Axel hesitated as he determined how much he should disclose. Gottfried recognized his reluctance and studied the open books on the table. "What is that you're reading?" he asked as he leafed through the books. "I've learned a lot, thanks to my innate curiosity. Sometimes it leads me to delve into controversial subjects that could get me into trouble. You wouldn't know anything about that, now, would you?"

The man was observant, with an affable quality that made Axel want to trust him. "Unfortunately, I'm all too familiar with that behavior. What is your intuition telling you now?"

Gottfried continued thumbing through the books. "You are interested in alchemy and botany, perhaps studying science. This book is specifically about aquatic plants, so I think you have something else in mind. Your uniform tells me you are a knight of Frostgarde. The king recently executed an alchemist, and that likely sparked your curiosity to learn more on the subject. I'm unclear why you're in Verone, though."

Axel explained his mission to escort Dirk. During his visit to Verone, he was to investigate any remaining books pertaining to alchemy at the library. Gottfried smiled with his eyes and nodded. "Okay, it's probably safest to stick to that story. Sadly, there is not much available about the subject. In fact, that book contains the only approved information on the topic. As I'm sure you've read, it was outlawed many years ago, and King Ferdinand barred the university from providing any further education on it. All books mentioning alchemy were removed from the library and burned. The king wanted it abolished and went to great lengths to ensure it happened."

Axel nodded. "Well, that explains why I haven't been

able to find anything useful. That's what Greta said, but I was hoping I'd come across something. What happened to the students that were studying alchemy?"

Gottfried released a long sigh and stroked his beard. "That's a rather unfortunate story. All the alchemy students at the university, along with their masters, were seized and turned over to the king. Although there was no official confirmation, it is widely speculated that they were quietly executed. The king ensured all the knowledge was destroyed and alchemy could no longer be practiced."

"That's awful. With no books or masters to preserve it, it's no wonder that there's nothing to be found." Axel hung his head, fearing he had reached an impasse.

Gottfried nodded in agreement, becoming quiet. He scanned the room before approaching Axel and whispering in his ear, "Rumor has it that an alchemist's apprentice escaped the university prior to their capture and smuggled a book out before fleeing the city. It is uncertain whether he managed to escape or was eventually apprehended."

Axel's interest was sparked. "Any idea where he went?"

"From what I heard, he fled north toward Coburg. However, he is long dead now, and whatever mysteries he held must have died with him. Unless he trained others in secret."

A rush of energy surged through Axel at the mention of Coburg. It was the same place the merchant had suggested. "Do you think it's possible he got away and started a secret society?"

Gottfried shrugged. "I don't know about a secret society, but considering an alchemist was just executed, it makes me suspect something was passed down."

His excitement was palpable. Gottfried's information was much more useful than anything he'd learned from the books. He considered how much trust he should place in the old man, but realizing he had nothing to lose, other than his head, he broached his next question with trepidation. "Have you heard of the Alchemist Creed?"

Gottfried's eyes gleamed, and a grin spread across his face. "That would explain why you are interested in aquatic plants. Prior to escaping, the apprentice left a mysterious message for his master, revealing how to find him. Despite the king's attempts to destroy it, the message survived and became known as the Alchemist Creed. How much do you know of it?"

Axel recited the verse, desperate to learn more about its meaning. "What does a lotus have to do with alchemy, and where would I find a field of them?"

"While I find the topic intriguing, I must admit my knowledge of alchemy is quite limited. I don't understand how it works. I do know there is another verse that goes:

> *In the mountain pass up high*
> *Through the stone up on its side*
> *Guarded by the pines in kind*
> *A hidden vale for you to find."*

Astonished, Axel gasped as another piece of the puzzle materialized. Coburg had been mentioned by two individuals, and beyond it, there were mountains that served as the boundary of the kingdom. "It appears my next destination is Coburg. You have been most helpful, Gottfried. It would mean a lot if you could keep this discussion between us. We inquisitive types need to look out for one another, right?" He gripped Gottfried's shoulder and gave it a friendly shake.

Gottfried shrugged, gesturing with his open palms. "I'm an old man who easily forgets things. It's doubtful I'll even remember meeting you." He gave a sly wink. "It's nice to be of use, and I'm delighted to help. I wish you the best of luck in your adventure, wherever it takes you."

Axel clasped his hand and shook it. "Goodbye, Gottfried. It was a pleasure meeting you." It was time to leave and find accommodations for the night. He'd gotten what he was looking for from the university and needed to think about his next steps.

As he left the library, his rumbling stomach reminded him he needed to eat. He still hadn't visited an inn since leaving Koenigsberg, and a hot meal followed by a comfortable bed sounded perfect. He asked the university guards for a recommendation, and they gave him a couple of options in Verone's main plaza.

Axel made his way back through the city by retracing his earlier route. After roaming through a narrow alley, he found an inn called The Eagle's Nest that looked quiet. A sign above the door advertised stew served in a bread bowl as their specialty. His mouth watered at the thought of a hearty dinner. On his way in, a familiar-looking face drew his attention around the corner of the building. A man with short black hair hurried down the alley. Axel wasn't interested in the affairs of others, but given his potential trouble, he decided to investigate. Now that he'd inquired about alchemy, he was becoming increasingly paranoid. Besides, there was something familiar about the man that he couldn't quite place. Since he had never been to Verone, it was unlikely that he knew anyone here.

With his hand resting on his sword, Axel explored the alley but discovered nothing out of the ordinary. Other than a beggar resting against the building, it was empty. He proceeded through the alley and cautiously glanced around the corner, uncovering no traces of anything suspicious. It had been a long, emotional day, and he must have been imagining things. He needed to relax.

The Eagle's Nest was empty except for a handful of university students. He sat at a table in the back and made himself comfortable. The waitress taking his order was both attractive and flirtatious. She pointed out how refreshing it was to serve a real man rather than the timid, scholarly type that frequented the tavern. Axel blushed but stumbled over his words as he attempted to flirt. She giggled and took his order for stew and a large mug of ale.

He settled in, feeling at ease, and pondered his next move. Insulting Amelia had landed him in trouble, but things would only get worse once Jurgen learned of his failure with Dirk. He would not appreciate hearing about another problem from Axel. The king was sure to find out as well. He wondered how he would be punished. Would they imprison or even execute him? Both seemed severe, considering neither Amelia or Dirk were done physical harm. They could rescind his knighthood and discharge him from Frostgarde. Ever since he joined the Black-Guard, he'd garnered nothing but negative attention. Jurgen likely believed he wasn't suited for the keep.

Dismissing him sounded like the ideal solution. He would no longer be there to cause trouble for the king. And if he was going to be dismissed, what was the point of going back to Koenigsberg? He had no purpose in life if he returned to Frostgarde as a failure. His only viable option was to focus on his quest and travel to Coburg. With nothing left to lose, he would head there in the morning.

The waitress returned with Axel's ale, which he promptly drained. He was in the mood to unwind, and getting drunk seemed like a good idea. He ordered another ale when she brought his bowl, still steaming hot. The spice of the meat and the thick broth of the stew was filling and delicious. He used the bread to soak up any remaining liquid and devoured the whole thing. The sign on the inn was indeed accurate.

He downed another ale before asking the waitress about a room. There was one available, so he took it, along with a bath to refresh himself. Aroused by the alcohol and emboldened by the waitress's flirtatious behavior, he asked her to join him. Her face flushed bright red, and she became apprehensive. Although she declined his advance, he remained in good spirits. He felt utterly drained, and the thought of a long, hot bath followed by a restful night's sleep sounded divine.

# Chapter 15

## *Retaliation*

Axel woke the following morning feeling revitalized after his first good night's sleep in weeks. He longed to burrow deeper in the cozy bed, but he wanted to get an early start. While lying awake last night, he'd made another decision: he would not abandon his post without advising Jurgen. Before leaving Verone, he would dispatch a raven, summarizing the circumstances with Dirk and emphasizing a much-needed break before he returned to Frostgarde. He hoped the detailed explanation would clarify the situation and allow them ample time to forget about him.

He started his day by enjoying a savory meal of smoked sausage and fried eggs. Once he hit the road, he would be relegated to dried meat and stale bread again. Unable to locate the waitress from the previous night, he asked the innkeeper where to find a messenger raven. The man suggested the baron's office if it pertained to the king's business, but after Axel explained it was personal, he was directed to the rookery used by nobles who didn't own their own birds.

He located the rookery and carefully crafted his message before sending it, ensuring it was directed for Jurgen's eyes only. Despite his skepticism about how his commander would react, he felt unburdened by informing him. He was told the raven would take a few days to arrive, but delivering messages to Frostgarde was common, so there shouldn't be any issues. His final stop was the city stables, where his horse was being kept. He left the palfrey that Dirk had ridden behind. The crown kept a strict count on all their holdings, including the livestock. Baron Helmuth would send a messenger to the king at some point, and the horse would be returned then. He paid the stable master before mounting his horse and heading north from Verone.

As soon as he left the stable, Axel sensed he was being watched. He kept his eyes open, scanning his surroundings for signs of potential danger. Even though he found nothing out of the ordinary, a lingering sensation in his gut suggested something was amiss. The feeling subsided once he left Verone, but he couldn't stop dwelling on it.

His initial thought was that Dirk's father had sent someone to monitor him. Perhaps they were suspicious that he was involved in something nefarious on the king's behalf. The prospect of being under the baron's surveillance intensified his fear. Baron Helmuth might have ordered it if his relationship with the king had deteriorated that much. If someone was tailing him, those would be the most likely reasons, but no matter how silly it seemed, Gunter always came to mind whenever he was paranoid. Of course, approval from Jurgen or the chancellor would be required for that. There was no reason to send another knight unless they lacked confidence in his ability to complete the assignment.

Gunter might have his own reason to spy on Axel, but for what purpose? Memories of the conversation he'd overheard at the queen's ball resurfaced. He'd been so engrossed in the merchants' gossip that he was oblivious to Gunter watching him. He became nauseous at the realization. Gunter suspected his interest in alchemy and could use it to get rid of him once and for all. He was spiteful, but Axel didn't think he would go to such lengths to track him. On the other hand, if he had credible proof of Axel's true intent, he could have been ordered to follow him. He cursed himself for being ridiculous. He was letting his contempt fuel his wild imagination. Had Gunter's vindictiveness escalated to the point of wishing him dead?

A xel was bored at his post on the Queen's Curtain. Although he appreciated the solitude, there were moments when he longed for the excitement at the Boar's Gate. Tonight, the sky was clear and illuminated with twinkling stars. While such nights were a blessing in the warmer seasons, they became a curse during the cold winter days. The cloudless sky allowed the daytime heat to escape, resulting in a sharp drop in temperature. As the highest point in Koenigsberg, the Queen's Curtain stood tall upon the hill, making it vulnerable to the biting gusts of wind that blew around it. Despite the lack of fresh snow, frost clung to the stone wall, causing it to glisten in the moonlight. To stay warm, he huddled near the roaring fire in his tower. It was time to embark on his hourly round along the freezing battlement.

He began his final patrol of the night—already one more than he'd been scheduled for. As his commanding officer, Gunter handled the schedule and had designated himself as Axel's relief. He abused his authority to torment Axel; not only was Axel given the least desirable shifts, but Gunter always arrived late, forcing him to work extended hours.

He stepped outside and was met with a gust of freezing wind that sent a chill through his body. With his wolf's pelt engulfing him, he navigated his way across the wall. The city possessed an eerie quietness at this hour. It was the dead of night, when the taverns had closed and the bakers and fishermen were still sound asleep. Only a few scattered lights flickered below, and without the moonlight, he would have been shrouded in darkness.

He took slow, deliberate steps, mindful of the frozen patches that dotted the walkway. Several knights had slipped and injured themselves. This was one of the first lessons he was taught when he joined the Watchmen. He'd heard the story of an inattentive knight who lost his footing, tumbled over the wall, and plunged to his death. Axel doubted its authenticity, suspecting it was a cautionary tale designed to encourage vigilance. A shiver ran down his spine as another powerful gust swept past. He was cold and tired and prayed Gunter would be there by the time he returned to the tower.

He finished his patrol to the opposite tower and headed back to his post. In his haste to escape the biting cold, he lost his footing on an icy patch. He tried to grab the parapet, but ended up cutting his hand on its rough edge. While trying to maintain his balance, he twisted his right knee and landed on his arse. He clutched his leg as a searing pain shot through it. He cursed his carelessness, massaging his knee until the shooting pain subsided, resentment simmering within him. Instead of being in bed, he was stuck doing additional rounds because of Gunter.

The cold chilled his bones, urging him to get inside near the fire. He pulled himself up, bracing against the parapet. With caution, he eased his weight onto his left leg while gently lowering his right foot. He agonized at the excruciating pain as he limped across the battlement, leaning against the wall for support.

Suddenly, a flash in the blackened sky caught his attention. As he peered over the wall, a faint outline of a large ship came into focus. Although ships rarely entered the port at night, it was not unheard of. However, this boat differed from any he had seen before. It appeared to be anchored in the bay rather than progressing to the docks. It wasn't a royal ship and bore no resemblance to any merchant vessel he had ever seen. Though it was probably nothing, his standing orders were to present anything suspicious to his shift commander. If his shift commander was unavailable, he should report to Commander Leopold.

Was it necessary to sound the alarm about a single unfamiliar ship? He wasn't sure. But he was incensed about his injured leg, so he decided to report the anomaly to Leopold if Gunter hadn't arrived yet. If the commander asked about Gunter, he would explain that his whereabouts were unknown. It was better to be cautious rather than regretful. In the worst-case scenario, he would be considered a fool. However, if it was something nefarious, he would be commended. In either case, Leopold would be upset Gunter wasn't there to handle it.

He quickened his pace, being extra cautious of other potential slick spots. His heart raced as he hoped Gunter hadn't reached the tower before him. This was a golden opportunity to seek revenge without being perceived as a snitch. It was frowned upon to inform on other knights unless there was compelling justification. He arrived at his station to find it empty. He rang the bell beside the staircase, signaling the Watchman below that help was needed. Those stationed atop the Curtain could not leave their post for any reason, so runners were employed to handle urgent communication.

The knight on duty rushed upstairs, demanding an explanation. Axel explained the situation and proposed that he corroborate it on his own. After the guard acknowledged it looked suspicious, Axel told him to notify Commander Leopold as soon as possible. The knight wanted to avoid waking their superior and asked where Gunter was. Axel explained he hadn't arrived and that protocol dictated they follow their chain of command. He promised the Watchman that he would take responsibility for disturbing Leopold. With the assurance that he wouldn't bear any blame, the knight consented before hurrying away to fetch their leader.

Axel took advantage of the fire to relax and soothe his throbbing leg. He massaged the aching muscles around his knee to release the pain while waiting for Leopold or Gunter to show up. It made little difference who arrived first at this point. Thoughts of vengeance raced through his mind as his plan to undermine Gunter was set in motion. With his reputation as one of the Knights of Frostgarde's finest swordsmen, Gunter enjoyed a certain leniency about his conduct. Even though he was difficult to manage, his extraordinary talent couldn't be over-looked, allowing him to exploit his status to the fullest. Everyone on the Curtain knew he was being groomed for the IceGuard. Not only would his swordsmanship be put to good use, but the removal of his tongue would make him far less disagreeable. He wouldn't dare misbehave in the king's presence.

After what felt like an eternity, Axel heard footsteps clambering up the stairs. He only heard one pair, so he assumed it was Gunter. He braced himself for confrontation as the door burst open. "There better be a damn good reason for rousing me in the dead of night," Leopold said, scowling at Axel through bloodshot eyes. He was still dressed in his rumpled nightshirt, struggling to wake up.

Axel winced as he stood to salute. "I apologize, sir, but

there is a suspicious ship anchored in the bay, and I felt I should bring it to your attention." He braced himself before limping toward the door that led to the battlement. "Follow me and I will show you."

Leopold looked at him with concern. "What happened to your leg?"

Blushing in embarrassment, Axel's expression shifted to one of pity. "I slipped outside when I spotted the ship. I've never come across a vessel like this, and in my haste, I stumbled and twisted my knee. There's no need for concern, sir. I'll take care of it when this has been addressed."

Leopold nodded. "Where is Gunter? Shouldn't he be on duty by now?"

With wide eyes, Axel shrugged, his hands lifted in a gesture of confusion. "I don't know, sir. He hasn't arrived for his shift yet. I have been maintaining the watch until he arrives. Perhaps he has fallen ill." He blew it off as if it was of little consequence. Planting the seed was sufficient. "Better grab one of those furs. It's freezing out there."

After Leopold bundled himself, they stepped outside and Axel showed him the ship anchored in the bay. The sun began to emerge on the horizon, casting a gentle glow that made it easier to see. It was still difficult to identify the ship, but it was definitely foreign. Leopold conceded he had seen similar ships and was positive it wasn't a war galley. However, the king did not allow unexpected visitors, so all foreign ships were required to send advance notice before reaching Koenigsberg. This ship was deviating from the established procedure.

Axel followed Leopold back inside. "Well, Axel, I don't think it is anything to worry about, but without advanced warning, one can never be too careful. Under the circumstances, you did the right thing."

Axel beamed with self-satisfaction. In a subtle manner, he'd made Leopold aware of Gunter's negligence while being commended for his own actions. He was looking forward to witnessing Gunter's reaction upon discovering the truth. Fortunately, he strolled up the steps just in time.

"So sorry to be late, Axel, but I was dealing with some officer business that you wouldn't—" Gunter stopped mid-sentence when he spotted Leopold. His eyes widened as he snapped to attention and saluted. "Commander Leopold, what are you doing here, sir?"

Leopold, now alert, confronted Gunter, his voice laced with fury. "The question is why weren't you here. Because of your tardiness, Axel had to wake me to report this suspicious activity. If you were on time, you could have dealt with this. We have had discussions about this before, Gunter. I told you that lateness will not be tolerated." He glanced at Axel with sympathy. "You've had a long night. Why don't you go get some sleep. Given the way you've been moving, I suggest you rest before having your leg examined. Good work today."

Axel grinned at Gunter before making his way downstairs. His face twisted with fear, and his eyes smoldered. He knew he was in trouble. Taking pleasure in the countless times Gunter had belittled and humiliated him, Axel chuckled as he descended the staircase. It was time for Gunter to endure his share of hardships.

Their relationship had always been strained, and the more they interacted, the stronger Axel's revulsion grew. He'd gotten his revenge by deliberately discredited Gunter, leading to his demotion by Commander Leopold. Gunter had never forgiven him and had promised Axel would pay when he least expected it. Yes, Gunter had a motive for wanting him dead.

# Chapter 16

## *Journey to Coburg*

Axel cursed his luck as rain poured down on him, soaking him to the bone. He was two weeks out of Verone, and his journey had been slowed by a storm for the past two days. The horse's miserable demeanor mirrored his own as they plodded along the muddy road. What had begun as a promising new chapter in his life, filled with hope for a brighter future, was transforming into yet another regretful choice, destined to bring only despair.

When he embarked on the road to Coburg, he'd felt a surge of confidence fueling his determination to pursue his dream, driven by a newfound ambition to learn alchemy. But his motivation waned as harvest season drew near and dark clouds loomed overhead. He wanted to be in Coburg before a storm arrived. He hated traveling in harsh weather unless it was absolutely necessary and tried to wait it out, but after losing a full day, he became restless and decided to push forward. At first, his horse was stubborn and refused to leave the jagged ledge where they'd sought shelter. After a great deal of cursing and tugging, the horse relented, but conveyed his dissatisfaction by walking at a slow pace.

Axel saw no further signs that he was being followed. He stayed vigilant, occasionally deviating from the road to keep an eye out for anyone approaching from the rear, but he found the idea of Gunter following him increasingly absurd. In spite of the trouble it had initially caused, Axel's snitching had ultimately benefited Gunter. Within a moon of being demoted from shift commander, he was promoted to the BlackGuard. The commander acknowledged Gunter's lack of leadership, but recognized his exceptional swordsmanship as an ideal fit for the IceGuard. His skill was being wasted on the Curtain. Axel's scheming only laid the groundwork for Gunter to become the youngest knight promoted to the BlackGuard in Frostgarde history. Although he used the promotion to further ridicule Axel, his thirst for retribution remained resolute. His elevated status inflated his ego to where he felt untouchable, immune to any serious repercussions. Circumstances seemed to conspire against Axel, as each new twist of fate only served to further fuel his resentment toward Gunter.

After a few hours of traveling at their plodding pace, the storm broke. Black clouds faded to a softer shade of grey as rays of sunlight peeked through. It was a good time to rest and allow his horse to graze. He hoped the destrier would be more agreeable when they resumed their journey. They paused beneath a cluster of trees whose leaves were transitioning to a vibrant shade of red. His horse nibbled on the wet grass while Axel stretched his legs and released the tension from his lower back.

His stomach was growling, so he ate what was left of his bread, along with a few pieces of jerky. He was tiring of eating the same food day after day. It had all gotten stale and difficult to chew. After choking down his meal, he rested against the trunk of the tree and shut his eyes. The soft sound of water dripping from the rain-soaked leaves created a soothing background that lulled him into a gentle slumber. The peaceful melody of chirping sparrows stirred Axel's imagination. He licked his lips, fancying a succulent feast of roasted pheasant beside a crackling fire. He was snapped back to reality by the distant sound of a horse's whinny. With his own horse grazing nearby, fears of being followed returned. He led his stallion further back into the trees and monitored the road.

A man on horseback appeared in the distance, following the same route as Axel. He squinted, attempting to identify the stranger. There was something familiar about his short beard and dark hair. Anxiety coursed through his gut as he again considered the possibility that Gunter was spying on him. As the rider drew closer, Axel realized that although he was of similar stature, it was not Gunter. The adverse weather and enormous stress he was under was contributing to his heightened paranoia.

Being in no mood to find out the man's intentions, Axel remained hidden and let him pass in silence. The rider stopped at the tree where he'd been dozing and examined the trampled grass. As Axel held his breath, a wave of nausea swept through him, making him light-headed. He gripped the hilt of his sword, ready to attack if necessary. After a long pause, the man urged his horse forward and continued on his way. Axel waited until he was out of sight to release a sigh of relief. He lingered for a while, allowing some distance to pass between him and the man, feeling childish for being so paranoid. With the storm clearing and his fear alleviated, his mood brightened.

He hoped to find an inn by the end of the day. After a couple of weeks on the road, he'd had enough of sleeping outdoors on the cold, unforgiving ground. His back and arse ached, and blisters had developed on both hands. He was not accustomed to such long trips. Regular travel hardened a man's body and spirit, and he recognized how soft he had become from his time on the Curtain. The lack of regular exercise had made it far too easy to add extra padding around his midsection.

He needed a comfortable place to rejuvenate himself and stumbled upon The Wild Raven a few hours later. It came sooner than Axel would have liked, as there was still plenty of daylight remaining to continue his journey. He opted to stop for a home-cooked meal before deciding whether to stay overnight or resume his trip.

He spotted a few horses tethered in front, but none

resembled the one that had passed earlier. A stable boy came outside to receive him and attend his horse. Axel was greeted by a musty odor and dimly lit room when he entered the inn. It was a well-worn and simple spot that served as a regular stop for travelers. The tables were weathered from years of abuse and spilled ale. Other than a group of three men seated at a large table in the center, Axel was the only patron. The barkeep stood behind the bar, wiping mugs and straightening up. A waitress burst from the back room, carrying two trays of warm bread and some type of sizzling roast. His mouth salivated at the smell of juice dripping off the meat.

"Take a seat wherever you like, honey. I'll be with you in a minute," the waitress said as she scurried past. He nodded and selected a strategic spot that provided an unobstructed view of both the entrance and the entire tavern. He watched her bring food to the other men before refilling their mugs, her mannerisms making his heart flutter. The way she carried herself reminded him of his former betrothed, Ysabelle. Her long brown hair framed her heart-shaped face, accentuating her striking jawline and button nose. As she approached, Axel noticed the differences more distinctly, enabling him to regain his composure. She said they had venison caught earlier in the day, accompanied by warm bread straight from the oven. It was exactly the kind of meal he had been hoping for. After he ordered his food, she brought him a tankard of ale and then left to prepare his plate.

He settled into his chair and allowed the warmth of the alcohol to take effect. Ysabelle's image remained imprinted on his mind, guiding his thoughts toward her. It was unfortunate their betrothal hadn't ended in marriage. Her absence had left a void in his heart that he couldn't shake. Their love was an enigma—a mix of fiery desire and never-ending arguments over trivial matters. Perhaps that was the essence of passion, elusive and untamed. When things were positive, they'd been intimately connected, as though they were two halves of the same person. Just looking at her had caused excitement to course through his blood.

Unfortunately, when they were not connected, their zeal had manifested in more destructive ways. Ysabelle's temper had the power to intimidate even the most resilient man, and her anger exploded whenever he failed to meet her ever-changing expectations. Anytime he felt like he had a handle on her emotions, she would remind him of something else he had messed up. Although she understood that Axel's primary responsibility was to the king, she lamented her sense of isolation and the burden of dealing with everything alone. He recalled the time he'd surprised her with a picnic in the countryside. He'd requested time off from her boss so they could go on a romantic date. Even though her boss had agreed and wished them a wonderful time, she'd shrieked at Axel for speaking to him without telling her. She'd rushed to the bakery and volunteered to work that afternoon. With nothing else to do, Axel had drowned his boredom by getting drunk, which led to yet another bitter argument that night.

As their three-year relationship progressed, the

pleasant moments dwindled and the arguments grew more hostile. Ysabelle dealt with it through avoidance, whereas Axel used alcohol to cope. Eventually, she got fed up with his drinking and boorish behavior and told him she was leaving Koenigsberg for good. Axel was heartbroken, but deep down knew it was the right decision. The relationship was making him miserable and interfering with his obligations. She moved back to her hometown of Coburg, leaving Axel to focus on his duties at Frostgarde. His urge to drink diminished as soon as they went their separate ways. Although he still turned to alcohol to ease his stress, it was nowhere near as excessive as it'd been when they were together.

He planned on visiting her in Coburg and hoped enough time had elapsed for their animosity to dissipate. If he was going to locate the alchemist, she would be his best option. He knew he could trust her with his secret. She might have despised him when they separated, but she wouldn't want to see his head upon the executioner's block. He trusted the love between them was still there, somewhere.

Carrying a generous portion of meat and a steaming loaf of bread, the waitress returned from the kitchen. Axel's stomach growled as she placed it before him. He dove right in, devouring the spicy meat and soaking up the pooling juices with the hot bread. The delicious meal revived his spirit. With a few more hours of daylight remaining, he decided to continue onward rather than spending the night. He was anxious to get there.

After another week of steady traveling, he finally saw

the small town of Coburg emerge in the distance. He was relieved that another stage of his journey was coming to an end. He arrived at the outskirts of town only to be met by a large gate. He didn't see a guard, but the gate was barred from the inside and he couldn't push it open. He shouted for help, hoping there was someone nearby. When no one answered, he pounded against the gate, demanding to be let in. After a few minutes, a spyhole slid open, revealing a face that asked his identity and purpose in Coburg. Axel explained he was a knight traveling to Ravenna and needed a place to rest for a few days. The man eyed him with suspicion before opening the gate to let him in.

As he entered, the guardsman greeted him and offered a brief overview of the town. It consisted of three taverns, one he recommended, two bakeries, a blacksmith, a cobbler, and an apothecary if he needed to refresh his supplies. He also mentioned a brothel in case Axel had other needs. Ask for Tilly if you want the best experience, he told him with a wink. Axel thanked him for his advice and set out to explore the town.

Coburg was small and easy to navigate. A grand manor stood in the center of town, serving as the mayor's residence and the central meeting hall for its townspeople. He headed toward the shops to find Ysabelle. She was an excellent baker, so he assumed he could find her at one of the bakeries. Although he didn't find her on his first attempt, he purchased a delicious fruit tart that he gobbled down. He had eaten nothing sweet since he left Frostgarde and savored in the sugary goodness.

Although the second bakery was farther away, the familiar scent of fried bread and sweet syrup confirmed he had arrived at the right location. Ysabelle's famous doughnuts were arranged on the counter with elegant precision. Fried balls of crunchy sweetness covered with powdered sugar. Fruity syrup dripped down their sides, pooling beneath them. He'd lost count of the number of those doughnuts he had eaten during their relationship.

The sound of clanging pots followed by a series of savage curses reverberated through the kitchen. Her voice brought back a flood of memories that brought nervous excitement to the pit of his stomach. He recalled those same words directed his way many times. Axel mustered up his courage and cracked open the kitchen door, peeking inside. His eyes teared when he saw Ysabelle working in front of the oven. She looked even more stunning than he remembered. Her hair was a darker blonde than before and pinned atop her head to prevent it from falling in her face as she baked. Her high cheekbones and dark, almond-shaped eyes still mesmerized him. An adorable button nose was accompanied by a pair of luscious red lips, so soft that they resembled velvet. Her sweeping neckline accentuated the graceful curve of her neck, showcasing her beautiful face. A small gold cross clung to her chest between a pair of beautiful breasts, perfect to rest his weary head on. Her simple light blue dress clung to her body, accentuating her voluptuous hourglass figure.

Axel stared transfixed, mouth agape, until he was brought back to reality by an emphatic gasp. Ysabelle stared at him in shock, fanning the sweat beading on her forehead. He didn't know if it was him or the heat from the stove. He entered the kitchen and with his most humble expression said, "Hello, Belle. I've traveled many miles, and I'm in desperate need of your help."

# Chapter 17

## *Ysabelle*

"I still can't believe you left Koenigsberg. You never took me anywhere." Ysabelle was preparing chamomile tea with a hint of lavender while Axel sat in silence near the stove in her small cottage. Hopefully the herbs would help them relax and ease the anxiety they both felt. Once her initial shock had subsided, she'd hugged him affectionately before fixing his hair. Since it was already late in the day, she'd closed the bakery and invited him to her place. She'd brought the doughnuts, allowing him to indulge in their delicious sweetness once again.

A surge of desire washed over him as he watched her move gracefully in her form-fitting dress. The way it hugged her body accentuated the seductive curves that had always enthralled him. He longed to taste her lips and bask in the warmth of her breath. He hungered to convey how truly beautiful she was and how much he missed their time together. However, fearing rejection, he chose to keep these thoughts to himself. "It's good to see you're doing well for yourself," he managed to say. "I'm impressed that you not only have a beautiful home but also own a bakery. I was worried about you when you left."

She rolled her eyes. "You never thought I could take care of myself. How could this poor woman ever survive without a man to look after her? The bakery isn't mine though. It's owned by a man who needed help after his wife died. Once he tasted my doughnuts, he offered me a job."

Axel cleared his throat, ignoring her passive-aggressive comments. It was typical of her to say something to provoke him, to elicit a reaction. She insisted that he struggled to forge meaningful connections with others, devoid of any genuine emotion besides anger. He knew this was untrue, as his emotions relentlessly gnawed at his insides. His challenge was finding a healthy means of expressing them. He smiled. "Of course he did. As I've told you, you're a great baker. I'm happy you rebuilt your life."

She snorted in laughter while he furrowed his brow in bewilderment. She grabbed his chin and said, "There's that confused look. You were always good about praising my baking. Too bad you never learned to compliment me instead of the food. Some things never change. So, tell me what I've missed since I left town."

Axel recounted everything that had transpired after she moved, how he was promoted to the BlackGuard and stationed inside the keep. He described life in the castle and passed along the bits of gossip he'd overheard. She was thrilled when he described Queen Helena's birthday ball, eager to learn every detail about the attendees, their attire, the couples, and all about the cake. It had always been her dream to bake for the royal family. He longed for something that could generate that level of enthusiasm in him. He had little interest in things that didn't impact him.

Ysabelle's smile widened, and she appeared more relaxed as she grew accustomed to his presence. These simple moments made him question why their relationship couldn't always be this way. He allowed himself to be more at ease while remaining vigilant for any pending signs of irritation. Ysabelle nibbled at a marionberry doughnut while sipping her tea. Her demeanor made it clear she wanted him to discuss the topic he was avoiding. She had a talent for sensing his apprehension, often picking up on it before him. She leaned on the table and studied his face. "Now that we have caught up, perhaps you'll tell me the real reason you're here. I doubt you came all this way to see me. I can always tell when something is bothering you." He envisioned her walls going up again.

A sigh escaped Axel's lips as he felt a growing uneasiness. He finished his doughnut and drained the rest of his tea. "You always know when I'm avoiding something. There is something I need your help with. Ever since I was promoted to the BlackGuard, my life has been nothing but problems."

He went into detail about his first two assignments,

recounting how he went about consoling Lady Amelia on her weight issue. Ysabelle only shook her head in disapproval as he explained his attempt to inspire her with his own story of overcoming adversity. He then recounted his trip with Dirk and how he'd tried relating to the boy's struggles at Frostgarde, how it had ended with him striking the lad for his condescending attitude toward the poor family that had been gracious enough to feed them and give them a place to sleep for the night. "After leaving the Queen's Curtain, my life has been plagued by constant drama. What I thought would be a wonderful opportunity to better my life has only led to more misery. These nobles constantly complain about problems they've brought upon themselves. Despite my attempt to show sympathy and understanding, I'm met with anger and scorn."

Ysabelle rolled her eyes as she massaged her temples. "Oh Axel, some things never change. Is it your job to offer advice to the people under your protection?"

He let out a frustrated moan. "So you're saying it's my fault? You're the one who told me to be more sensitive to others' feelings. You always find fault with everything I do."

"I'm not aware of the details of your conversations, but it seems like you have a habit of trying to solve other people's issues, even when they may not want your assistance. It drove me crazy. I wanted you to be present and listen, but you approached everything as a problem that demanded your involvement. Not everybody is asking for your opinion."

He rubbed his face in annoyance. This sounded like a familiar argument they'd had countless times before. "I can't help it. If I see someone in need, my inclination is to lend a hand. Why is that wrong?"

On the verge of getting upset, Ysabelle rose to pour herself more tea. "Let's move on from this subject. We both know how it ends. Regardless of who was at fault, you're in trouble. That doesn't explain why you came here when you left Verone. Why didn't you return to Frostgarde and explain yourself? It's clear that they deemed this boy to be troublesome, otherwise they wouldn't have sent him home. You can't escape your troubles by running from them."

Axel paused and glanced around, making certain that there was no one else nearby. "Are you familiar with alchemy?"

She chortled. "The magical ability to transform metal into gold? I know it's illegal and punishable by death."

He nodded and proceeded to share his account of the alchemist's execution. "That people are being murdered for it suggests that it could be possible."

"I think it's superstitious nonsense. They use public executions to stoke fear."

Axel stood up and began pacing the floor. "It also puts the idea in their head. Prior to the execution, I hadn't heard a whisper of alchemy in years. Now it's the buzz of the city. I overheard a merchant mention the Alchemist Creed at the queen's ball. Apparently, it's an encoded message that reveals how to find them. He pointed out that after alchemy was outlawed, an alchemist fled north.

The man was intoxicated but nervous, leading me to suspect there might be some truth to it."

"Of course he was anxious. He was foolish enough to discuss alchemy at a royal event. Did he know the creed?"

Axel recited the first verse he'd heard of the Alchemist Creed, then summarized his trip to the university to learn about alchemy and the lotus. He revealed what Gottfried had shared about the alchemy student who'd fled to Coburg and provided another verse of the Alchemist Creed.

*In the mountain pass up high*
*Through the stone up on its side*
*Guarded by the pines in kind*
*A hidden vale for you to find*

He shrugged. "Since I'm already in trouble, I decided I might as well take a detour to learn the truth."

Ysabelle raised her arms in exasperation. "You came all this way to find the alchemist and learn how to make gold? Are you mad?"

His face reddened in embarrassment and irritation. "If I was rich, I could quit my job and leave Koenigsberg for good."

"How will gold solve your problems? Dealing with people doesn't get easier when you're rich. It's probably worse. Many will take advantage of you."

Axel glared at her in righteous indignation. He pointed his thumb at his chest and gestured repeatedly. "Being wealthy means I won't have to answer to anyone.

Gold will give me the freedom to live life on my own terms. I'll buy some land and live a quiet, peaceful life away from all the arseholes."

"It's possible to do that without being rich. Look at me."

"You work for a baker, which means you plan your life around his schedule. You serve him to support yourself."

Ysabelle looked down and shook her head in disbelief. "Baking is my passion. My boss is kind to me, and I experience little stress. He bears the risk, not me. I appreciate my simple life."

Axel released a long sigh and stared out the window. "I struggle to find happiness in the simple things. You work well with people, while I find ways to keep them at a distance. I end up annoyed or unintentionally upsetting them."

She gazed at him with sympathetic eyes. "That's because you want everyone to think like you. You insist on being right and belittle anyone who disagrees. I felt it and tried to tell you, but you were too stubborn to listen."

He groaned. "Yeah, I've heard this all before. I'm interested in finding out if you have any knowledge about a lotus field. Have you heard of that discussed here?"

Ysabelle scratched her head as she considered the question. "I've never heard of a lotus field. From what little I know, they grow in water. I'm not sure where they can be found in a field."

He nodded. "That's what's so strange. They also bloom in warm weather. Why would they grow up north where it's cold? It makes more sense to be south of Verone."

"That's likely the intention. A secret wouldn't remain hidden for long if it were easy to find. My friend, Zsu, owns the apothecary. If anyone in Coburg would know of lotuses nearby, it would be her."

Axel was disappointed, but at least he had a new lead to pursue. "It's not exactly what I had in mind, but it's a start. I'll stop by tomorrow morning. I saw the shop near your bakery."

She shook her head. "Oh no you won't. I'll speak to her. Your approach toward others needs work. Any talk of alchemy will only frighten her. It's not a subject folk here want to discuss."

He stroked his beard in agreement. "It makes sense for you to come along. You can introduce us and put her at ease."

Ysabelle's response was forceful, her raised voice filled with frustration. "You're not listening. I'll go alone. Keep your distance, and I'll update you on what I find out."

After arguing, he agreed to let her go alone. She accused him of underestimating her abilities. Even though he knew it wasn't true, he decided to go along to avoid further conflict, resisting the urge to say she might overlook something important without him.

Axel left Ysabelle's cottage, in search of lodging. He followed the guard's recommendation and chose The Frosty Fox. Prior to retiring for the night, he enjoyed a savory pheasant's leg and washed it down with a few mugs of dark ale. After enduring weeks of sleeping on the cold, wet ground, the bed was a welcome oasis of comfort.

He ended up sleeping later than he had planned, but he felt refreshed and in high spirits. Later that afternoon, after her work, he was supposed to meet Ysabelle to discuss the details of her visit. Although he was tempted to go to the apothecary, he resisted the urge and accepted the fact that he would have to wait. After eating breakfast, he considered having a few drinks, but knew it would be a mistake to show up drunk later. Since Ysabelle was doing him a favor, he resisted ordering an ale and instead asked the innkeeper if they had any books. The man handed him a book titled The Dragon's Hoard, which told the story of a courageous knight embarking on a quest to slay a dragon and steal its treasure. Axel took it to his room and began reading, but it triggered thoughts of the futility of his own quest. He placed the book on his chest and drifted off to sleep instead.

He woke that afternoon thinking Ysabelle should have been to the apothecary by now. Although he wanted to stop by the bakery, she had explicitly instructed him not to disturb her, so he decided to explore Coburg instead. He discerned a few things about the small town. Inland and isolated in the far north, Coburg existed in its own bubble, shielded from the current trends. The city's architecture and fashion brought back memories of his childhood. He'd watched Koenigsberg grow and evolve like other large cities. Its large seaport allowed for exotic goods and introduced new styles from distant lands. Coburg was small and outdated in comparison. It only took a short time to explore the whole town, and he quickly lost interest.

Axel strolled along the river that served as the primary trade route in Coburg. It was just large enough to accommodate the river barges that traversed the waterway between Verone and Ravenna. The water was crystal clear, free from the grime that plagued larger cities. It was also a favorite spot among the locals, where they fished for fresh trout. The fishermen had already finished their work and left for the day, producing a serene atmosphere as the gentle sound of the river washed over the rocks near the shore. Axel stopped to reflect on his situation before being interrupted by a couple arguing upstream. From a distance, he thought the woman's mannerisms resembled Ysabelle when she was irritated with him. He laughed, glad he didn't have to deal with that anymore.

As he studied the couple, he realized it was Ysabelle. Overwhelmed by a nauseating sense of worry, he ran to her. "Leave her alone!" he yelled. She was blocking his view of the stranger, but dread was building within. "Get the fuck away from her or I'll kill you." She was shoved to the ground, giving him a clear sight of Gunter.

Rage overwhelmed Axel as he drew his sword. "Get away from her, Gunter. She has nothing to do with this. This is between you and me."

Gunter regarded him with a devilish grin as he yanked Ysabelle to her feet and held his sword to her throat. "Stay back, piggy, unless you want me to cut her pretty face. You know I'll do it."

Ysabelle's eyes were filled with tears, revealing her

unmistakable fear. Axel swallowed his rage. He couldn't put her in further danger. Despite his urge to lash out, he lowered his sword. "Alright. Let her go and tell me what you want."

Gunter kept a tight grip on her while maintaining a wicked smile. "Why, to see your head on the executioner's block, of course. I always knew you were a traitor, and now I have proof."

Axel's stomach churned as he fought back the urge to vomit. "What are you talking about?"

"Don't play coy with me. I knew from the time I caught you at the queen's ball that you were interested in alchemy. I watched you eavesdropping on those drunks' conversation. You were so enthralled that you didn't even realize I was nearby. Ever since you were promoted to the BlackGuard, you have been nothing but an incompetent laughingstock. Why they had you escorting that whiny bastard to Verone is beyond me, but I knew you would bungle that too."

Despite his crushing anxiety, Axel struggled to maintain his composure and remain confident. "So it was you following me. I thought I saw you in Verone, but I never thought you would stoop to stalking. I'm flattered you're obsessed with me. Perhaps you have unresolved feelings, and this is your way of expressing them. I should warn you, I am not that easy." He winked.

Gunter's nostrils flared, and his cheeks flushed red with anger. Ysabelle was horrified and scowled at him. "He has a sword at my neck. Don't encourage him, you arse!"

Gunter chuckled. "You should listen to your lady, Axel. She always was the smarter one. It's a shame that you ruined your relationship like everything else in your life. You wouldn't fight for her when you were together. What makes you think you are capable now? I remember defending her more than you did."

Axel was livid. His forehead was covered in sweat, forcing him to wipe it away before it reached his eyes. The fear plastered on Ysabelle's face was the only thing holding him back. Gunter grinned at Axel's discomfort and continued, "After convincing the chancellor you were deserting to pursue alchemy, I took a boat to Verone and waited. I paid a man to tail you when I thought you recognized me. I figured that once you saw him, your guard would drop and give me an opportunity. You are so predictable."

"That proves nothing. I have no experience with alchemy or any involvement with alchemists. I've done nothing unlawful."

Gunter scoffed. "I would expect a knight of Frost-garde to be more familiar with the king's law. You don't need to practice alchemy to be found guilty of treason. You just need to make inquiries into it. From what I over-heard you tell Ysabelle, I have all the proof I need."

Ysabelle exploded with an anger that Axel had been the recipient of many times over. "I can't believe you had the gall to spy on me in my home." She thrust her fist backward, targeting Gunter's groin.

Startled, he let her go before bending over in pain and clutching his genitals. Ysabelle scrambled away and ran toward Axel, and he seized the chance to get rid of Gunter for good. Gunter was a superior swordsman, so he needed to strike while he was incapacitated. Screaming at Ysabelle to stay back, he rushed forward while Gunter was still grimacing from the hit to his nether region. He lunged with his sword, only to have Gunter parry and turn him aside.

Gunter laughed. "You'll have to do better than that if you want to beat me. Surrender and I will leave Ysabelle alone. If you insist on making me kill you, I will channel my frustrations onto her."

Lost in a state of panic, Axel impulsively launched another attack, but Gunter's speed proved too much for him. He danced aside with ease, recovering quicker than Axel had anticipated. He slashed again and again, yet Gunter brushed aside his wild swings. His emotionally charged assault only drained his energy and intensified his frustration. Gunter was playing with him, opting to taunt rather than retaliate.

Axel stepped back to gather his wits and take a breath. Gunter hadn't broken a sweat and regarded him as he might a fly. "Stop fighting and be a smart piggy, before you make me angry."

Axel knew he couldn't beat Gunter in a duel. Rather than put Ysabelle in harm's way, he threw down his sword. "You win, Gunter. I surrender. Now leave her alone."

Ysabelle screamed as Gunter howled in celebration. As he drew close, Axel pulled his concealed dagger and slashed at his exposed throat. Gunter was too quick in deflecting the attack, causing it to slice into his forearm instead.

He gasped in pain, thrusting his sword into Axel's shoulder. Axel shrieked as blood ran down his arm, and Gunter got a demonic expression in his eye. "You've been a fucking thorn in my side my entire life. I've had enough of you and your insolence. I'm going to enjoy killing both of you."

Axel retrieved his sword just in time to deflect Gunter's flurry of blows. While he managed to block a few slashes, many broke through his defense, and the cuts on his body multiplied. Gunter continued to rain blows upon him, driving him back toward the river. Just as he was convinced he was about to meet his end, Gunter let out a painful scream and retreated. There was mud on his face—Ysabelle was trying to blind him. Taking advantage of Gunter's distraction, he attacked and slashed him across the stomach. Blood poured from Gunter's midsection, causing him to drop to one knee.

"It ends now, Gunter," Axel said as he swung his sword at his exposed neck.

Gunter deflected the attack and dove into the river. The rapid current carried him downstream. Axel tried running along the bank but was in too much pain. He abandoned his efforts and watched as Gunter was swept away.

Ysabelle ran to him, tears streaming down her cheeks. "Oh no. Let me help you."

He hung his head, feeling immense shame for putting her in danger and exhausted from the fight. "I'll be alright. All the cuts are shallow. I'll be in a lot of pain, but I'll live. Let's just go home and you can treat them."

"What about Gunter? Will he live?"

He shook his head. "I doubt it. If he doesn't handle it soon, that gut wound should bleed out. Even if he escapes the river, I don't think he can stop the bleeding without the proper means."

Ysabelle shrugged. "Alright, let's head to my place, where I can treat these wounds." She supported him as they walked back, handling him with gentleness and patience. Axel understood the wounds were a small price to pay to be rid of Gunter forever. All he could do was hope that it was true.

# Chapter 18

## *A Path Forward*

Axel drummed his fingers on the kitchen table as Ysabelle made breakfast. The savory aroma of sausage filled the cottage as it sizzled atop her stone oven. In the past, he'd had little patience for her meticulous meal preparation. She insisted on perfection, making sure that the presentation was flawless before serving. He used to complain about the time she spent, knowing that it would all end up in his stomach. As long as it tasted good, he didn't care how it looked. Today was different, however. Today, he found comfort in her purposeful approach to preparing their food.

His injuries showed signs of improvement after a restful night of sleep. Ysabelle had brought him back to her house and washed his wounds before dressing them. She'd prepared a soothing herbal compound to relieve his pain and speed up his body's natural healing process. A strong lavender and valerian root tea allowed him to sleep through the night uninterrupted. She'd insisted he use her bed while she slept on the floor. He'd tried to argue, but she dismissed his appeals. Once he stopped resisting, she relaxed and became more pleasant. He didn't want to be stubborn, but he couldn't ignore his chivalrous tendencies. It was frustrating how often their arguments stemmed from his attempts to be a gentleman.

Ysabelle served the food, and Axel admitted it looked appetizing. The dish was a perfect balance of flavors. The rich, fatty sausage and poached eggs satisfied his salt cravings, while the strawberry tart added a touch of sweetness to each bite. He washed it down with cold water, brought fresh that morning. She avoided giving him anything with alcohol. After finishing the last of his tart, he rested his hands on his stomach and sat back, satisfied. "Your cooking is as delicious as ever. It's comforting to be in such capable hands."

Ysabelle blushed as she fluttered her eyes. "Thank you. It's nice to be appreciated. I'm glad to see you're feeling better." She absentmindedly wiped away the pastry flakes that had accumulated on his shirt. "You still make a mess when you eat." With a gentle touch, she grabbed his chin and ran her fingers through his beard before collecting the dirty plates.

"So, what did you learn from your friend at the apothecary? I need to consider my next steps. I hope you found a lead, otherwise I'll have to explore other options."

She was so taken aback, she almost dropped the dishes. After putting them down in the wash bin, she threw up her arms. "You can't be serious. You're still going ahead with this absurd quest? I thought you would abandon this silly notion after reaching a dead end. That was before you almost got us both killed. You heard Gunter. If you continue down this path, it won't end well."

Axel pulled his hair in frustration. Just when things were going well, she had to stir things up. "Look, Belle, you may not agree, or even understand, but I have to pursue this. What other option do I have? There is nothing but trouble waiting for me in Koenigsberg. If the chancellor thinks I'm engaging in alchemy, I'm already a dead man. Even in the best-case scenario, leaving my position could cause me to lose my knighthood or be thrown in the dungeon. I thought we discussed this."

"You are too damn stubborn for your own good. Despite your intelligence, your pride continues to cloud your judgment. Maybe you don't have to go back to Koenigsberg or find the alchemist. There are other options."

The conversation made Axel uneasy. He didn't like where it was headed. "What other choice do I have? Remain in Coburg and argue with you? I will always love you, but we both know the outcome if we get back together."

"I wasn't suggesting that!" Ysabelle said in an emphatic tone. She was wound up, coiled like a snake about to strike. "What makes you think I want to be with a stubborn arse like you? I'm happy with my life and don't need you ruining it. You haven't changed a bit. You're the same selfish man who can't see beyond his own needs."

Though frustration boiled within him, Axel forced a smile and bit his tongue, determined to avoid any outbursts. This was how their fights began. He would say something harmless and she would take it personally and overreact. As his stomach churned, he became dizzy and his head spun. The nagging anxiety he felt during their relationship was rising. He didn't want a fight, and getting defensive would only exasperate the situation. She was scared, and provoking him was her way of putting distance between them. He took a deep breath and gazed into her eyes. "Belle, I don't want to fight, but this is something I have to do. It's my only chance for freedom and happiness. I confess the chances of success are small, but there's something inside propelling me forward. This quest has given me purpose, reinvigorated me. I need to do it."

Her face softened, and she leaned in closer. Her eyes watered, but no tears fell. Taking his hand, she nodded and said, "Okay, Axel. I may not understand, but I haven't seen you this determined since you first started courting me. I will do what I can to help."

She then recounted her visit to the apothecary. Zsu had confirmed everything Axel already knew about the lotus was accurate. As an herbalist, she resourced plants from all over Vilsheim. She gathered locally grown herbs personally, but relied on traders to bring her the more exotic species. One was a boy, Erich, who came every few months with an abundance of lotus petals, which reduced swelling and aided in digestion. Unfortunately, Zsu didn't know much about him other than he appeared slow-witted. He spoke little and was difficult to understand, but he brought a letter detailing his inventory and what he wanted in exchange.

Zsu had mentioned that while it was not uncommon for merchants to sell lotuses, it always happened during the summer when river barges traveled from Verone. She found it odd that Erich brought such large quantities throughout the year. He refused to tell her where they were grown. She'd considered following him, but couldn't afford to close her shop for an extended period.

Axel listened, debating his options. It wasn't what he'd expected, but it was another lead. "If this Erich brings lotuses on a year-round basis, it makes sense his source would be near Coburg. If she's too busy to follow him, perhaps I can."

Ysabelle nodded. "Zsu was hoping you would. She will help if you share your findings. She wants to learn the secret to growing lotuses in this climate so she can do it herself."

Despite his effort to suppress his excitement, Axel couldn't help but smile. He still had hope. "This is great, Belle. When does she expect him back in town?"

"Erich's last visit was almost two moons ago. If he sticks to his current schedule, he'll be here any day."

Filled with excitement, he leaped out of his chair and made his way toward the door. "We better get over there. I don't want to miss my chance." He paused at the door and motioned for Ysabelle to follow.

She sat with her arms crossed and rolled her eyes. "Relax, there's no hurry. Zsu is gathering herbs today, so the shop is closed. Erich won't be able to sell his merchandise until it opens tomorrow. She always closes the store when he sells his stock, as the transaction is time-consuming. When the shop is closed, the open banner below the apothecary sign is removed. Since the bakery is nearby, I'll keep an eye out. As soon as the banner comes down, I'll come get you from the inn. You'll wait behind the shop until he leaves and then follow him. He travels on foot, so you'll need to leave your horse."

With a plan in place, Axel breathed a sigh of relief. Ysabelle needed to open the bakery, so he accompanied her on his way to the inn. He was still in a fair amount of pain, so he wanted as much rest as possible before resuming his journey. He needed to be ready to leave at a moment's notice, so he packed his belongings. When he was done, he removed his boots and lay on the bed to rest, imagining what he would do with all his gold as he drifted off to sleep.

Axel dreamed he was having a relaxing day fishing with Stefan in the Koenigsberg harbor. He was reeling in a large bass when an errand boy told them they needed to report to Frostgarde right away. Baron Helmuth had arrived from Verone to report on Axel's mistreatment of Dirk. The errand boy told him he needed to hurry or he would be late. Axel was still struggling with the fish and did not follow, and the boy panicked and yanked on him, pleading with him to get up.

He opened his eyes to find Ysabelle tugging his arm, trying to rouse him. "Wake up. Wake up! Zsu is stalling, but you need to get to the apothecary before Erich leaves."

As he sat up, he felt a lingering drowsiness, realizing he must have been sound asleep. Ysabelle threatened to throw water on him, to which he replied, "I'm up. No need for that." He jumped out of bed, grabbed his travel sack, and followed her.

He told the innkeeper he was leaving and paid the remaining silver he owed. Ysabelle led him down the main road, through the town square, and past her bakery. The apothecary was on the far end of the plaza from The Frosty Fox. She motioned for Axel to go behind the shop and wait. She would go in and confirm Erich was still there. He went into the small alley that separated the apothecary from the cobbler next door. The owner was working in the back of his shop, so Axel crouched behind a stack of crates and waited. With his limited view, he settled himself in and waited for Ysabelle's return.

He stood by for several minutes, seeing no sign of Erich or Ysabelle. A sound from behind startled him, and he drew his sword. His heart skipped a beat, fearing Gunter had arrived to sabotage him. He gasped with relief when he saw it was only a piebald cat with black markings on its face. It gave him a curious glance and meowed before dashing into the apothecary.

Axel didn't know if he was supposed to keep waiting or if that was his cue that Erich had left. Rather than miss his opportunity, he crept out from the alley and peered down the street. He noticed a large blond boy carrying a battered leather sack. He assumed it was Erich, but ducked into the store to confirm.

The scent of herbs filled the apothecary as he navigated through the maze of strange-looking vials and empty jars that cluttered the room. Plants hung from the ceiling and lined the shelves that butted against the walls. He found Ysabelle conversing with a disheveled woman, her clothes covered in dirt and leaves. "Is that him? The blond kid with the big bag?"

Ysabelle nodded. "We didn't want to arouse suspicion, so Zsu sent Hazel to alert you. You better not stand around too long or you'll lose him."

Axel, full of excitement, hugged both women. "Thank you both."

Zsu pulled away, her eyes narrowing with a stern look. "You can thank me by learning how he grows his lotuses. Now get out of here before you ruin everything."

He smiled, staring at Ysabelle. Would he ever see her again? She gave him one final squeeze and told him to go. He scrambled out the door and raced in Erich's direction. But when he got to the end of the plaza, the boy was nowhere to be found. He sprinted toward the northern exit, adrenaline coursing through his veins. He shouted at the guard on duty to open the gate and let him pass. As it opened, he caught a glimpse of Erich shuffling along the main road and immediately set out to pursue him.

# Chapter 19

## *Applefest*

Axel yawned as he watched Erich break his fast before beginning another long day. He was used to waking before dawn, ensuring the boy didn't leave without him. He'd been keeping his distance, and Erich had shown no sign of detecting his presence. Over a week had passed since they'd left Coburg, and the weather was getting colder. Patches of frost covered the ground and a crisp chill filled the air. He guessed they would reach the snow-capped mountains off in the distance within a few days and prayed they wouldn't have to travel much farther north as he wrapped his cloak tight around his body. Just looking at the wintry landscape made him shiver.

His thoughts wandered, as they often did when performing mundane tasks. He worried Gunter was still alive and what he would do to Ysabelle if he discovered Axel had left town. He weighed the potential repercussions of going back to Koenigsberg and how his colleagues would respond. Would Gunter's sudden disappearance raise suspicions of Axel's involvement? He thought of Ysabelle and all the ways their relationship could have unfolded differently. When it was working, Axel had never felt happier. But when they fought, he experienced such misery that he'd entertained thoughts of suicide.

He daydreamed of what to grow on his farm—he fantasized about obtaining land away from the politicking of the large cities. The closer he got to civilization, the more he felt the suffocating grip constricting his freedom that he longed to escape. He was fond of trees and decided to grow apples, picturing an orchard full of apple trees, their branches heavy with plump fruit, ready to be transformed into delectable pastries and other sweet treats. He loved apples, particularly in pies and spiced cider. Ysabelle baked the best apple pie he had ever eaten. They were in high demand during harvest season. She'd always had a way of keeping one for him whenever he visited.

Thoughts of apples and Ysabelle brought back vivid memories of the Koenigsberg Applefest they had attended a few years ago. It was a day he would never forget.

Ysabelle was caught off guard when Axel showed up at her place ahead of schedule. It was the first day of the annual Koenigsberg Applefest, and he was fortunate it landed on his day off. Anticipation filled him as he was eager to spend a day with his beloved, enjoying all the yummy apple delights. For the past two days, Ysabelle had been tirelessly baking her famous apple pies and was permitted the day off to enjoy the festival before working it the remainder of the week. He knocked and heard a profanity-laced tirade before she opened the door. "You're early," she said while motioning him to enter.

He realized she was still getting ready, as she wore nothing but her undergarments and her hair was pinned atop her head. "I'm sorry, but I was excited to see you. Is there anything more enjoyable than a day full of food, music, and a lovely lady by your side?"

He held her waist, drawing her near, and they shared a passionate kiss that she reciprocated with a soft, open mouth. A surge of arousal overcame him, prompting him to kiss her with a newfound fervor as he moved along her neck.

"Okay, enough, Axel." Ysabelle giggled while nudging him away. "I need to finish getting ready. We have time for that later. The quicker I am done, the sooner we can leave."

He sighed, dejected, as he took a seat. "It's always later. I prefer to begin our day intimately. It helps us stay connected."

"And I like to be wooed first. I am not a man who succumbs easily to arousal. I want an emotional connection before we make love. It's not solely about fulfilling your desires. Now, hush. I need to finish preparing myself so I'll look my best for you."

As he gazed at her, Axel couldn't help but be seduced by her beauty. With her hair pinned, her slender neck was on full display, tempting him to run his tongue along it. Her face was already powdered, and she was applying rouge to her lips. Even without cosmetics, her natural grace was evident. "You know I don't think you need any of that stuff. You're perfect as you are."

She waved him off, but he caught her blushing. He knew it was best to be patient. Any attempt to rush her would result in irritation, quickly turning her mood sour. He questioned his decision to hurry here. Waiting on her always left him frustrated.

When she was done with her face, she donned a festive red and green dress. It was her favorite autumn attire, designed to show off her ample bosom and sleek waistline. It made her breasts look like two ripe apples that Axel hungered to bite into. Ysabelle gestured for him to secure her dress, and he pulled it snug, then tied a bow to keep it in place. She grunted and smacked his hand. "Not so hard. You're making it too tight."

Axel examined her closely and noticed a small tear running along the side seam, causing him to grimace. "I'm doing it like I always do. I think the dress is getting old. It has a tear under your arm." He pointed to the hole.

Her face twisted in horror and chagrin. "You arse, you ruined my favorite harvest dress."

He felt his enthusiasm slipping away. "Don't worry about it, Belle. It's hidden beneath your arm where nobody can see it. You can fix it later. Don't let it bother you now."

She ignored him as she felt the hole and ran to her looking glass to get a better look. "I can't wear a dress with a hole in it. I'll be a mocked by the other women. How could you do this to me?"

Before she could undress, Axel reacted swiftly, his hand shooting out to stop her. "If you keep your arm down, no one will notice. The dress fits perfectly and accentuates your best features. You look stunning."

Ysabelle was preoccupied with examining her reflection from every angle. "Do you really think so? Maybe if I secure it with a pin, it will last the day."

He took her in his arms and gazed into her eyes. "You are the most beautiful woman I've ever seen. Be prepared to turn heads." He leaned in to kiss her mouth.

She returned the kiss with velvety soft lips and pulled him close. He pushed his tongue into her eagerly waiting mouth. Their passionate kiss reignited Axel's arousal, and he pulled back, saying, "We should get going before my excitement gets out of hand."

With a seductive gaze, she ran her fingers through his beard, further stirring his passion. "We have a few extra minutes. You may lift my dress, but don't make me have to reapply everything. And don't make this hole bigger!"

He lifted her and brought her to the bed. He removed his pants and pushed her dress up as he climbed on top of her. Pleasure coursed through his body as he made passionate love to her before finishing with a powerful shudder. With tenderness, they kissed and expressed their love for each other before getting out of bed.

Ysabelle moved to the mirror to straighten her dress and make minor alterations to her hair. She smiled as she reached for his hand, and he gladly grasped hers back. "We better be on our way. It's going to be swarming with visitors, and I want to avoid the crowd," he said.

He felt much better after bonding with Ysabelle. He noticed a slight look of annoyance on her face but dismissed it. As long as they beat the crowd, it would be a wonderful day. They walked out the door arm in arm to enjoy the festival.

The road was filled with fairgoers, becoming more congested as they approached the entrance. Although other cities held their own celebrations, Applefest was the largest harvest festival in all of Vilsheim. The changing tree leaves along the avenue created the illusion of walking through a river of red. Autumn was a popular time of year and excitement filled the air. Folks dressed in the traditional fair colors of red and gold pushed their way forward. They were inclined to overlook the jostling that often happened when large crowds gathered. However, as the day wore on and the attendees indulged in sugary food and drink, their moods soured.

Axel was annoyed when they got stuck behind a sizable cluster of out-of-town guests. The parents seemed unfazed as their children darted between the other attendees, and the group took up the entire thoroughfare, making it impossible to pass. Frustrated by their complete disregard for others, Axel grew impatient and pushed his way through, dragging Ysabelle with him. He heard mumbles about rudeness and received a few dirty looks, but pressed forward anyway. They had a lot of nerve claiming he was the rude one.

Ysabelle pulled her hand away and flashed an angry scowl. "Slow down. Do you have to twist my arm and drag me through a mob? If you keep letting these people get under your skin, you'll ruin the day for us both."

He glared at her. "You were the one that took so long getting ready. If we'd left sooner, we could have avoided this."

Shaking her head, she couldn't hide her frustration. "You were the one who wanted to partake in other activities before we left." She softened her shoulders and pleaded with him. "You're so uptight. Try to relax. I want to enjoy my time without you grumbling about the other people all day."

Axel knew she was right. He wanted to savor their time together too. "I'll try to focus on you rather than all the arseholes."

In a loving gesture, she showed her appreciation by intertwining her arm with his and drawing herself closer.

There was already a long line at the entrance. Axel ignored his restless thoughts and fixated on the great food he was going to eat. His dry mouth salivated as he imagined all the cider he would soon be drinking. The most popular libation was watered-down wine infused with chunks of apple, which gave it a crisp, refreshing flavor that complemented the smorgasbord of sweets. Ysabelle would probably keep a close eye on his drinking, so he'd have to search for the most potent blends surreptitiously.

He spotted Gunter near the front and held Ysabelle back so they wouldn't be noticed. He was the last person he wanted to see while enjoying his day off. She looked confused before she recognized Gunter and rolled her eyes. They waited for a few others to pass before entering the festival and heading in the opposite direction.

To Axel's dismay, Ysabelle headed straight to the jewelry vendors selling cheap harvest trinkets. He shook his head with disgust while she perused the gaudy pendants and brooches, and he whisked her away before she asked to see anything, guiding her toward the food vendors. "You don't need any of that cheap shit."

She glanced back at them. "They're festive. Besides, it's all I can afford."

"It's overpriced gold-plated bronze for fools who are easily duped. One day, I'll save enough to purchase a beautiful piece of real gold jewelry adorned with black opals to complement your eyes."

The food promenade was bustling with activity as vendors hustled to serve their fare to the lines of waiting guests. A rich aroma of sweet and savory scents mingled together, and Axel didn't know what booth to visit first. The open grass area nearby was filled with tables for the common people, while tents had been erected for the nobility. Later this evening, King Otto would make his grand entrance to mark the official start of the week-long celebration. Apple-shaped lanterns hung from ropes strewn across the veranda to illuminate the festival when dusk drew near.

Ysabelle mentioned she was thirsty and suggested splitting a carafe of apple wine. She found a seat while Axel waited in line. After he ordered, the merchant had him try their new apple schnapps. It was the most potent drink at the fair and only offered in small quantities. He knocked back a sample, and as the burning in his throat subsided, a warm euphoria washed over and relaxed him.

He found Ysabelle at the end of a full table, saving a spot for him to squeeze into. They poured the wine and toasted to a day of pleasure and tranquility. As he'd expected, the wine was sweet and easy to drink. She promptly drained her cup, proclaimed it delicious, and Axel refilled hers before topping off his own. They sat in silence, watching the crowd that flowed through the dining area. Attendees were already getting unruly. They overheard a dispute over who'd taken whom's seat and why someone had left without cleaning their table.

"The behavior at this festival gets worse every year," Ysabelle said as she put her cup down. "I would expect people to be more joyful and kind to one another. Instead, they argue over the most petty things."

He nodded. "I agree these people are arseholes, but I can deal with it as long as they don't bother me."

She studied him skeptically. "You're annoyed with just about everyone. Pour me some more wine, sweetie. I'm going to need it."

"Why do you think I see so many arseholes?" He

laughed while emptying the rest of the wine into her glass.

Ysabelle giggled as he flashed a foolish grin. She reached across the table and gently stroked his arm. "Let's go find something to eat before this wine gets to my head." They left the table and headed for the meat vendors as two women argued over who would get their seats.

They shared a pheasant leg, along with a loaf of bread to soak up the alcohol in their stomachs. Ysabelle was in a festive mood and didn't appear concerned with how much they were drinking. After their meal, they sampled a few meads and Axel even convinced her to try the schnapps. He was thoroughly enjoying himself as he wandered carefree through the fair, finding it easier to laugh things off that usually annoyed him. The alcohol had soothed him, and his connection to Ysabelle remained strong. This was the way life was meant to be.

After haggling with vendors over an autumn-themed scarf, they watched a puppet show chronicling how the Koenigs had fought off an overseas invasion. Minstrels sang and poets recited embellished stories as the two of them continued drinking their cares away. Arm in arm, they laughed at the peculiar people they encountered.

Later that afternoon, they headed toward the dessert vendors, where bakers from across the realm offered their delightful apple treats. Ysabelle's bakery had a long line, and her boss told them her pies were once again a tremendous success. Due to the high demand, she was asked to show up early the next morning and bake additional batches. She was thrilled when she heard the news and glowed as they perused the competitions' offerings. There was an entire section of booths dedicated to selling a variety of tarts, cobblers, crisps, cookies, and doughnuts. While they all looked tempting, it was a merchant selling apples on a stick that was garnering the most attention. The apples were coated in a sweet syrup, followed by a generous roll in a blend of almonds and walnuts. Axel tried one. The flavor was delightful, but the sticky nuts kept clinging to his back teeth.

Ysabelle was interested in the other apple pie vendors. As a perfectionist, she had to be sure her pies were the absolute best. Axel thought it was silly that she worried so much about other people's opinions. Everyone had different tastes, so someone claiming another pie was better than hers was nothing to fuss over. They'd had this discussion on multiple occasions, and it almost always resulted in an argument. They stopped at a popular booth where the baker had traveled all the way from Ravenna. Ysabelle scrutinized the pies, commenting on how similar they were to her own. She asked for a sample and a woman cut her a small square. She popped it in her mouth and rolled it around as if she was trying to determine each individual ingredient. Her eyes widened in shocked recognition, and she grabbed Axel. "Tell me that doesn't taste like mine. I don't understand how this is possible."

He asked for a sample and gobbled it down. He noticed the spiciness of the same flavors he recognized in Ysabelle's pies. Cinnamon, nutmeg, and ginger were all common factors in apple pie, but her secret ingredient was not. "I sense cloves. You're the only person I know who adds cloves to their pie. I thought it was strange at first, but after a couple of bites, I found the pungent flavor pairs well with the apple."

"I knew it!" She grabbed the baker's attention and demanded to know the ingredients used in her pie.

The woman laughed and told her, "It's an old family recipe that was passed down from my grandmother's grandmother. I'm afraid I can't tell you. Otherwise, everyone would bake them this way and leave me with nothing to sell."

Her anger intensifying, Ysabelle began shouting. "Don't you tell me it's your family recipe! You stole it. It tastes like my pie."

The baker was surprised by the attack but lashed back at her. "How dare you accuse me of stealing! I've been selling these pies in Ravenna for fifteen years. I was told pies this good should be at Applefest. If you're not going to purchase a pie, then please step aside."

Ysabelle remained unfazed, stating she had proof and then storming off toward her booth. Axel scrambled after her, trying to calm her. "She's from out of town. You never know where folks get their recipes. Why are you so angry? Your boss said yours are selling so well, you need to make more in the morning. Please let it go."

She stopped and jabbed a finger in his chest. "Don't you dare take her side. This is exactly what we've talked about. You need to support me, not try to placate me. I don't want your advice, so stop being an arse."

When they got to her booth, she explained the situation to her boss, who was also troubled. He cut a slice and encouraged her to show the woman who the true baker was. Ysabelle went back to the other booth and thrust her sample into the woman's hand. "Try this and tell me it's not similar."

With each bite, she savored the flavor, trying to identify the individual ingredients. She eyed Ysabelle with intense focus. "I confess they're similar, but not quite the same. The distinction lies in the apples. I detect the flavor of a lighter, sweeter apple found in the south with a touch of cloves to strengthen it. I use the tarter, green apples grown in the north. They're already pungent, so fewer cloves are needed. Both pies have a strong flavor, but mine comes from the apple while yours is from the spice."

"So you admit it's the same recipe!" Ysabelle fired back.

"I admitted they're similar. However, I use the spice to enhance the apple flavor while yours is used to dampen it. My compliments on the pie, though. You did the best you could with what you had to work with. Now if you'll excuse me, please, I have customers to attend."

Ysabelle cursed at the woman, garnering the attention of the surrounding crowd. She became more infuriated when Axel apologized to the baker on her behalf. A voice from behind them suddenly spoke. "It appears what you need is an impartial judge. I would be delighted to provide my opinion."

Axel was horrified when he saw Gunter staring at him

with a mischievous smile. He requested a sample of the merchant's pie and the remainder of Ysabelle's portion.

The baker agreed and provided the samples. Gunter tried hers first and nodded approvingly as he savored the taste. "This one is quite good." He then took a bite of Ysabelle's, and his eyes lit up. "While I admit there are similarities, the first one was much too tart. The combination of sweetness and spice in this one is a perfect balance, making it more enjoyable. They are distinct, and Ysabelle's is unquestionably better."

With relief on her face, Ysabelle replied, "Thank you, Gunter. I appreciate your unbiased opinion."

He smiled in a manner that conveyed concern. "Of course, dear. I'm certain Axel said something similar."

She glared at Axel. "He told me I shouldn't worry about it and then apologized for my behavior. I think I've had enough of the fair today. I have a long day tomorrow." She left the booth and headed for the exit.

Axel unleashed a string of curses at Gunter before running after her. Gunter had only sided with her to provoke him. He had always undermined Axel, but now it was bleeding into his relationship. He caught up to her near the exit and tried to embrace her, but she spat at him as she pushed him away. "I despise you! You treat me like I'm crazy. Just once, I wish you would support me like Gunter and my boss did. Instead, you make me feel worthless!"

Axel had reached his breaking point. "Gunter only sided with you to get under my skin. He didn't mean that. Whenever things don't go your way, you get resentful and direct your anger at me. Now you're asking me to be like the man who made my life a living hell. I've done nothing wrong, and I refuse to be your scapegoat!"

Their judgment was impaired because of all the alcohol they had consumed. Although he was not in the mood to tolerate her abusive behavior, he didn't want to argue. Taking a deep breath to compose himself, he made another attempt. "Belle, I love you. There's no need for things to be like this. Please, come and give me a hug." He extended his arms, pleading for her.

Instead, she stared at him with disgust. "Fuck Apple-fest and fuck you. I'm going home." With fists clenched, she stormed off. Axel attempted to follow her, but she told him to leave her alone. Finally, he gave up and headed back to the festival to seek solace at the schnapps vendor.

Axel's head drooped over his slouched shoulders as he continued to fall further behind Erich. The memories of that day weighed heavily on his heart, pulling him into a deep melancholy. It was a day that encompassed both the best and worst aspects of their relationship. At the start, he had felt so alive and full of love, but it ended with him passed out in a cow pasture on the outskirts of the festival. Ysabelle appeared to be thriving without him, and Axel desperately hoped that Erich was leading him to the alchemist. If this plan didn't work out, he didn't know what he'd do.

# Chapter 20

## *The Lotus Field*

After trekking along the main road for three more days, they arrived at the foot of the colossal mountain range, which served as the northern border of Vilsheim. Axel had hoped to steer clear of them, but an increasing sense of unease settled in his stomach as they drew nearer. The ground had now become blanketed in snow, growing thicker with every league they ventured northward. The sun's rays reflected off the icy peaks, creating a blinding glare that made it difficult to discern what lay ahead.

He suspected he made a mistake following Erich. With the decrease in temperature and rising snowfall, the chances of finding a suitable spot to grow lotuses seemed more and more improbable. He still was unsure if Erich was aware of his presence, but at this point he didn't care. Exhausted from traveling, he longed to reach their destination, wherever it may be. He cursed himself for going this far, but had no other options. He felt stupid for ever beginning this ridiculous quest. Ysabelle must have thought he was a fool. She'd saved herself a lot of grief by ending their relationship when she did. But the prospect of going back to his miserable life was even more discouraging. It was better to risk everything for a chance at happiness than spend his life full of regret.

To his surprise, Erich deviated from the main road and turned onto a small trail that veered to the right. Axel let out a sigh of relief, grateful that they wouldn't have to scale the peak. This narrower path wound its way along the side of the mountain. Fallen trees were scattered across the pathway, creating obstacles he needed to navigate through. As they continued, the terrain became unsteady, with sharp rocks jutting out from the snow. He stumbled into hidden potholes, causing his legs and back to ache, and he slowed his pace, fearing that he might twist an ankle. Erich's familiarity with the terrain allowed him to move faster, leaving Axel to rely on his footprints to stay on the right path.

With the remaining daylight hours waning, he expected they would find a place to camp soon, but he didn't know how far behind Erich he was lagging as he trailed through a long, serpentine corridor carved in the mountainside. Despite the imposing cliff walls on both sides, he was thankful for the solid support they provided as he leaned against them. Once he made it through a tight corner, he was thrilled to find that the road opened up. The feeling of being trapped vanished as he took a moment to enjoy the breathtaking view that surrounded him. Snow-covered fir trees littered the landscape stretched out before him. Off in the distance, a rock formation resembled a massive wolf howling at the daytime moon. As he readied himself to press on, he noticed that Erich's footprints had vanished. In a panic, Axel scoured the area for signs of him. It was odd that there were no impressions, considering it was the only viable path. Perhaps he'd realized he was being followed and had taken steps to cover his tracks.

He continued combing the ground, hoping there was something he'd missed, but found no indication Erich had been here. He walked toward the cliff's edge, gazing upon the picturesque setting, and noticed movement along the cliff wall below. When he squinted, he could just about make out a figure moving in the distance. Erich was treading a slender trail that snaked alongside the mountain. Axel searched his surroundings, trying to find out how he'd gotten there. He concluded he must have overlooked something, and he retraced his steps through the narrow passage. While he noticed small depressions along the wall, he found nothing resembling an alternative path. He continued searching for footprints and found where they stopped. At first glance, there was nothing visible, but upon closer inspection, he discovered a crack in the wall that appeared to be large enough for him to squeeze through.

Axel removed his backpack, trying to make himself as small as possible. He held his breath and turned sideways to squeeze through the narrow opening, inching through the crack. After running out of breath, he found himself stuck during his inhale. At the end of the fissure, he spotted a path that ran along a small ledge on the cliff side. He knew he was close, if he could only get loose. He took in a deep breath, feeling the wall tighten around him, before forcing all the air from his lungs and driving himself forward. His clothes were torn and his chest was pierced by the coarse stone, but he forged ahead, determined to push through. When he emerged, he saw the ledge was not wide enough to walk straight ahead without losing his balance. He needed to sidestep across with his face or back pressed to the wall. Neither option was appealing, but the thought of seeing the sheer drop below made him queasy. He threw his pack on, pushed his stomach against the wall, and inched his way onto the ledge.

Despite the raging fear pulsating through his body, Axel discovered the ridge was stable and had ample room to slide across. His feet found a secure foothold, with no part dangling off the edge. Tracing his hands along the smooth stone, he discovered a convenient groove that acted as a miniature handrail, providing support that he gripped with his fingertips. With his body pressed against the wall, he eased along the ledge.

With each step, he gained more confidence. Fueled by determination, he quickened his pace and found his stride. Right foot, right hand, left hand, left foot, right foot, right hand, left hand, left foot. He refused to look down and kept his eyes fixed on the wall. Just as he was getting comfortable, he shuffled his right foot and found no place to put it down. Overwhelmed with panic, he clutched the ledge and yanked his foot back. He glanced over and saw a two-foot gap where the ledge had collapsed. He put both feet together and positioned his right hand over the crevice. With a firm grip, he stretched his right foot over the gap until he reached solid ground on the other side. He then extended his right hand farther down the handrail until he was spread over the chasm.

When he lifted his left foot, he lost his balance and snatched it back, securing it on the ledge. Intense fear surged within him, and even though it was freezing, sweat beaded on his forehead and trickled into his eyes. The salty sting made him instinctively close his eyes and drop his head. He cautiously opened them, only to be greeted by the sight of sharp rocks protruding from the gap below. Terror engulfed him as his stomach churned, and he fought back the urge to vomit. The weight of his impending death pressed down on him, suffocating his every breath. He had no desire to die, but perhaps the world would be better off without him. It seemed so effortless to let go and drop into the void. No more pain or judgment from those seeking to control him.

He didn't know how long he remained frozen, but once his thoughts had run their course, he refocused on the problem at hand. If he was going to die, it wouldn't be because he'd quit without a fight. He took a few deep breaths to regain his composure and slid his left hand until it was almost across the gap. With a firm grip, he maneuvered his left leg over and slid his hand the rest of the way. His tension eased as he planted his foot on the other side.

As he pressed on, he kept an eye on the ledge, scanning for further signs of instability. His uneasiness was nothing compared to the sheer terror he felt when looking straight down. He reestablished his rhythm of right foot, right hand, left hand, left foot and continued onward. He looked ahead to gauge the remaining distance, but there seemed to be no end in sight. The sun was beginning its slow descent, and he didn't want to be out here when it became dark. The mountain curved, giving him a glimmer of optimism as he rounded the corner, but to his dismay, it stretched on. Axel paused, searching high and low, hoping to find Erich. Farther ahead, he noticed a small bluff jutting out from the cliff, towering above the ledge.

When he was right below it, he found small indents hollowed out in the wall, forming a crude ladder. He used the footholds to establish his position and, grabbing the stone rungs, pulled himself upward. The well-positioned grooves made it easy for him to ascend the wall. When he reached the top, he used a rock to pull himself onto a ridge. He stood up to stretch his sore muscles and discovered an entrance to a small cave. It appeared that Erich was now gone for good, so he had better be in the right place.

He entered the cave, looking for signs of the boy, but found nothing but a scattering of loose rocks. There was no indication to suggest that anyone had been here. The ceiling was low, giving him little room to stand. He traced his fingers along the walls, hoping to find clues of a hidden passage. Detecting none, he unleashed a barrage of expletives and slammed his fists against the wall. His words reverberated within the confined space, surpassing his expectations for a cave this size. He shouted again and heard his voice reflected three times, fading with each repetition. There had to be some kind of opening causing that effect. He yelled again and followed the sound toward the back of the cave. Upon closer inspection, he spotted a large boulder leaning against the wall. He called out, and his heart jumped when he heard an echo coming from behind it.

He went to the side of the rock and pushed with all his might, but it refused to budge. Despite continuing until he was out of breath, it was all in vain. His efforts were only pushing the rock further against the wall. He berated himself for his foolishness. He moved to the other side and noticed a trench etched in the ground. With a gentle nudge, he guided the boulder into the slot, effortlessly sliding it into place. He let it go, and it rolled back, wedged against the wall once more. Undeterred, he repeated the process and spotted a small opening behind the rock, just large enough for him to squeeze through. Pushing the boulder as far as it would go, he positioned himself on his hands and knees, bracing for impact as the rock crashed against his body, pinning him to the wall. He summoned all his strength and forced himself through the opening, causing the rock to snap back into its original position, trapping him inside. Impenetrable darkness enveloped Axel, his heart racing with the terrifying thought of being buried alive.

He crawled through the narrow corridor, occasionally pushing against the low ceiling, hoping it would open up. Eventually, his head bumped the wall, and his hands searched blindly until he felt the tunnel change direction, curving to the left and rising. The whisper of a slight breeze provided a glimmer of hope that an outlet lay ahead. Axel did not know how far he had crawled when he caught a faint trace of light. His knees were sore and his back screamed in protest as he struggled forward. As the ground leveled, he spotted an opening where the light was coming from. He burst out of the tunnel and rolled onto his back, gazing at his surroundings.

Thick stalactites hung ominously from the ceiling while loose rubble cluttered the floor. He found the source of his guiding light on the opposite side of the cave. To his surprise, there was an exit that opened to the moonlit night. A brisk breeze entered the cavern, bringing a chill to the air.

He stood up and tiptoed over the rugged terrain. Despite stumbling multiple times, acquiring additional bruises, he reached the exit and gasped at the sight that unfolded before him, leaving him speechless. A hidden vale, inaccessible to the outside world, sat nestled within the heart of the mountain. The moon, perched high above, cast its rays onto the glade. Tall pine trees stretched toward the light, while berry-filled shrubs and colorful pansies flourished nearby. In the middle of the clearing, a large pond mirrored the glowing sky above. A wooden shelter on the far side grabbed Axel's attention. Smoke billowed from the stone chimney, and a warm light shone from a fire, glowing through its windows. He recalled the second verse of the Alchemist Creed.

*In the mountain pass up high*
*Through the stone up on its side*
*Guarded by the pines in kind*
*A hidden vale for you to find*

This had to be the right place. Overwhelmed by emotion, Axel buried his face in his hands while tears of relief flowed down his cheeks. After a long and arduous journey, he had arrived at the end of his quest. While he was no longer worried about being noticed, he was in no condition to meet anyone, so he elected to spend the night in the cave. He reasoned he would have a better chance of explaining himself after sleeping. Once he found a flat spot, he stretched out his tired limbs and rested his head on his pack. Despite his excitement, he succumbed to sleep within minutes of lying down.

Upon waking, Axel was greeted by the sight of a massive stalactite hanging just above him. He panicked until his moment of disorientation passed and he remembered where he was. Although fatigue had enabled him to sleep uninterrupted, it had also left his joints stiff and backside aching. His stomach was growling, so he choked down a hunk of stale bread while preparing his appeal to the alchemist. He decided to be transparent about the long journey he had undertaken. Axel had no ambition for power or using wealth to achieve it—he yearned to be free of the people who abused those things. His only desire was the freedom to live life on his own terms. Surely, someone living in isolation would understand that.

The sun was shining as he stepped out of the cave, giving him a clear view of the glade. The sight of the pond in daylight took his breath away. Instead of clear blue water, there were hundreds of lotus blossoms floating on its surface. These flowers were much more colorful than the ones at Martene's. Not only were some white, but others shimmered with hues of gold, lavender, pink, and blue lapis. As he gazed upon the lotus field, he understood why it had earned its name—it was the most breathtaking sight he had ever seen. He experienced a profound sense of fulfillment, knowing he had discovered what he had been searching for.

"Excuse me, young man, but is there something I can help you with?" a calm voice said from behind him. Startled, Axel turned to find an elderly man, wearing a black cloak with a golden shoulder cape. His long white hair hung in a single braid, complementing his chest-length beard. Wrinkles ran in abundance along his forehead, and crow's-feet framed light blue eyes that bored into Axel.

He was caught off guard and fumbled for the right words. "I'm sorry, sir, I didn't mean to intrude."

The man smirked. "You didn't mean to intrude? What were you hoping to find when you followed my apprentice here?" His eyebrow lifted, revealing a hint of curiosity.

Axel's face flushed with embarrassment. "I suppose

that was a silly response. My name is Axel, and I traveled all the way from Koenigsberg to find you."

The man assessed him while nodding. "Yes, I see you are wearing the uniform of a king's knight. Have you come to arrest me?"

He clutched at his chest, horrified. "No, that's not what I meant. You're the man I've been searching for. I'm here to learn alchemy."

The man ran his fingers through his beard and hesitated before saying, "In that case, welcome to my home. You must be hungry. We were just about to have breakfast and prepared extra when we saw we had company."

Axel was stunned. It was as if the man had a touch of magic in his very being. "You were expecting me?"

The old man chuckled. "We saw you arrive last night. You needn't be so shy. We could have given you a more comfortable place to sleep. You must be covered in bruises."

Axel blushed and rubbed his sore arse in acknowledgment.

They crossed the glade to the dwelling on the far side. Upon seeing it in daylight, he realized it was a small cottage surrounded by gardens in every direction. In front, a beautiful display of pansies stretched out, while on either side, vegetable gardens thrived with radishes, peas, cabbage, and carrots. They stepped into the cottage, which was more spacious than its outside appearance suggested. Erich sat near the hearth, tending a cauldron that rested upon a blazing fire. He flashed an impish smile and nodded at Axel as they entered, before turning his attention back to the pot. The table had already been prepared with three settings. Two smaller rooms branched off from the main chamber. Through the open door of one, he saw two beds and a writing desk. The other door was closed.

The old man motioned for him to sit. Axel's mouth watered at the smell radiating from the cauldron. "I hope you like rabbit stew. We caught a few plump ones this morning. Allow me to introduce myself. I'm Balthasar, and I assume you are already familiar with my apprentice, Erich. Welcome to our table."

A sense of relief washed over Axel as he exhaled. Things were going much smoother than he'd predicted. He relaxed in his chair as Balthasar filled their mugs with fresh water. After the stew finished simmering, Erich spooned it into their bowls and they enjoyed their meal. Axel was unaware of his ravenous hunger until he took his first bite. He devoured the stew, letting the flavorful broth trickle down his chin, which he crudely wiped with his sleeve. He ate two additional bowls before being satiated.

After eating, he was ready with a flurry of questions. "Maybe it's because I was so hungry, but damn if that wasn't the best stew I've ever had. This vale is remarkable. I'm having a hard time understanding how a place like this is even possible."

The old man put down the bowl he was working on and gave Axel a brief explanation. The surrounding mountains trapped heat in the vale, giving life to things that were normally impossible in the snow-capped mountains. Its primary heat source came from the hot springs that ran underneath, creating a temperate climate. Warm water drizzled into the lotus pond, increasing its temperature, while the cool air balanced it, maintaining the pond's ideal conditions. The glade received ample sunlight and retained a significant amount of heat because of the surrounding mountains.

Axel furrowed his brow as he considered the explanation. "So that's how you're able to grow lotuses this far north. I heard they grow in the south where the water is warmer. It sounded inconceivable that they would prosper in the cooler temperatures. I see this climate allows you to grow vegetables as well."

Balthasar bowed his head slightly. "Indeed. This ecosystem is also home to an array of wildlife. The ancient pine trees are a magnet for birds, and Erich's skill with a bow has provided us with plenty of meat. In addition, small game such as squirrels, rabbits, and even badgers find their way here." He finished his soup and motioned to Erich that their meal was over.

Erich gathered the dishes and went outside to clean them.

"Now that we are alone, perhaps you can tell me why you're here. You mentioned you want me to teach you alchemy. Why don't you start by telling me what you know about alchemy and what you think it can do for you."

Axel explained that alchemy was the transmutation of base metals into gold. A hundred and fifty years ago, Vilsheim was facing a devastating famine. King Ferdinand von Koenig was determined to avoid a revolt, and desperation led him to try drastic means, including magic. He summoned the most skillful alchemist from the University of Verone and demanded a demonstration. After one of his many failures injured the king, he was beheaded.

King Ferdinand was a vengeful man and decided if the alchemists could not make gold for him, then they would not make it for anyone. He outlawed alchemy and discontinued the program at the university. The alchemy students were captured and never heard from again. It was rumored that one student escaped with a stolen manual before he could be captured. He fled north to a remote location and created a riddle known as the Alchemist Creed, which led only the wisest and most determined to find him.

"The lotus field in the Alchemist Creed must be referring to your pond. Therefore, you must be the alchemist, and I want to learn from you." Axel eyed Balthasar, looking for any sign that he was correct.

Balthasar rested his hands across his stomach and settled back into his chair. "You believe I fled the university a hundred years ago?"

It was unclear to Axel whether he found it amusing or offensive. He shrugged his shoulders and replied, "As I mentioned, I know little about alchemy other than turning lead into gold. I don't know what else you can do with it. I thought perhaps you used it to increase your lifespan."

Balthasar burst into a deep, jubilant laugh. "You really do know little of alchemy. Some of what you say is true. The king was using the alchemists to solve his problem, and when he saw its capability, he had them killed. It was my master who vanished during that time. Many years ago, I deciphered the Alchemist Creed and found him in this very spot. I begged him to teach me, and after weeks of proving myself worthy, he agreed."

Axel's heart overflowed with joy. The arduous journey, filled with pain, anxiety, and relentless struggle, had all been worth it. With utmost humility, he made his plea. "As you did many years ago, I humbly request your guidance in the art of alchemy. Please, accept me as your apprentice and teach me the secrets of transforming lead into gold."

Balthasar gazed at him with sympathy. "I know you traveled a long way and overcame many hardships to reach me. Unfortunately, I cannot teach you how to turn lead into gold. That part of your story was true. The alchemists could not fulfill King's Ferdinand's request. I'm sorry, but it's only a myth." He rubbed Axel's shoulder in comfort.

Axel's enthusiasm morphed in to devastation. "What! That can't be true. I traveled all this way for nothing. Against all odds, I succeeded in this absurd quest, only to find out it was a myth!" His face turned bright red, and his eyes bulged from his skull. Overcome with grief and rage, he lost control. He paced the floor in a panic, tears streaming down his cheeks as he cursed his stupidity. He became lightheaded, and the room spun around him. His legs grew weak, and he lost his balance, collapsing next to the table and hitting his head on its hard surface. As blood seeped from the gash, it blended with the tears that continued spilling from his eyes. His vision blurred, and a sense of numbness overcame him. Filled with bewilderment, he couldn't remember who he was or his reason for being here. He fell into a state of unconsciousness, and everything around him became silent.

# Chapter 21

## *A New Hope*

When Axel fluttered his blurry eyes open, he was disoriented by the unfamiliar surroundings. Nausea twisted his innards, and his brain pounded inside his skull. As he reached for his sore head, he felt a wool bandage wrapped around it. He sat up and realized he was in one of the beds he had seen earlier. On a nearby table was a jug of water and a mug already filled to the brim. His memory of what had happened was returning. He was in the alchemist's cottage, recovering after blacking out. It was worse than the most intense hangover he had ever experienced. Shooting pain radiated through his head as he reached for the water. He managed a few sips before the agony forced him to lie back down. The effort triggered a wave of nausea, prompting him to close his eyes and let the urge to vomit pass.

He was in no condition to see Balthasar, so he tried to fall back to sleep. Unfortunately, he couldn't stop ruminating over his situation. His life was hopeless. The woman he loved drove him crazy, and exposing her to danger filled him with unbearable guilt. His thoughts returned to Gunter and what would happen if he was still alive. Axel didn't think he could survive a gut wound, but history had taught him that Gunter was resourceful. What if he threatened Ysabelle again? Disgusted with himself, he pushed them both out of his mind, hoping to avoid further angst.

He thought about his next steps. His goal had been to find the alchemist or die trying. He had not expected to find the alchemist, only to hear the transmutation of gold was just a myth. So what did he do now? There was nothing waiting for him at Frostgarde. If Gunter had warned the chancellor about Axel's interest in alchemy, they would expect a report from him. Axel returning without him would only further those suspicions. They could also punish Axel for deserting his post, including dismissal, imprisonment, or worse. The thought of it sent a shiver through him. He would rather die here than suffer humiliation in front of his colleagues.

He was frustrated and wanted retribution, but didn't know who to blame. Balthasar had been nothing but kind to him, and the old man couldn't teach him something he wasn't able to do himself. His thoughts wandered to Kasper, the drunk merchant at the queen's ball. He was the arsehole who'd planted the idea in the first place. That was also when Gunter had become suspicious of him. Axel wouldn't be in this mess if he hadn't eavesdropped on that conversation. He fantasized about getting revenge. Kasper had mentioned he traveled north as part of his business. Perhaps Axel could track him down and slice his throat. As a final insult, he would leave a lotus on his dead body. The fiendish idea pulled his thoughts away from self-loathing and allowed him to drift off to sleep with a wicked smile.

When he opened his eyes again, Balthasar was sitting at the foot of the bed, smiling. His water jug had been refilled, and steam billowed from a fresh bowl of stew. The spicy aroma made Axel realize how hungry he was. Balthasar patted his leg as he stood up, promising a tea that could alleviate his headache. Axel inched himself toward the headboard and settled into a seated position. His head still pounded, but most of the blurriness had subsided. He gulped the water before sipping the stew's savory broth. It warmed his insides, settling his stomach. After a few more sips, he took the spoon and ate small bites.

Balthasar returned, carrying a tray with the teapot and an extra mug. He poured Axel a full cup. "Here, drink some tea. It should help with your recovery. How are you feeling?"

Axel drank the tea, detecting an unusual taste. "My head is still pounding, but I no longer see two of everything. This tea has an interesting flavor. What's in it?"

Balthasar chuckled, his laughter echoing through the room. "Why, lotus, of course. It's a wonderful herb with many uses. It should help with the swelling in your head. Be sure to finish it all. I was worried you might be more seriously hurt. That was quite a tumble you took."

Axel lowered his head in shame. "I'm sorry about

that. I don't know what came over me. There was so much hope riding on this quest. I went from being over-joyed to devastated in an instant. It's tough to accept that I reached my destination without finding what I was searching for. I let my anger get the best of me."

The old man smiled and nodded. "And what was it you were seeking?"

Axel let out an exasperated sigh. "As I mentioned earlier, I wanted to learn how to turn lead into gold."

"Yes, I remember, but you never revealed why you want to learn that."

Axel became irritated as Balthasar failed to see the obvious. "I want a better life. If I was wealthy, I could avoid returning to my awful situation. I wanted to buy a small farm in a quiet place, where I could live in peace. I yearn to be the master of my destiny, free from the influence of others."

Balthasar furrowed his brow and looked at him, confused. "Are you not the one in control of your life? What is stopping you from finding that place now?"

"I'm a knight. My orders come from a chain of command that starts with my commander and goes all the way to the king. If I had gold, I could quit my job and discover a life that belongs to me."

Balthasar stroked his beard. "I assume you interact with a lot of affluent nobles at Frostgarde. Do they seem happy? Does their wealth enable them to live the carefree life you desire?"

Axel mulled it over. He thought of Amelia and Annaliese and their difficulty finding husbands. They feared they would never experience true love and end up as miserable spinsters. Dirk wasn't happy either. He was overwhelmed by his fear of being rejected by his family and was on the brink of being disowned. "I guess not. Even with all their wealth, they still had problems. If I'm being honest, I didn't envy the nobles. Their lives were too complicated."

Balthasar nodded. "That's my experience as well. The gold you seek is merely a means to an end. It's the potential you believe it has for you. So I will ask you again: what is it you truly want?"

Axel pondered the question as he took another sip of his tea. "I guess I want to be happy. I want to be in control of my life and no longer feel like a servant to my ever-changing emotions."

"You see, you just needed to give it some thought. The answers will come. I cannot teach you how to transmute gold, but I can show you how to take control of your life and walk a path of peace and happiness. Finish your tea and try to eat more. The nausea may continue, but it should pass in a day. Reflect on what I've shared, and let's continue the discussion tomorrow. You've had a long couple of days, so for now, get some rest." Balthasar exited the room and left Axel alone with his thoughts.

The following morning, Axel opened his eyes to sunlight flowing through the window. He must have been in bed for an entire day. Although he enjoyed the rest, he was not accustomed to being idle for so long. His head still throbbed, and now his back and neck were stiff from lack of movement. His anger had waned, and he was no longer consumed with despair. Balthasar was offering a glimmer of hope, and Axel was eager to learn more about it. He pushed himself into a seated position and poured a fresh cup of water to soothe his dry throat. Taking a deep breath and wincing as he rose, he stretched his arms to loosen his tight muscles. His garments were folded at the end of the bed, and their offensive odor had been replaced with a flowery fragrance. He dressed and left the bedroom.

Balthasar was in the main room with a platter of fresh fruit and warm bread. Axel took a seat, and the old man beckoned him to eat. Ravenous, he dove right in. The sweet juice from the fruit was refreshing, and the bread warmed his insides. Balthasar let him finish eating before saying, "It looks like you are doing better today. Your body needed the rest, and it's good to see your appetite has returned. How's your head?"

Axel replied that his headache lingered, prompting Balthasar to prepare more lotus tea.

"I gave some thought to last night's conversation," Axel said. "You were right. I pursued gold as a means to achieve happiness. Even though my memory is hazy, I remember you mentioning that you could teach me how to regain control of my life. I'm interested in learning how to do that."

Balthasar contemplated his words, as if evaluating their sincerity. After a moment of silence, he smiled. "I thought that might be the case, once you had time to reflect on it." He rose from the table and made for the front door. "Let's take a walk outside. The fresh air and sunshine will do you good. Erich is cultivating lotuses in preparation for his next trip to Coburg."

They strolled through the glade, basking in the comforting warmth of the sun. The soft wind created a pleasant contrast, offering a refreshing pause. Filled with newfound hope, Axel enjoyed the beauty of the small valley, marveling at its incredible allure. Majestic pines extended toward the sky, while apple and plum trees adorned the bank of a meandering creek. The air resonated with melodious birdsong, creating a serene ambiance. He couldn't help but feel a tinge of envy toward Balthasar, who resided in such tranquility. They arrived at the pond, where Erich was gathering the lotus blossoms that dotted its surface. He was using a long pole with a metal hook to retrieve the flowers and bring them toward him.

The two men watched as Balthasar explained why the lotus was used as a symbol for alchemy. A lotus began its journey by taking root in the sludge that accumulated at the pond's bottom. In order to survive, it must ascend above the murky waters and emerge onto the surface, where its beautiful flower could bloom. Despite growing in muddied surroundings, the blossom opened in pristine condition, shielded from any trace of dirt.

"This is analogous to what we are attempting with alchemy. The bed of the pond represents the physical world that your life is buried in. It too is filled with muck, and if you cannot rise above it, your life will remain stagnant. The goal of alchemy is to overcome this struggle. To transcend the frivolities of our physical reality and embrace our authentic selves. The seed of your flower is planted within you. You simply need to awaken it and let it grow beyond your perceived limitations."

Axel listened intently. It was nothing like he had imagined, but it piqued his curiosity. "So my life is full of shit, and I need to learn how to grow beyond that?"

"In a sense. Something inside all of us seeks a higher purpose. However, we are too engrossed in our everyday lives to perceive it. Most of us are so stuck in our ways that we can't imagine it any other way. We become trapped in a lifetime of suffering and can't understand why life is so unfair."

Axel was very familiar with that feeling. His entire life had been plagued with one unfortunate situation after another. But perhaps there was hope after all. "That's been my experience. Most of the lotuses are white, but there are pockets of colored ones. Does each color have a unique significance?"

"An excellent question. They signify the different aspects of alchemy. White is the most common color, exemplifying purity of mind. We want to purify our minds and become enlightened expressions of ourselves. Yellow represents the mental clarity and wisdom needed to achieve it. Blue is for the serenity and peace we seek to attain. Red embodies love for yourself and a passion for life. Purple, the rarest color, symbolizes a higher state of awareness beyond your physical surroundings. It is the awakening of your true self."

Axel examined the pond. The white blossoms were scattered all around, creating a visual contrast with the other colored flowers, which appeared to be avoiding each other. "They are so beautiful. It is a shame that Erich needs to disturb them with his harvest."

"Erich does what is required to maintain them. He is not doing them any harm. During their brief blooming period, he waits for the flowers to show signs of wilting before cultivating them. If he was not clearing them, the pond would be overwrought with decay, making it more difficult for new ones to bloom. Watch as he uses the grappling pole to pull any loose flowers toward him. Unless the blossom is ready, it won't be easily removed. Our primary source of income is derived from the petals. We rely on them to purchase goods from Coburg."

Erich extended the pole and tested the hook against a cluster of lotuses. If a blossom did not release with a slight tug, he would move on to the next one. His collection was organized into colorful piles, one large white mound flanked by two smaller stacks of red and blue. He was now working with a patch of yellow flowers, inching one toward him.

As they watched, a renewed sense of hope surged within Axel. He yearned to discover ways to improve his life and find genuine happiness. With a firm determination, he said, "Thank you for showing this to me. Like the lotus, I aspire to transcend the boundaries of my physical existence and unravel the true essence of life. I want to become your apprentice so I may gain these skills. Will you please teach me?" He lowered his gaze and bowed his head.

A gentle smile spread across Balthasar's face, lighting

up his eyes. "I expected nothing less. I accept you as my apprentice. You have just completed your first lesson. Let's help Erich gather these flowers so they can dry. Your next lesson will begin tomorrow, when I will teach you the true nature of alchemy."

# Chapter 22

## *The Laws of Alchemy*

With bloodshot eyes, Axel stared at Balthasar as they shared their morning meal. The piercing sound of chirping birds and the bright morning sunlight were like a hammer to his skull. Last night, sleep had come fast; he'd drifted off the moment his head touched the pillow. Becoming the alchemist's apprentice had him hopeful about his future for the first time since he was promoted to the BlackGuard. His renewed optimism led to a pleasant dream about returning to a better life in Koenigsberg. Sadly, his tranquil dream had morphed into a horrifying nightmare, leaving him terrified and unable to go back to sleep.

It had begun with Stefan and Jurgen welcoming him back to Frostgarde with open arms. His past transgressions were forgiven, and he was given a fresh start. Word of Gunter's dead body, found in the river far downstream from Coburg, had relieved his worry about any future confrontation between them. But no sooner had he lowered his guard than the IceGuard swooped in, seizing him without warning. They'd uncovered his involvement in alchemy, and he was arrested for treason and thrown into the dungeon to await punishment. He dreamed of another execution—only this time his head was on the chopping block. He'd awoken with a gasp as the executioner's axe blade was inches from his exposed neck. It was impossible to get any sleep after that. Not only did the nightmare haunt him, but he was second-guessing his decision to learn alchemy. His mind grew heavy with morose thoughts, interpreting it as a clear sign to proceed at his own peril.

Balthasar studied him as he nibbled on an apple slice. "You look terrible this morning. Maybe your head injury is worse than I assumed."

Axel winced as he sipped his tea, hoping to ease the pain. "I had a disturbing dream that kept me up for half the night."

Balthasar chuckled. "The bane of every insomniac: an active mind unable to settle down. Tell me about this dream."

Axel was not sure how to disclose his apprehension about alchemy. He didn't want Balthasar doubting his commitment, but he knew lying was a poor way of starting his apprenticeship. He decided it was better to be honest, so he described his dream and how it had shifted into a nightmare. "You're the alchemist. Do you know what it means?"

Balthasar stroked his beard as he considered the possibilities. "It could mean several things. Alchemy has been on your mind for months now. Since you're from Frost-garde, I assume you're aware that an alchemist, poor Lucian, was recently executed. You witnessed firsthand the severe consequence of practicing it. When asleep, your mind conjures its own projections, weaving them into intricate dreams. With your newfound commitment to studying alchemy, coupled with your fears, it's no wonder you would feel this way."

Axel's eyes grew wide in understanding. "Lucian? So you knew the alchemist that was executed."

Balthasar nodded. "Lucian was a former student of mine. When he left, I warned him to be careful with whom he shared information. Unfortunately, he was stubborn, and I feared he would speak carelessly around the wrong person. I'm not surprised his life ended tragically. Suppose that hadn't happened, though. Would you be here? I assume you used his clues to find me. Everything happens for a reason; every effect has its cause. But I am getting ahead of myself."

Axel hadn't considered that possibility. Had Lucian not been caught, would he have shown any interest in alchemy? Even though he'd been aware of it, the execution had brought it to the forefront of his mind. "I interpreted my dream as an omen of what could occur if I start down this path."

"While it's certainly possible, it is nothing to fret about. There are a myriad of other possibilities that could just as easily prevent it. My interpretation is just as probable. However, I have another explanation. Today marks the start of your training, and it was your dream that triggered this conversation. It's an excellent place to start your first lesson. Dreams are analogies of our perceptions of the physical world. Your mind created an example to help you understand this. The universe presents lessons that help us grow. You merely need to keep an open mind to receive them."

Axel's eyes narrowed as he pondered this. He never considered other options. There were unlimited possibilities, but he only focused on the worst potential outcome. He admitted he engaged in narrow thinking.

Balthasar clasped his hands together and rested them on the table. "While you were having this nightmare, did you know you were dreaming?"

"Not until I awoke in a panic. It took me a moment to realize it was only a nightmare, but it didn't prevent me from obsessing about it for the rest of the night."

"So while you were dreaming, it seemed like you were actually experiencing it?"

Axel nodded. "I was terrified I was about to die. When it began, I was excited to celebrate my return with Stefan. I remember the scent of honey from the mead we drank and the chill of the dungeon as I awaited execution. As they forced me onto the headsman's block, I distinctly recall the stone pressing against my head, providing a momentary coolness against my flushed face."

Balthasar fiddled with his beard. "The mind uses thoughts, memories, and beliefs during sleep to construct a dream so authentic it becomes nearly impossible to distinguish it from reality. That's the power of the mind. In fact, it's doing that right now. This discussion is a similar creation of your mind. The only difference is the primary elements used to create this experience are your senses. What you see, hear, smell, feel, and taste are simply tools the mind uses to construct your physical reality. This leads us to the seven alchemical laws that govern the universe. By understanding the true nature of reality, we can learn to alter it. The Law of Mentalism states the universe is entirely mental. It's the first law and the foundation for everything else."

Axel's jaw dropped in disbelief. "You're saying this is all in my head? I'm still dreaming? That makes no sense."

"A dream is more of an analogy that makes the law easier to comprehend. Your physical reality exists, but you experience it within your mind. Let's take a step back. Everything in the universe, seen and unseen, is made of energy. Everything from this chair to the sounds we hear and the air we breathe consists of a life force called Oüd. Even your thoughts are composed of Oüd. Your mind is so powerful, it consolidates this energy to create a mental projection where you can exist."

With a sigh, Axel crossed his arms and leaned back in his chair. "If everything is made of this Oüd, why does it take on different textures and sensations? Why do I see some things rather than hear them?"

"This is the second alchemical law, the Law of Vibration. Oüd is energy, and energy is constantly in motion. That motion creates a vibration, and its frequency determines its density. The slower its vibration, the lower its frequency and the denser it becomes. Take water as an example. When water is cold, its rate of vibration slows, causing it to solidify. What happens when you apply heat?"

"It melts back into water."

"And if you continue to apply heat?"

"It turns to steam and disappears."

Balthasar smiled. "Exactly. Increasing the heat increases its vibration, making it less dense, until it transforms into gas and is no longer visible. Of course, it's still there. It's not visible, but you still notice it. Picture those hot, muggy days when the air's so thick it's like trudging through mud. Your senses attune to different rates of vibration. Lightning is another example. There are distinct moments when you see it and when you hear it."

Axel nodded, his eyes reflecting his understanding. "That's right. I recall storms when I was atop the Queen's Curtain. I would see lightning in the distance, but it took a few seconds for the sound of thunder to reach me. That makes sense, but how does it apply to me?"

"You must understand the true nature of reality to evoke lasting change in your life. Otherwise, you wind up repeating the same experiences. Have you ever felt that no matter what you do, your life remains unchanged?"

He was all too familiar with that struggle. He recalled his time with Ysabelle. Despite his attempts to be understanding of her needs, what he said or did often resulted in arguments. He recalled a time when work had overwhelmed her and he'd taken a day off to assist. All she'd done was complain about him being a bother and tell him to stay out of her way. "I made numerous attempts to transform myself, but more often than not, I ended up nursing a drink and lamenting about life's unjustness."

"That's because you don't understand the universe and attempted to alter the wrong thing. The third law, the Law of Correspondence, reveals that your physical world is subject to your inner self; as within, so without. Since your outer world is merely a projection of your mind, you must look inward to change your life. Many people waste time attempting to change their outside world and avoid what's happening internally. Think of a romantic relationship that starts off with passion but eventually loses its spark. Over time, the same behaviors become evident and you reach a point where you can't bear each other."

A lot of this was ringing true. Axel thought back through his relationships with women. They started out amazing, full of hope and enthusiasm. As time passed, they would fight more often, until the relationship ended. He'd had hopes for a different outcome with Ysabelle, but it had ultimately ended in the same way. He expressed to Balthasar that he assumed he was choosing the wrong person.

"That's my point. You may substitute the women in your relationships, but if you change nothing about yourself, then you repeat the same patterns. If you've ever had an experience where someone had a completely different perspective on a situation than you, that's because indeed they did. The way our outside world appears is primarily influenced by our beliefs, how we choose to direct our attention. Take this hidden vale as an example. One person may think it's a sanctuary filled with beauty that provides everything needed for a fulfilling life. Another may think it's cold, dreary, and isolated from civilization. When looked at without personalization, it's simply a clearing in the mountain. The rest is our own biased projections. Think of the outside world as a mirror that reveals your inner self. Your beliefs about the world are reflected back to you. If you wish to change what you see in the mirror, you don't alter the reflection; you must change what you place in front of it. To do this, you must change the focus of your attention. Using the example of how one might perceive this glade, what do those distinct impressions say about the person who is observing it?"

Axel scratched his head as he considered the question. "I would say the one who thinks it's a sanctuary is at peace with themself and appreciates the beauty of the world around them. It's clear that the other person is unhappy and preoccupied with their own problems."

Balthasar concurred with a nod. "Let's take this a step further. Tell me what you thought when you arrived. What does that say about you?"

"When I saw the lotus pond, I felt successful. I'd set a goal, and I'd achieved it. I was relieved that my journey was over and I was beginning the next phase of my life. That lotus pond was the most beautiful thing I'd ever seen. When I learned I could not create gold, I felt hopeless and foolish. While lying in bed, I still thought it was pretty, but the luster was gone. The destination wasn't worth the effort of the journey. I wanted to leave and put it behind me."

Balthasar's face lit up with an enthusiastic smile.

"Good, you are understanding. There have been no physical changes since you arrived here. Even the weather has been consistent. The only change was internal, and that was reflected at you. What do you see now?"

"I think it's a peaceful place where one can relax without fear of being disturbed by others. Even the lotuses are more beautiful since you explained their symbolism. I can see the struggle they go through to display their flower, and it fills me with hope."

"You are keeping yourself open to new possibilities. You came here seeking physical alchemy, the transmutation of material things in the outside world. However, alchemy is really about transforming your inner self. By understanding the true nature of reality, you can free yourself from the fears and limiting beliefs that confine your potential. The aim is to transform your experience of reality through the power of your mind. The goal is to live in the present moment, connect with the world, and create more joy. By mastering our minds, we can choose to live the purpose-filled life we desire."

Axel contemplated the idea while gazing out the window. He stretched his arms and let out an enormous yawn. The lack of sleep from the previous night, along with the intense discussion, was catching up to him. Balthasar took notice of his lack of concentration. "Well, I can see you are wandering, and this requires your full attention. This is a good place to stop. Reflect on what you have learned and how to apply it to your own life. Pay attention to your feelings, and we can discuss them in our next lesson. I need to help Erich prepare for his journey."

The old man left to find Erich. It was time for him to take a fresh supply of lotus petals to Coburg, and with Axel here, they needed to stock up on additional food and supplies. He stepped outside to take in his environment with a new perspective. A sense of optimism washed over him as he realized he had everything he'd ever wanted inside him. As his belief flourished, he understood the serenity that the valley offered. The birds sang cheerfully to each other while two squirrels chased each other through the trees. The vibrant colors of the floating flowers burst from the tranquil pond. Even the air carried a fresh scent as the light breeze gently carried the perfume in his direction. He took in a deep breath and slowly exhaled. This place truly was a hidden sanctuary.

# Chapter 23

## *Instinctive Nature*

Axel sat near the lotus pond, waiting for Balthasar to finish his chores so they could begin their next lesson. Erich had left for Coburg a few days earlier, and the old man was busy without his assistant there. Despite Axel's attempts to help, Balthasar had insisted that overseeing his work would be more time-consuming than doing it alone. Axel provided support by taking care of basic responsibilities, like preparing meals and cleaning.

After their first lecture, Axel had assimilated the information and become more comfortable with the concepts. Eager to continue his studies, he'd badgered Balthasar about his next lesson and was advised to show patience. It would present itself at the right moment. He was instructed to focus his attention on something else. But the more he fixated on it, the longer the delay seemed. Balthasar pointed out that he had the power to shape his own experience.

Just after midday, the alchemist joined him by the

pond and asked if he had stopped obsessing about the lecture. Axel admitted he'd tried, but his mind kept drifting back to it. No matter how he'd sought to distract himself, something would trigger thoughts of training. Balthasar stared at the lotuses floating on the water. "Controlling your focus, where you direct your awareness, is difficult for the untrained mind. Tell me what sets humans apart from other animals."

Axel scratched his head and furrowed his brow as he considered the possibilities. It seemed fairly obvious, so he thought it might be something he wasn't expecting. He shrugged his shoulders before listing the ability to speak, create tools, and cook food. Balthasar gazed at a nearby pine tree, where two sparrows were singing to one another. "Animals have other ways of communicating. Their chirps can function as a mating call or a warning of a nearby predator. One of the key distinctions between us and other living creatures lies in our ability to be self-aware. We are conscious of our awareness, and our intelligence allows us to choose where we direct that awareness. The key to transforming something lies in our ability to pay conscious attention to it. Without utilizing our self-awareness, we're no different from animals, driven by instinct. Our instinct operates beneath our awareness without requiring deliberate thought. It enables us to breathe effortlessly and walk without concentrating on each step. All living things are created with innate survival and self-protection skills. Let's use an example from the plant kingdom. How was this pine tree created?"

Axel was uncertain about where this conversation was going, but the answer was clear. "From a pine cone."

"True, but what causes the pine cone to transform into this magnificent tree that bears no resemblance to its original seed?"

Axel specified soil and water, and Balthasar responded, "Yes, but there's something inherent in the pine cone that knows how to use those resources and grow into a tree. That natural instinct is part of every living thing's inherent nature, facilitating its ability to survive."

Axel didn't understand how that related to animals. "I can see what you're saying about the tree, but aren't animals different? Humans train dogs, horses, and birds to do our bidding. They wouldn't be able to follow our direction if they weren't intelligent."

"When you train an animal, you're not imparting a lesson for its understanding. Instead, repetition is used to create a pattern for its mind to follow. When you train an ox to pull a wagon, you start by getting it to move when you whip its haunches. Eventually, it learns to move when it feels the sting of the whip. If it doesn't move, it will be whipped again. Its survival depends on pain avoidance. The power that distinguishes humans from every other living thing is the ability to choose where to direct our attention. If we are not actively focusing our attention, something will unconsciously direct it for us. When that happens, humans live no differently from animals, mindlessly clinging to instinctive behaviors deemed essential for survival."

Axel reflected on his own life. Was he living like an animal, impulsively reacting to perceived threats in his environment? He recalled when he'd punched Basel at the brothel. It had never occurred to him to question why Basel was talking with Mistila. He'd assumed it was to humiliate him and his instincts had taken over.

Balthasar waited for Axel to reflect on those comments before continuing. "Let's put this in context with what you learned the other day. If you recall, there were two main points. The first was that the physical world, as you experience it, is a projection of your mind. It's a combination of what your senses perceive and what your mind believes to be true. The second is that everything in the universe is composed of an energy called Oüd. The energy is processed by your mind and presented in a way that allows you to interact with it. If you are not actively paying attention to your thoughts, your mind will present you with an experience that is consistent with your beliefs. Reflect on how this relates to your experience of waiting for this lesson."

Axel recalled how his hunger to learn had only made the delay more difficult. The more he'd tried to avoid thinking about his lesson, the more it had consumed him. He told Balthasar, who nodded. "Your mind doesn't recognize when you tell it not to do something. Instead, it increases your focus on it. Oüd flows where your awareness goes. If I tell you not to think of a purple lotus when you look at the pond, what do you see?"

Axel tried to avoid the purple lotuses as he scanned the pond of vibrant flowers. While purple was the least prevalent color, they still stood out vividly. "It's ironic. I'm drawn to the purple flowers. The more I try to avoid them, the more noticeable they become."

"That's right. Oüd is the energy used by your mind to create your outer world. What it consumes is determined by your thoughts. When you think, Oüd emanates from you as thought waves. Those thought waves attract the experience your mind creates. Oüd is derived from your conscious and unconscious thoughts, beliefs, and emotions. This is referred to as your aura. While your body occupies a certain amount of physical space, your unseen aura emanates an additional two to three feet beyond that. Your aura emits an energy that attracts the experience your mind will project as the outside world in which you live. This brings us to the fourth law of alchemy, the Law of Causation. It states that every effect has its cause, and every cause leads to an effect. Life is nothing but a series of causes and their ensuing effects. An effect in one situation will be a cause in another. There is no luck or chance. Let me demonstrate."

Balthasar removed a silver coin from his pocket and showed the two sides as heads and tails. He flipped the coin, allowing it to fall to the ground, where King Otto's profile was facing up. "While it may appear as chance that it landed as heads, it was actually a sequence of cause and effects. Which side was up, how many rotations it made, and the angle at which it was thrown were all factors in determining which side it landed on. The Law of Causation, when considered alongside the other laws, brings us to the pivotal point of this lesson. Your aura, derived from your thoughts and beliefs, attracts the Oüd your mind uses to create your everyday experience. Therefore, your thoughts and beliefs lead directly to your experience. You are the cause, and your life is the effect. Living from this vantage point puts you in control of your life. Unfortunately, most people are unaware and live their lives believing the opposite. Life presents a never-ending series of problems that must be overcome. They can't be happy because it seems like life is always conspiring against them."

Axel gasped in horror. That sounded like his own life. The memory of upsetting Amelia and the consequences that followed came rushing back to him. He'd found her constant whining repulsive, thinking it would be better if she just took action to address her weight. By sharing his own story, he'd assumed he was being helpful. He had a natural inclination to help those in need, regardless of whether they wanted his assistance. In fact, it bothered him when they did not show appreciation for his efforts. If he'd remained silent, as he was instructed, he never would have upset Amelia and been forced to leave Frost-garde. Yet he'd held her responsible for overreacting to advice she'd never asked for. He'd blamed everyone but himself because he believed his actions were justified. He'd repeated this pattern with Ysabelle throughout their relationship. As their relationship grew more serious, his fear of her having an emotional meltdown became more intense. Therefore, he was at least partially responsible for creating the drama that he blamed on her. He buried his face in his hands, ashamed.

Balthasar chuckled to himself before rubbing Axel's back in sympathy. "Don't be too hard on yourself. Everyone I've taught has the same realization. People form their personalized view of the world based on their unconscious beliefs, and they resist any efforts to change it. They live in an illusion of their own creation, so pervasive that it's the only thing that makes logical sense. The mind perceives what it needs to be right so that it feels safe. This habit reinforces those beliefs, strengthening the illusion. People suffer because they view life as the cause and its impact on them as the effect. We know this as martyr mentality. It puts your experience out of your control, allowing you to blame others and avoid taking responsibility. As alchemists, we see ourselves as the cause and our life as the effect. This means taking responsibility for everything that's occurred in our lives. Whether we were aware of it or not, the outcome remains the same. Your life is no one's responsibility but your own. However, with that understanding comes the power to change it. This is creator mentality. Over time, you will come to realize that the only problems that exist are the ones we create ourselves. With martyr mentality, the problems never end. Do you want to be a martyr, continuing to blame others, or do you want to be a creator who takes control of his life?"

Balthasar rose from the bench and headed back to the cottage, leaving Axel to reflect on their discussion. It disturbed him that he was to blame for everything in his life. He had always considered himself accountable and often chastised Ysabelle for whining like a martyr. He harbored resentment toward those who didn't behave according to his beliefs. It had never occurred to him that he was a martyr. He sighed and went inside to join Balthasar.

Axel's alchemy skills developed in the weeks that followed. Balthasar continued reinforcing his foundational knowledge while laying additional concepts on top. His new understanding of how his outside world was shaped allowed him to see things he had taken for granted in alternative ways. Once Axel felt comfortable with the basic concepts, Balthasar introduced him to meditation.

Meditation served as a technique to calm his mind amidst the unrelenting stream of thought. Axel learned to ignore his inner critic, which Balthasar defined as his personal ego, and connect to his true self. The goal of meditation was to raise his level of awareness to a point where he could identify with his unconscious mind. He gained the insight to observe his inner world as an unending river of thought that was always flowing and changing. At first, it was difficult to develop patience while meditating. He struggled to ignore his thoughts and avoid getting swept away by them. By fixating on his breath or repeating a brief mantra, he learned to maintain his concentration. As he progressed, he watched his thoughts pass through his awareness and could observe them without judgment. They were merely a product of his unconscious mind, designed to keep him imprisoned within the illusionary world he had spent his entire life building. It dawned on him that his reasoning mind was not the trusted companion he'd always assumed. Under his conscious control, it served as a powerful tool, but when left unchecked, it drove him to dark places and amplified his deepest fears.

Balthasar taught Axel about the Law of Creation. The fifth alchemical law stipulated that the feminine and masculine aspects of Oüd were essential for creation. In the physical world, human life was created when a man fertilized a woman's egg. The same concept was used to manifest an idea. The feminine represented the seed of an idea, while the masculine was the force that brought it to fruition.

Axel applied this concept to his relationship with Dirk. Before he met the boy, Jurgen had asserted he was a spoiled brat. This created Axel's underlying belief, establishing the foundation of their relationship. All of his subsequent interactions with Dirk had reinforced this belief because he was unconsciously seeking validation supporting it. Axel had shared Dirk's frustration with the foul weather and his eagerness to find an inn, but rather than evoking sympathy, it had only strengthened his contemptuous view of him. His personal bias had overshadowed his judgment, stirring bad feelings that led to him striking the boy. Like the pine cone that grew into a towering tree, the negative seed planted in Axel's head had evolved into a self-sabotaging situation he'd used to blame others. His journey might have ended differently if he'd challenged that initial belief and replaced it with the realization that Dirk was returning to an abusive family.

To create a new reality, Balthasar taught him to envision the life he desired as if it had already happened, rather than focusing on how to change the life he had. Through persistent visualization, his vision would be internalized by his unconscious mind, creating automatic patterns that worked toward its realization. Axel visualized himself standing tall, exuding self-confidence, and commanding his own destiny. The opinions and approval of others no longer concerned him. He envisioned a state of serenity flowing through his entire being, allowing him to remain calm in any situation. Throughout it all, Axel's hope of transforming his future blossomed like the lotus flower.

# Chapter 24

## *Rhythm of Life*

A xel had just finished his morning meditation under the canopy of an apple tree when Balthasar approached, carrying a small bag. He looked happy, probably because Erich's return was imminent. Axel understood how much the boy meant to him. Not only did he depend on his help, but it was the old man's hope that when he passed, Erich would continue to maintain the vale for future visitors. He'd never expected Axel to stay, saying he was meant for a greater purpose than a life of isolation here. Given his position at Frostgarde, he could be a facilitator of significant change in Vilsheim. Axel remained skeptical. He hadn't come here to change the world; he just wanted to retake control of his life.

Balthasar placed his bag down and took a seat. "Today, I am going to introduce the last two laws of alchemy. These laws demonstrate how change is necessary to achieve balance. The first one we will discuss is the Law of Polarity, which states everything comes in pairs.

Opposites are identical in their nature but differ in degrees. Tell me the opposite of cold."

"Hot," Axel replied.

"Yes, hot and cold are two ends of a spectrum we know as temperature. At what point does something cold turn hot?"

Axel weighed the options for a sensible temperature. "This sounds like a trick question. Freezing is zero degrees. That seems like the logical point. However, I think it gets hot when it's closer to twenty-five degrees."

Balthasar acknowledged his claim. "I'm accustomed to the chilly mountain air, so fifteen degrees feels warm to me. That's my point. There is no hot or cold temperature, just degrees of relativity. Twenty-five degrees is hotter than fifteen degrees, but colder than thirty degrees. The Law of Polarity is about relativity. Without knowing hot, we can't understand cold. Can you think of other pairs?"

"North and south are opposing directions, while night and day are differing degrees of sunlight. More personal to me is the concept of fat and thin. I remember when I enlisted as a knight—they forced me to lose weight. Within a few weeks, I had dropped a stone in weight and noticed a significant change in my body, but my squad still called me fat."

"Those are fine examples from the physical world. Can you give me some emotional ones?"

Axel had to give it some thought. "I suppose happiness is the opposite of sadness, as cowardice is the opposite of courage."

Balthasar agreed. "Polarity, in emotional terms, is a

primary focus in mental alchemy. Other important pairs include calm and anger and, of course, love and hate. This law generates the most confusion with alchemy. Much like you first did, many believe alchemy is the transformation of lead into gold. However, with mental alchemy, we are learning to transmute our lower, negative emotions into their higher, positive counterparts. To accomplish this, you must consciously shift your attention toward the opposite emotion you are feeling."

Axel's brow furrowed, so Balthasar continued. "Remember that Oüd flows where your awareness goes. In moments of rage, our tendency is to justify our behavior, boosting its intensity. By fixating on that anger, the unconscious mind activates a behavioral pattern that our instincts rely on for self-preservation. This leads to overreaction, emotional outbursts, and antisocial behavior. Instead, focus on remaining calm. Imagine your thoughts, body language, and breathing as if you were at peace. Because calm is on the same spectrum as anger, you are transmuting your negative emotion into a more positive one. Direct your energy on envisioning the person you want to become, rather than dwelling on your current circumstances."

Succumbing to his negativity was something Axel understood all too well. When he got angry, he usually exacerbated the situation by justifying his sentiments. Balthasar pointed out he was succumbing to his automatic thoughts. "If you want to change your behavior, you must control your mind. Do not allow your thoughts to run unchecked. Relax and observe them as they pass through your awareness."

Axel considered how the Law of Polarity had influenced his life. The notion that opposites were similar led him to question whether he and Gunter shared more in common than he'd presumed. Both had escaped their abusive fathers and sought refuge in Frostgarde. While Axel had been compelled to do so, Gunter was excited for the opportunity. Their personalities diverged, with Gunter being outgoing and impulsive, while Axel remained reserved and contemplative. Axel believed in adhering to rules as long as they made sense, whereas Gunter would enforce or break them, depending on how it furthered his own interests. Both harbored underlying anger issues. Axel internalized his resentment, leading to excessive drinking and ensuing blackouts. Gunter, unafraid of confrontation, would engage in arguments and physical altercations with anyone who disrespected him. Axel sought personal growth by embracing a new perspective, whereas Gunter craved validation from others, evident in his desire to become the youngest knight in the IceGuard.

Axel shared his realization with Balthasar, who concurred with his assessment. He underscored the value of being proactive and taking action, reminding Axel that he had a choice: whether to continue being a victim of his circumstances or to make the adjustments to improve them. If he refused to change, he would fall back into his old routines and experience the same outcomes.

This led to the Law of Rhythm, the seventh alchemical law. The Law of Polarity explained that everything had its opposite, while the Law of Rhythm established that balance was maintained through the constant swinging between these opposites. A swing in one direction was followed by an equally unconscious swing in the opposite direction. Balthasar used breathing as an example. A corresponding exhale followed every inhalation of breath. In a larger context, animals took in oxygen and breathed out carbon dioxide. Plants took in that carbon dioxide and released oxygen, perpetuating the cycle.

Axel was asked to provide other examples of rhythm. "Given my prior example, night and day follow a similar pattern. Day emerges from the darkness of night, only to give way to nightfall again. The longer days in summer are offset by the shorter days in winter. That means that changing of seasons is another."

"Excellent. You called out another key point. Rhythm's balancing act is not always immediate. In the summer, you have long days and short nights. When you analyze this within a single day, it appears out of balance. It is not until you view it within the context of an entire year that the rhythm becomes clear." He continued with a history of the rise and fall of human civilizations. Although the Koenig dynasty had reigned for almost five centuries, there were empires before them, just as theirs would one day fall. "What can be inferred about the future of the Koenigs, considering their long-standing rule?"

Axel's lips curled into a sinister smile. "They will face a severe and agonizing decline."

The old man's eye sparkled with giddiness. "Yes

indeed. One that is much needed and long overdue." Balthasar reflected for a moment before brushing it aside. "Like polarity, rhythm affects emotions, too."

Axel leaned forward, eager to share. "This is something I am familiar with. The moment I step into the tavern and have a couple of pints, my mood brightens and a wave of euphoria washes through me. The following day, I'm exhausted, irritable, and filled with shame. I've always shrugged it off as the price I pay for a good time. Now I understand why."

"And the more you drink, the more severe the hangover."

Axel nodded. "When I get angry, I feel a surge of energy. Sometimes it's so much that I can't control it and it leads to outbursts. It eventually burns out and I'm drained. I want to be left alone so I can decompress."

Balthasar smiled. "Have you ever known someone with elaborate mood swings? Full of passion and joy one moment and then angry or depressed in another? Some individuals have a wide gap between their emotional poles. Those who are overly enthusiastic will face equally strong repercussions in the opposite direction."

Axel didn't need further explanation. He had witnessed this firsthand with Ysabelle. The reason he'd fallen in love with her was her intense passion. There was no one he enjoyed being with more when she was on the upswing. Unfortunately, she had her dark side. When she was in a foul mood, she could be outright nasty, calling him horrible names and attacking his deepest insecurities.

He often wondered if she had been consumed by an evil banshee.

"My former betrothed had wild mood swings. I wished to be as passionate about life as she could be. She belittled me, saying I was an ice golem, devoid of emotion. Although I couldn't reach her levels of enthusiasm, I also avoided falling into her deep depression."

"This leads to our last exercise of the day." Balthasar reached into his bag and pulled out a tarnished bronze pendulum dangling from a thick chain. He gave the ball a soft push, causing it to sway back and forth before coming to rest. He pushed it again, this time with more force. The ball soared as high as his hand before reversing course and reaching the same height in the opposite direction. "What did you notice about those two swings?" he asked.

"The first one was short and didn't go very high and came to a sudden stop. The second one went higher and swung longer."

Balthasar pushed the pendulum again. "Your betrothed's emotions are more akin to the second swing, while yours are closer to the first. The larger the gap between the two poles, the farther the pendulum must travel to counterbalance it. With mental alchemy, we seek balance. Extremes toward either emotional pole can be detrimental. Take courage and cowardice. Nobody wants to be so timid that they become paralyzed by fear. However, an individual who expresses such heroic bravery that they become reckless and arrogant can be just as dangerous. Love is a universal pursuit, but we must be mindful not to let it become an unhealthy obsession that controls our lives."

"So my emotions are more stable than Ysabelle's. Does that mean I can't achieve happiness without triggering significant mood swings?"

"Absolutely not!" Balthasar said as he held up his hands. "Think of a spectrum with love on the right and hate on the left. There is no set point where hate turns into love. If point A is to the right of point B, then A is more loving than B, just as B is more hateful than A. That doesn't mean point B is hateful. What if point C is much farther left than B? B looks quite loving in comparison. As alchemists, we strive to move the pivot of the pendulum farther to the right, toward love, while keeping the swing as short as possible. Your moods may be balanced better than Ysabelle's, but if your pivot is on the far left of the spectrum, you are likely living in a state of misery."

That resonated with Axel. Prior to finding the alchemist, he'd been suffering. "That sounds accurate. So while I have balance, I am positioned on the negative side of the spectrum. How do I stay balanced while moving my pivot to the right?"

"By living with intention and purpose. As thoughts pass through your awareness, observe them for what they are: creations of your unconscious mind used to trap you in your illusionary world, safe from your fears, which were created by beliefs you hold as truth. Do not succumb to them. If a strong negative emotion pulls at you, polarize your mind to its positive equivalent. Learn to change your beliefs through meditation and powerful affirmations that benefit you. Think and act like the man you seek to be, as if it has already transpired. Control your mind and you will control your life. I suggest you meditate on what we have discussed. Keep your mind open and trust your intuition."

Balthasar returned to the cottage, leaving the pendulum behind. Axel flicked the ball and watched it sway back and forth, transfixed by what he'd learned. He repeated this process, keeping his eyes focused on the swinging ball. It brought a sense of tranquility. He'd have to be more vigilant of his emotional state from now on. When he was anxious or feeling down, he needed to remember it was only the temporary backswing of the pendulum and things would eventually turn around. He had the power to master his emotions.

# Chapter 25

## *Vengeance*

Axel's dirty-blond hair blew in the breeze as he culled the wilting lotuses from the pond. Balthasar had taught him the technique after Erich left, and he'd been doing it ever since. He enjoyed collecting the flowers and maintaining the beauty of the pond. It brought back a sense of purpose that had been absent since he left Koenigsberg. The difference he felt between his old role and this task was impossible to ignore. Whereas he'd been bored on guard duty, he now felt a sense of peace. He appreciated the experience rather than fretting about when his work would end.

He'd been excited about today's lesson ever since Balthasar prefaced it by emphasizing the need for confidentiality. Axel had laughed, assuring him he had no intention of divulging anything, especially with the threat of execution hanging over his head. The old man had remained unfazed, prompting Axel to promise that he would be serious. As he pulled another blossom toward him, he speculated on what the secret could be. Perhaps it was a new perspective on the world or a way to enhance his meditations. That would be helpful, considering he wasn't always able to relax enough to clear his mind. Sometimes his thoughts swept him away, making it challenging to concentrate. Balthasar assured him that this was normal and that it required consistent practice. There were times even he struggled to maintain focus. There was no cause for concern. The unconscious mind could be stubborn.

He took stock of the inventory once he was satisfied he had gathered all the withering lotuses. Only seven flowers, all white. There were others on the brink of fading, but he decided to wait until his next harvest. He brought them to the cottage, where he would remove the petals and lay them out to dry. Balthasar was waiting inside and motioned for Axel to join him at the table. He poured a cup of hot tea, which Axel gratefully accepted. Even though it was warmer by the pond, there was a chill to the air that permeated the glade. He took a hearty sip, the pleasant aroma of lemongrass filling his nostrils. The soothing warmth filled his belly, putting him at ease.

Balthasar asked him to repeat why King Ferdinand had banned alchemy. Axel summarized the story of the alchemists, who were unable to turn lead into gold and paid the ultimate price. Balthasar nodded, acknowledging it was the prevailing narrative embraced by most of the population. "However, it is not the full story. It's true that Ferdinand called upon an alchemist to create gold for him. There was a group of them who were adept in chemistry and believed this sort of physical transmutation was possible. They had tried for years at the university but failed many times over. The king's desire, coupled with his boundless resources, presented an unprecedented opportunity in their eyes. Unfortunately, their lack of resources was never the problem.

"Ferdinand's frustration mounted as the alchemist continued to fail, time after time. However, the alchemist was so convinced of his eventual success that he staked his life on it. The king agreed, but the failures continued and his patience grew thin. If it weren't for the chatter around Frostgarde, he might have let them continue. But his subjects mocked him behind his back and rumors of madness spread. Upon hearing the whispers, Ferdinand summoned his alchemist and unleashed his fury. He accused him of being a deceitful fraud out to steal his gold while demanding an explanation for the sort of alchemy they were studying at the university.

"The alchemist knew he had reached the end of the king's patience and was compelled to divulge alchemy's true purpose. He revealed the secrets of mental alchemy, imparting the same principles I am sharing with you. He educated him on the natural laws of the universe and how to transcend them. Ferdinand gained proficiency in meditation, visualization, and how to shape his own reality. The alchemist showed him how anyone has the power to master their own mind and experience true freedom, regardless of their circumstances. It's what ultimately led to his demise."

Axel rested his head in his hands, hanging on

Balthasar's every word. He found the actual story fascinating. Even after he'd learned the true purpose of alchemy, it had never crossed his mind that the Koenigs would have had access to this same information.

The alchemist took a sip of tea before continuing. "King Ferdinand was a shrewd man with an open mind. He was an excellent student and quickly absorbed everything he was taught. His image improved, and he regained the respect of his court. His newfound optimism allowed him to see the famine in a new light. He negotiated new deals with the other kingdoms by promising favorable trade conditions in the future. He experienced the immense benefits alchemy could bring to everyone in Vilsheim and conveyed how grateful he was for the profound change the alchemist had brought to his life.

"Ferdinand's final words were along the lines of 'You have revealed the truth to living a joyous, peaceful life. One that will allow all my subjects a life free from fear and filled with love. But a population full of hope is difficult to rule. A king's subjects must endure a life filled with hopelessness and despair. They may despise me, but they must fear and respect me as the one who holds their salvation. Without it, I am powerless. Therefore, I sentence you to death.'

Axel led out an audible gasp as he clutched his chest. That explained why Otto had been so angry during the execution. When Lucian mentioned the art of transformation, he was revealing the secret to everyone. Axel had used those words to fortify his belief that alchemy was transforming gold, but the king understood what he was really implying. It was all making sense.

Balthasar stared into his cup and sighed. "The IceGuard stormed the chamber and butchered the alchemist. Ferdinand had already sent ravens to Verone, and that same day, the alchemists at the university were arrested and had their tongues removed to prevent them from revealing the truth. They were taken to Koenigsberg and discreetly executed. The king issued a decree stating that alchemy was black magic and anyone practicing it would be publicly beheaded.

"However, one young student was not captured. Upon hearing information about suspicious events occurring at the alchemists' enclave, he fled north to evade persecution. He gathered provisions in Coburg and embarked on a quest to discover his own paradise. During extended periods of meditation, he searched for guidance, until the path to this hidden vale appeared before him, bathed in golden light."

Axel's stomach churned with a sickening feeling. He'd expected to learn something that would help with his studies. It had never occurred to him that everything he knew about the history of alchemy was built on a lie. "So the transmutation of gold was nothing but a myth to keep people from knowing the truth? It's appalling how this could help so many who are suffering, yet it's purposefully concealed so the Koenigs can retain power."

With sorrow etched across his face, Balthasar lowered his head. "It's even worse than you think. This brings us to the lesson that I've been waiting to teach until you had a stronger grasp of the fundamentals." He reiterated that the world Axel perceived was a projection of his mind, influenced by the sensory inputs he received and his unconscious thought patterns. "There is another input, derived from the collective consciousness of society—the thoughts and perceptions of all individuals in an environment. People's lives are consumed with thoughts of fear, anger, and greed, and the resulting Oüd amplifies their prevailing negativity. Think back to an incident when you were able to see this with your own eyes."

Axel leaned forward, stroking his beard, and recounted his experience at Lucian's execution. "It was a strange day. The city was buzzing with excitement. The atmosphere was lively and celebratory, like a festival. Executions are rare, and everyone wanted to be a part of the historic event. A vibrant crowd filled the town square, imbibing in drink provided by vendors who lined the plaza. However, there was an unspoken anger simmering just beneath the surface, ready to be released at the slightest provocation. The thought of trying to control a riot with that many people made me anxious."

Balthasar nodded. "Yes, that's mob mentality. People will do to things in large groups that they would never do alone. During war, it is not uncommon for both sides to lose sight of the fact that they are fighting against fellow human beings with families. When the battle begins, bloodlust fills the air as survival instincts and the desire for victory take over. This happens in our daily lives as well. The prospect of a poor harvest, increased taxes, or rising crime rates can bring about a sense of gloom. The threat of a foreign enemy can also add tension. Folks are especially vulnerable when they think their livelihood is in jeopardy. When faced with threats, people develop new beliefs and adopt new patterns of behavior. It's a remarkably effective tool for manipulating the masses."

Axel sat back in his chair and crossed his arms. "That explains how the Koenig dynasty has lasted so long. As far as I know, it's the longest dynasty in history. Most crumble within a few hundred years. Their power is so entrenched in the kingdom's history that nobody disputes their divine mandate to rule."

The old man grimaced. "During my life, the Koenigs have only gotten stronger. Once the famine had passed, even those trade deals that Ferdinand negotiated benefited the crown and not the people. Recently, I've heard murmurs about a baron who is plotting to secede and establish his own kingdom, but he lacks the courage to challenge the king openly. You've witnessed how sinister the Koenigs are firsthand. Their actions are more than just withholding knowledge that could benefit the realm. They use their power to numb and exert control over their subjects."

It dawned on Axel how little influence he was exerting over his own life. "I understand why it's crucial to pay attention to the internal dialogue occurring in my mind. I have often given into errant thoughts and wondered why my life was out of control. It doesn't matter whether my unconscious thoughts are derived from my beliefs or placed there by society—I must remain vigilant and take action when my mind wanders."

As Balthasar watched his apprentice, a proud smile spread across his face. "Indeed you do. However, it does not have to be strenuous. Allow yourself to relax and observe your thoughts in their purest form: Oüd passing through your awareness. Remember the Laws of Rhythm and Causation. Change is always happening, like the ebb and flow of the tides. Be mindful of it, but do not magnify its significance. Embrace the present moment, unburdened by past frustrations or future worries. Trust that everything is happening exactly as it should and your outside circumstances will have little effect."

They sat in silence while Axel considered his master's words. He had always struggled to live in the moment. He anticipated his future, planning the most mundane tasks in painstaking detail while devising strategies to tackle potential challenges that might arise. Most mornings, he would picture several outcomes for his day and plan accordingly in case something unexpected happened. In the back of his mind, he worried about trivial matters, like when he would eat if his shift went long. He never considered the time he wasted devising solutions for nonexistent problems or the stress he was causing himself from anticipating them. The slight relief he received from an uneventful day did little to ease his constant anxiety from expecting the worst.

Balthasar put the kettle on the fire and began slicing fruit. "I heard something outside. Erich must have returned. He's always hungry after his trip, so I like to have something prepared for him."

Axel strained his ears, listening for any sign of his

approach, but the only sound was the occasional caw of a crow. The door burst open with a crash, and to his surprise, it wasn't Erich but a knight with his sword drawn. Sunlight reflected off the blade, creating a glare that obscured his vision—but he recognized the familiar figure by his dark hair and pointy beard. He rushed to his room to retrieve his sword.

Gunter stepped into the cottage, his face twisted into a maniacal grin. His gaunt appearance revealed the toll that the gut wound had taken on him. With a pained expression, he eased into the cottage, his arm bracing his stomach. "Ah, there you are. You won't get away this time. You must have thought I was done for, but you'd be amazed at how much a burning desire for revenge can push a man beyond his limits."

Balthasar moved to the far side of the cottage, huddling in the corner. "What have you done with Erich? Where is my boy?" His face contorted, panic-stricken, as tears welled in his eyes.

Axel whisked across the room to guard him.

Gunter stared through bloodshot eyes. "I'm sorry about your boy. He was a fine lad. He led me straight here. It's a pity I had no further use for him once we arrived. Of course, I couldn't risk him getting in the way, so I had to take precautions. After all, there is only one of me and there were three of you."

Balthasar screamed as he brushed past Axel, attempting to run to Erich. Gunter grabbed his arm, preventing him from leaving. "Not so fast, old man. While I was outside, I couldn't help but overhear a fascinating conversation. The gods must be smiling upon me. I had hoped to return to Frostgarde with a false alchemist, but finding an authentic one far surpassed my expectations. When the king learns I have the master alchemist, I'm sure he'll promote me to the IceGuard. I'll wager he'll even let me keep my tongue. I'll be the most decorated knight in Frostgarde history, celebrated throughout the realm."

Gunter reversed his sword, using the boar's head pommel to deliver a powerful blow to Balthasar's head, rendering him unconscious. Blood leaked down his face and pooled on the floor.

Axel cried out as he charged. Gunter raised his sword to deflect the attack but couldn't prevent Axel from crashing into him as they tumbled through the open door. Both men jumped to their feet and started trading blows.

Gunter's laughter rang out as he defended himself against Axel's onslaught. "Since I no longer have use for you, I'm afraid it's the end of the road for you, piggy. The old man is a far more valuable prize. I'll have my revenge and earn my just reward. After all the pain you've caused me, I deserve it." He unleashed a flurry of strikes that Axel struggled to block.

Gunter moved fast, but his wounds slowed him a step. There was no one to divert his attention, so if Axel was going to win, he needed to do it alone. Circling around Gunter, he swung his sword low, attempting to stab him from behind. Gunter shifted his feet while gracefully dancing away from the attack. They traded blows as Gunter hurled insults. Axel couldn't believe he could fight with such ease while continuing to disparage him. In that moment, he understood what he needed to do.

Memories of his meditation training flooded back, reminding him of the pitfalls of intense concentration. He was analyzing every swing, seeking to anticipate Gunter's next move. But it was only when Balthasar instructed him to stop trying and quiet his mind that he'd achieved success. He let go of all mental chatter and yielded to his instincts, allowing his training to guide him. In an instant, everything seemed easier, as if time had slowed down. He deflected Gunter's attacks with ease while anticipating his next move. He noticed a subtle shift in his opponent's eyes. Gunter's steadfast confidence wavered, leaving him uncertain. He hesitated, giving Axel an opening in his once-impregnable defense. As their swords clashed, Axel closed the distance between them. He hooked his right foot behind Gunter's, causing him to lose his balance and topple to the ground.

Axel towered over him, his sword pressed against his chest, drawing blood. A deep-seated hatred contorted Gunter's face as he came to terms with his defeat. He unleashed a torrent of curses at Axel, fuming with anger. "I should have killed you when we were kids. Your incompetence made us lose that tug-o'-war match. My father and I could have feasted on that ox for months. He brutally beat me—I couldn't get out of bed for a week. I still have pain in my wrist from where he broke it! You've been nothing but a nuisance. I would have been much better off if you'd died then."

Axel's face twisted into a grimace of frustration. He

wanted nothing more than to kill the man for all the pain he had inflicted over the years. Unfortunately, Gunter was right. His father was the worst. Axel had often seen Gunter covered in bruises or bandages. He felt sorry for him, and it was unnerving. But if he killed in cold blood, then he was no better than Gunter. If he was to embark on a path toward a better life, it needed to start now. He looked at him with empathetic eyes. "It doesn't have to end like this, Gunter. You don't have to remain angry at the world, blaming your father or me for your miserable life. Trust me, I know the feeling, and it drove me to some dark places. There is a better path, and I can guide you if you let me. Let's bury the past and walk toward a new life together."

Axel removed his blade from Gunter's neck and resheathed it. He extended his hand and pulled him to his feet. Gunter's eyes remained locked on him as he considered the offer. Then his lips curled in a wry grin as he said, "I'd rather die than take advice from a pig."

He snatched his sword and thrust it toward Axel's chest. Axel had given him the benefit of the doubt but was not foolish enough to let his guard down, and he grabbed Gunter's wrist, twisting it so the sword was pointed back at him. They lost their balance, but Axel shifted so his full body weight fell on Gunter, driving his own sword deep into his chest. Blood spilled from Gunter's mouth, his vacant eyes were transfixed on the open sky. As he untangled himself with a mix of disbelief and relief, Axel checked his neck for a pulse and confirmed that his longtime nemesis was dead. He remembered Balthasar and hurried inside.

The old man was still lying the same position. The bleeding had stopped, and the oozing blood had congealed in a pool surrounding him. Axel shook him, tapping his face, as though waking him from a deep slumber, but Balthasar did not stir. He looked at his head wound and realized Gunter's pommel had caved in the side of his skull.

Axel was horrified. It was hard to believe that it had ended like this. Everything had been going so well. He embraced his master, holding his weight against his chest. Consumed with grief, he wept over Balthasar's lifeless body.

# Chapter 26

## *The Return*

Axel's descent down the mountains was a slow and somber one. Winter's arrival had transformed the landscape outside the vale into a snow-covered wonderland. The road leading to Coburg was eerily silent, devoid of any signs of life. Balthasar's untimely demise had left his emotions in a constant state of turmoil, like a relentless storm raging within him.

His initial task was ensuring the bodies were properly buried. Axel discovered Erich's corpse slumped over a boulder in the cavern bordering the glade. The dried blood covering his clothes and the surrounding area was gruesome. Gunter must have slashed his throat when he found the cottage and had no further use for him. Axel fought back the urge to vomit as he hauled Erich away. The poor boy was about the same age as he'd been when his father abandoned him at Frostgarde. He was too young for his life to have ended in tragedy.

Axel dragged his body to the lotus pond, as it seemed

the appropriate spot to lay Balthasar and him to rest. He dug a grave large enough to accommodate both of them and laid them inside with great care. He put a blue lotus across their chests, ensuring a peaceful rest, followed by a white lotus placed delicately upon their faces. Once the burial was finished, Axel meditated near his master's resting place, seeking peace and clarity.

Gunter's remains were buried against a high cliff wall that enclosed the vale. He didn't deserve to be anywhere near the pond, and Axel wanted him far away from Balthasar. He threw a red lotus in his grave so that he might find love and compassion for others. The act of burying Gunter stirred up a wave of unexpected emotions. They had been in each other's lives for so many years, and never had he shared such an intimate moment. It dawned on him that everything had happened for a reason. While he didn't feel remorse for slaying Gunter, Axel detected a slight void inside himself. Without Gunter's constant tormenting, he might never have sought the alchemist and discovered a new perspective on life. It would always be a source of gratitude for him.

After tending to the deceased, he restored the glade to its original state. He cleaned the cottage before the blood could seep into the wooden floors, but it was impossible to remove it all—bloodstains were notorious for leaving specks behind. He harvested the decaying lotuses a final time, gathering petals to bring back to Zsu, as well as collecting seedpods in every color so she could grow her own. To ensure he had enough food to make it back to Coburg, he hunted rabbits and brought down a few birds.

He took one final pass through the cottage before leaving. As he went through Balthasar's room, he noticed an assortment of scattered papers and a curious collection of quills and ink jars. Within the stacks of paper, Axel came across a document containing the complete Alchemist Creed.

*Seek the truth beyond your eye*
*Find the place within the sky*
*Illusions formed will disappear*
*Reality no longer feared*

*To the north where winter blows*
*Gold is found where knowledge flows*
*Within the lotus field found*
*An open mind no longer bound*

*In the mountain pass up high*
*Through the stone up on its side*
*Guarded by the pines in kind*
*A hidden vale for you to find*

He collected the papers, along with a few quills, and stuffed them into his sack. He also took the pendulum to remind him never to dwell on his negative emotions, as they would eventually swing toward the positive. Once the clutter was removed from the desk, he could see the words etched into the wood and sealed by flame: **KNOW THYSELF.** He made a mental note to consider this message in the future.

He meditated near the lotus pond one final time, filled with immense gratitude toward Balthasar for teaching him a new perspective on life. In learning the true purpose of alchemy, he'd broken free from his mental prison and begun to build the life he'd always desired. His father's voice, once a constant presence, finally fell silent, relieving him from the burden of feelings of inadequacy. He was thankful that he had summoned the courage to overcome his fears and leave the comforts of his predictable life to pursue his dream. Axel took one last look at the valley before departing. The memory of the vibrant lotuses adorning the tranquil pond would forever be ingrained in his mind. He would always remember the noble fir trees and the valuable lesson of the pine cone. Even the cottage elicited a warmth and coziness that made him smile. It was a paradise he would visit during every meditation.

Axel arrived at Coburg late one evening under the light of a glowing moon. He hurried straight to Ysabelle's house, fearing that Gunter might have hurt her while he was searching for him. A sense of relief flooded through him as he caught a glimpse of light shining behind her drapes. After straightening his hair and smoothing his surcoat, he knocked. He heard the faint sound of shuffling feet and muffled curses before she peeked out from behind the curtain. Their eyes connected, and a smile lit up her face. She rushed to the door, and he scooped her up, spinning her in his firm embrace.

Tears streamed down their cheeks as they clung to each other for comfort—each had assumed Gunter had injured the other. Ysabelle prepared tea while Axel recounted his story. The news of Erich's passing left her melancholy, but she was relieved that Gunter would no longer be a problem for them.

She shared the details of Gunter's return. Following Axel's departure, he'd turned up at her house, looking pale and distraught. He'd threatened to beat her, and she disclosed their plan. He dragged her to the apothecary, where he assaulted Zsu. Gunter forced the two women to wait at the shop until Erich returned, demanding that Ysabelle tell her boss she would not be available to work for a while. When Erich arrived, Gunter bullied him, but the boy stood his ground and didn't reveal Axel's location. It wasn't until he threatened to hurt Zsu that Erich gave in. He promised to take Gunter if he left the women alone. They'd left that day, and it was the last she'd heard from them.

Any remorse he'd had for killing Gunter vanished as Ysabelle told her story. Axel's only regret was putting her in danger. He apologized for not being there, just like he hadn't been there for her in their relationship. He now understood that his perception of Ysabelle was an illusion of his own creation. Balthasar had taught him to be a creator, responsible for everything that happened in his life. He'd recognized he had been living as a martyr, and there was no more obvious example than his relationship with her.

He told her that when they were together he became anxious and would scrutinize her demeanor, searching for signs she was in a good mood. He remained guarded, anticipating that her perfectionism would materialize, leading her to criticize something insignificant. His fears contributed to his unconscious belief that she should view the world as he did. She used to say he lacked empathy, and he now realized why. Viewing her problems through his own perspective had only exacerbated them. She had her own unconscious beliefs that he would never understand. However, knowing she had them allowed him the patience to listen without judgment.

Ysabelle was dumbfounded as she listened to his confession. "I never imagined you could escape your own stubbornness. Your rigid thinking made it difficult to connect with others."

Axel let out a heavy sigh at all the pain he had caused. "It was impossible to love others when I never learned to love myself. I viewed myself as a continuous set of problems that I needed to correct. In my misguided attempt at personal growth, I focused on resolving the very issues I created for myself. I was trapped in a self-imposed prison, suffocating under the weight of my own convictions. I considered fixing my problems an aspect of self-love. So I expressed my love for you the only way I knew how: by trying to solve your problems. In my warped perspective, I believed I was helping. It never occurred to me I was undermining your self-esteem."

She reached across the table and caressed his arm with tenderness. "I'm glad you see that. I thought you criticized me because I was a burden. The more I attempted to please you, the more it seemed to bother you. I dreaded our time together for fear of constant judgment. It was more stressful to be with you than be alone. It was as if I was losing my grip on reality."

As Axel listened, his heart ached with the pain he'd caused her. It had always been his intention to make her happy, but he'd never told her that. He pulled her into his arms in a loving embrace. "I think you are not only beautiful, but caring, considerate, and full of passion. I tried to build upon your perfection to prove my worthiness. Instead of acknowledging what you are, I was fixated on what you were not. Please forgive me."

Her head tilted upward, and she kissed him with a deep sense of love and tenderness. Axel's mouth hungrily pressed against hers in a fiery exchange of passion. She removed her dress and led him to her bed. He disrobed and sank into her open arms. They made passionate love, as they had when they first met. While he was inside her, he felt them connect as if merged into one. Axel opened his heart and allowed her fully within. Following their shared climax, they fell asleep in a loving embrace.

The following morning, Ysabelle prepared a delicious strudel, filling the kitchen with the enticing aroma of baked apples and cinnamon. With great enthusiasm, Axel asserted it was one of the best pastries she had ever made, making her blush. Their conversation was lighthearted, yet there was a newfound sense of openness that had been absent for years. The anxious knot in Axel's stomach was gone, and Ysabelle admitted he seemed more relaxed. They planned to visit Zsu today, as he needed to deliver the lotus petals and inform her of Erich's passing.

After they finished eating, he collected the flowers and they strolled arm in arm to the apothecary.

Zsu burst into tears when she learned of Erich's death. She'd always had a fondness for him and enjoyed his visits. She was relieved to hear Gunter was dead. "That arse kicked my Hazel," she said while petting her cat. "Never trust a person who isn't kind to animals. How a person treats something weaker than them reflects their true character."

Her spirits lifted when Axel handed her the sack of lotus petals, along with the seedpods. He explained how they'd grown in the heat of the hot springs below the pond, which warmed the water and the surrounding air. "I don't know how it's possible to reproduce that environment here, though."

Zsu's eyes grew distant, as if she was already grappling with the problem. She noticed him staring and said, "Don't worry about that. I already have a couple of ideas in mind. If there is nothing else to discuss, I would appreciate some time alone, as I need a moment to grieve. Thank you for stopping by."

Axel stayed with Ysabelle for the next couple of weeks. The connection they shared surpassed anything they had ever experienced during their relationship. They spent their time enjoying each other's company and made love often. Axel couldn't resist indulging in her baking, savoring each bite and complimenting her on the deliciousness of her sweets. He praised her for her imaginative ideas, sharp wit, and exceptional style. He enjoyed watching her eyes light up whenever he complimented her beautiful face and alluring physique.

Sadly, it wasn't meant to last. Despite their improved relationship and genuine affection for one another, the weight of their shared history hung heavily between them, casting a shadow over any possibility of starting anew. She'd built a life in Coburg, and Axel had no intention of living this far north. It was much too cold for someone who'd spent their entire life near the southern sea. He felt he needed to return to Koenigsberg and confront whatever fate had in store for him. He let go of his fears and surrendered to the unfolding of events, allowing himself to be carried along by the current of life. A barge en route to Verone was expected to make a stop at Coburg within a few days. His return trip would be much quicker traveling along the river.

A week passed before the boat arrived. The temperature plummeted, and the snowfall was heavy during that time. There were concerns the river would ice over, but fortunately, it didn't. Ysabelle accompanied Axel to the docks. Although it tore at his heart, he knew leaving was the right decision. When they'd first separated, Axel had sensed there was something unfinished in their relationship. Their reconnection had allowed them to find closure and move on from the past. He would love Ysabelle for the rest of his life. After a tear-filled goodbye, he summoned the strength to board the barge. It was more difficult than he'd expected. He watched Ysabelle grow smaller in the distance as he sailed down the river. Once she was out of sight, he found a comfortable spot against the cargo and closed his eyes.

The journey to Verone was rather uneventful, and the crew left him to his own devices. The only meaningful conversation he had was with a well-dressed merchant, whose presence exuded an air of opulence, as he escorted his goods from Ravenna. Axel recognized him as Kasper, whom he had first heard recite the Alchemist Creed at the queen's ball. Kasper confided in him about a once-in-a-lifetime opportunity he'd been offered by an overseas investor to export goods. If successful, it would make him wealthier than he'd ever dreamed. Unfortunately, his business partner wanted no part in it and threatened to dissolve their partnership if he pursued it. Moreover, the deal would require him to be away from Vilsheim for months at a time, causing further strain on his already troubled relationship with his wife. Kasper grumbled everyone close to him was against his chance to strike it big. Axel couldn't help but chuckle. Kasper's pursuit of riches had come at the cost of true happiness. He felt immense gratitude that Balthasar had taught him something far more valuable than the mere transmutation of gold.

As they neared their destination, Axel asked the captain about finding another boat to take him to Koenigsberg. The captain warned him about the escalating tension between Verone and the capital city, implying it might be difficult. Although there were plenty of ships heading in that direction, Axel wearing the king's colors would make people wary, if not outright hostile, toward him.

He kept this in mind as they anchored in Verone. The captain provided a list of traders who might offer him passage. Unfortunately, only one of them was in port at the moment. After a wary glance at his uniform, the merchant said, "Sure, I'll take you to Koenigsberg. I'll need to adjust the cost to cover the taxes that the king has forced upon me. I'm sure he can afford to cover the passage for one of his guards."

Axel declined and looked for other options. The barge captain was correct about it being difficult. One person ignored him as he turned his back, while another had the nerve to spit at him. Axel stayed optimistic and made a deliberate effort to combat the frustration that was creeping up on him. He tried not to take it personally. It wasn't him but what he represented they despised. The king was inflicting hardship in their lives, so it was natural to associate those feelings with a symbol of that suffering. He was certain that he would find a boat that was meant to take him home.

He realized how much he had grown since visiting the alchemist. The old Axel would have been exasperated at these people and the rudeness shown to him. In the past, he would have succumbed to anger and likely threatened violence to deal with their disrespect. It was that martyr mindset that had led to his outbursts and the ensuing trouble. His patience paid off when he found a female captain named Winfrey who agreed to take him.

"How much for passage to Koenigsberg?" he asked.

She smiled as he approached, eyeing him up and down. "One gold piece will suffice for such a handsome man."

Despite it being more than he should have paid, a single gold piece was still a considerable discount compared to the other offers he'd gotten. His face softened with relief as he agreed. She smiled at him as she tugged at her lip with her finger. "I reckon that's the cheapest fare you've heard all day, wearing that uniform. But I don't have the luxury to turn down business. I need to work twice as hard for half the amount as any man. Besides, I may have a special duty you can perform for me." She gave him a knowing wink that Axel met with a nervous smile.

Winfrey gave him a quick tour of the boat and showed him the tiny cabin where he would stay. The room was empty except for a narrow cot that Axel struggled to fit his broad physique into. He opened the small porthole, allowing light to enter and clear out the musty odor. He shut the door, grateful to have a private cabin to himself.

Within a week, they reached Koenigsberg. Axel stood at the bow of the boat as the city came into view. The wind tousled his blond hair, and the familiar scent of the sea welcomed him home. He'd never realized how much he had missed that salty smell. On a clear day, the powerful wind would sweep away the stench of the city's decay, leaving behind a refreshing, natural fragrance. In the distance, Frostgarde stood atop its fortified hill, casting a sinister shadow over the city below. The Queen's

Curtain enveloped it, shielding it from the outside world. From the highest tower, the black boar's standard rippled in the gusting wind, as it had done for many centuries. While seasons changed and generations passed, the boar's sigil remained unwavering.

When they docked, Axel bid farewell to Winfrey. True to her innuendo, she'd attempted to seduce him during their voyage. He'd politely refused, but made amends by dining with her on multiple occasions. Winfrey was lonely and looking for companionship, and he enjoyed getting to know her while consciously avoiding any thoughts of being intimate. He thanked her for the ride and proposed that they meet up the next time she was in town, to which she eagerly agreed. They hugged, and Axel stepped into Koenigsberg for the first time in over half a year. Inhaling a deep breath of ocean air, he headed straight for Frostgarde.

# Chapter 27

## *Before the King*

Axel took a deep breath to calm himself as he approached Frostgarde. On the boat, he'd groomed himself to ensure he looked presentable. He'd polished his mail until it gleamed in the afternoon sun and tied his hair into a warrior's braid that extended to his neck. His beard was combed and glistened with a touch of oil. He envisioned himself as a knight of the BlackGuard, returning after completing a crucial mission for the king, and despite his mind's efforts to convince him otherwise, he dismissed any thoughts of failure or abandonment. He remained vigilant, refusing to be lured into the anxious, guilt-ridden version of his former self.

The guards watched with little interest as Axel approached the Boar's Gate. With an air of confidence, he stood tall and introduced himself, stating his intention to report to Commander Jurgen. His uniform served as a sign of his superior rank, prompting them to salute and welcome him home. After they let him pass, he strove with purpose up the hill, bypassing the smaller gate at the Queen's Curtain with no issues. He had yet to run into anyone he recognized.

That scenario shifted as soon as he reached the keep, where two knights from the BlackGuard were stationed. They looked at each other, confused, before the larger one spoke. "We didn't expect to see you again. Heard you ran into trouble with the baron's nephew. We surmised the boy's insolence had gone too far and you let him know it. Everyone thought you were dead."

Axel looked remorseful. "I admit I had to hold myself back a few times, but I didn't harm the lad. After meeting his family, I realized he would endure far greater misery with them than any pain I could have caused." The guards laughed. "It's good to be home. If you'll excuse me, I need to report to Commander Jurgen."

The guard nodded, but mentioned he was required to escort him. Axel followed him through the familiar hallways of Frostgarde Keep. Things had changed little while he was gone. Routine was a constant companion within these walls, never faltering. Its residents changed with each generation, but the traditions and customs endured. It dawned on him that this was one way the Koenigs cultivated the steadfast belief in their right to rule. They found Jurgen in the familiar surroundings of his office. When he saw Axel, his brow furrowed, but a smile crept across his lips, reflecting both relief and worry. He invited him to sit as he dismissed the guard.

"So you've returned," he said. "I'm glad to see you

well. When I didn't hear any further from you, I feared you'd either deserted your post or were killed."

Axel nodded as he cleared his throat. He'd already decided to be honest about his assignment, aside from his detour to the alchemist. "Thank you, sir. I had concerns about returning home after offending two of the most powerful men in the realm. Once I delivered Dirk to his family, I knew I was in serious trouble, so I was in no hurry to return. I decided to visit my former betrothed in Coburg. It would give me a chance to clear my head and consider the consequences of my actions. Of course, there is a reason she is my former betrothed, and I knew I had to leave at some point. I'm not one to abandon my duty, and it was always my intent to return. I assume you got my message?"

Jurgen's eyes narrowed as he considered Axel's explanation. Following a tense pause, he shook his head and threw up his arms. "Women! Over fifty summers, and I'm still not a day closer to understanding them. I've quit trying to relate to them and simply appreciate all they do for us. I learned to enjoy the results without questioning the reason."

Axel chuckled and nodded in agreement. They traded stories about the women in their lives before Jurgen's face took on a grave expression. "King Otto wants to see you. He instructed me to inform him as soon as you returned." He sent a guard to advise the chancellor that he would escort Axel when the king was ready.

Axel swallowed, feeling his mouth go dry as he pushed away thoughts of why the king wanted him. His hands turned clammy, and tiny beads of sweat formed on his forehead. He allowed his emotions to flow through him, recognizing that whatever ensued was meant to happen. While they waited, Jurgen apprised him of what had transpired during his absence. Another training class had begun, along with formal promotions of several men in their order. All knights had been instructed to be on high alert for any discussions pertaining to alchemy.

A servant arrived soon after to inform them the king was ready. Axel was to be escorted to the sitting room inside the royal chamber.

Jurgen accompanied him through the dining hall to the empty throne room. They proceeded to the royal quarters by passing through the hallway behind the throne. The IceGuards, dressed in pristine white uniforms, guarded the entrance. The walls were lined with portraits of former kings who reigned during the Koenig dynasty. Axel counted over twenty before finding the imposing gaze of King Otto. His picture depicted a youthful man, free from the excess flesh that now sagged beneath his neck. They continued in silence until they reached a heavy oak door guarded by another IceGuard. "Commander Jurgen of the BlackGuard escorting Axel Albrecht at the king's request," the older man said.

The guard's eyes remained fixed on them as he knocked at the door behind his back.

Chancellor Heinz opened the door, dressed in a formal blue robe buttoned to his chin and extending to the floor. He flashed an impish smile. "Commander Jurgen, thank you for escorting your knight here. You're dismissed." He reached for Axel, drawing him into the room before closing the door behind him.

Axel entered a posh room, marveling at the sheer opulence of the Koenigs' wealth. Luxurious silk tapestries adorned the walls, complemented by intricate silver trim on the finely crafted oak furniture. A roaring fire blazed in a grand stone hearth across the room. A solid gold boar, its ruby eyes glowing as the light from the fire struck them, rested on the mantel. Two exquisite steel swords, their hilts embellished with rubies and diamonds, hung crossed above it. King Otto, seated in a plush velvet chair near the fire, faced Axel. His golden crown rested slightly askew atop his head, and his robe hung open, revealing his impressive chest and stomach. He was an imposing figure, known for his prowess in his younger days, when he would spar with multiple opponents in the practice ring. His broad shoulders and thick legs bulged with muscle that were said to possess the strength of a boar. Although age had softened him, hiding his muscles beneath layers of fat, his strength remained evident. He took a sip of wine from a jewel-encrusted goblet and studied Axel.

He approached the king at the chancellor's request, his heart pounding as he knelt down and lowered his head in a humble bow. "Your Majesty." He hesitated before glancing up to find Otto scowling at him.

The king put his wine down and pressed his fingers together. "So you're the knight who has been causing trouble for my barons. I'm sure you're aware I have a tumultuous relationship with them and don't need to give them any more reasons to take my crown. Your role is to stand guard, vigilant and in silence, no matter the task at hand. Stay quiet unless spoken to and take action if there's a threat. Despite any personal annoyance you may feel, you have a duty to fulfill. It's really quite simple unless you choose to make it difficult. It appears you prefer it complicated."

The tension in the room was palpable, and Axel felt the negative energy creeping into his psyche. The king was a powerful man who determined what was right and what was wrong. His way was the only way. Axel sensed Otto was provoking him to determine how much influence he had exerted. He put his negative thoughts aside and concentrated on being in control of the situation. The king wanted him to react, and he couldn't let that happen. He steadied his breath and remained silent.

"Do you have anything to say for yourself?" Otto said, slamming his fist on the armrest.

Axel, still on one knee, said, "If their children are anything like them, I understand why you have such a negative opinion of the barons." He flashed a charming smile before continuing. "Lady Amelia of Wismar complained of being too fat to attract a husband. I simply told her that there are methods to lose weight if she wanted to. I described how your generosity allowed me access to the knight's training program, where I lost weight. She lamented that she would never have an opportunity like that and I was rubbing her nose in it. I told her I did no such thing, but she was offended and expressed her grievances to her father.

"As for Lord Dirk, he's a conniving bastard that you should be wary of. During our travels, we were fortunate to find hospitality with a family in the Verone countryside. They voiced their complaints about Baron Helmuth's negligence of the roads, and the boy attempted to shift the blame onto you. They knew I was a king's man and asked that I deliver the information to Frostgarde. Lord Dirk took it as a personal insult when they showed disrespect toward his uncle and sought your help instead. There is a great deal of animosity for you in Verone. There were whispers of rebellion and trying to break away from Vilsheim."

Otto eyed the chancellor, who nodded back. They were already aware of the temperature in Verone. He motioned for Axel to continue. "I admit, I became frustrated during my transition to the BlackGuard. I never expected to be babysitting spoiled children. So after I completed my assignment in Verone, I decided to take some personal time to visit my former lover in Coburg. I'm sure you've already deduced from my interaction with Amelia that I am coarse around women. It goes without saying that our relationship didn't succeed this time either. I also needed to update Commander Jurgen about what I observed during my trip. I was delighted to hear that I would report to you directly."

The king snickered before releasing a booming laugh and relaxing in his chair. "I will concede that you do seem a bit boorish. Even I would never be so crass as to mention a woman's weight. The information you gathered from Verone is disturbing. There have been rumors of discontent, and this confirms it. Baron Helmuth will fulfill his obligations or I'll have him removed. I have no tolerance for disobedience." He took a long sip from his goblet before asking, "Did you encounter any other knights on the road?"

Axel knew he was referring to Gunter, and if he was being strictly honest, he'd only seen him in Coburg and in the glade. "While I didn't come across any other knights on the road, I can confirm that it's more dangerous than it once was. A lone traveler, even a knight, may not be safe. I returned from Coburg by boat. I didn't trust the roads."

As Otto's mouth met his wine goblet, he said, "It's all in how you perceive the Oüd, eh?"

A perplexed expression crossed Axel's face, his forehead scrunching. "Forgive me, Your Majesty, but I am not familiar with that term."

The king took another sip and waited. He then shrugged it off and said, "It's nothing, just an old family term. Forget you heard it. Now, the question is, what do I do with you? You have disrespected two barons, who blame me. I could have you executed or thrown into the dungeon. But reports indicate you have been loyal for a long time and served me well. I could discharge you and leave you with nothing, but I appreciate your directness and courage in speaking your mind. With the insight you gathered from Verone, I see you as someone who could be of great use to me. I believe it would be wise to keep you around."

"Your Majesty, a word, if I may?" the chancellor said

as he cut in. Otto obliged, and Heinz whispered something in his ear.

The king broke out in a broad smile, nodding his head. "You will be demoted to Watchman and resume your previous post on the Queen's Curtain. You won't be able to disturb my guests, but you'll be close by in case your help is needed for any future assignments."

Axel let out a sigh of relief before bowing again. "Thank you, Your Majesty. You are most generous, and I am grateful for you leniency."

With a wave of his hand, the king dismissed him, leaving the chancellor to escort him from the room. "During your absence, talk of alchemy has decreased significantly. Make sure it remains that way," he said before closing the door behind him.

Axel breathed a sigh of relief as the IceGuard accompanied him to the main hall. He wasn't sure where to go next, so he headed for Jurgen's office to fill him in on his demotion. He was relieved that his punishment was manageable, and they hadn't probed further into his trip to Coburg. The king's powerful presence and mention of Oüd convinced Axel that he had been trained in mental alchemy. He wondered who had taught him and if Queen Helena and their children were educated in it as well. It was likely a secret of royal lineage, passed down through generations. In order to be sure, he knew he had to keep his guard up around all of them.

When he got to Jurgen's office, he was surprised to find Stefan conversing with his former commander. With an impish grin, he knocked at the open door before entering. Stefan smirked and pulled him into a tight bear hug. "Ax, you have returned! I'm so relieved to see you. You must fill me in on what you've been up to."

Axel released him and patted his shoulder. "I've missed you too, old friend. I have much to tell you, but first I must speak to Jurgen about my meeting with the king. If you're available tonight, let's meet at The Badger and the Boar for a tankard, where I can apprise you of my trip."

"That's an excellent idea. I need to be going back to my post now, anyway. I'll see you there this evening." On his way out, he slapped Axel on the back. "It's good to have you back."

Axel was moved. It felt good to be missed, and he was looking forward to reconnecting with Stefan. He remembered Jurgen and saluted. "Commander, I must inform you that the king demoted me and ordered that I return to the Queen's Curtain."

He stroked his chin. "That's interesting. I thought you would be discharged or thrown in the dungeon for a spell. Fortune must be smiling upon you."

"Yes, sir. I shared some valuable information I picked up in Verone that proved helpful. The people there have contempt for the crown and hold a rather low opinion of the Koenigs."

Jurgen did not seem surprised. "Perhaps that's why the baron's nephew was such an unruly bastard. I'm relieved he's gone. We can't have that sort of attitude tainting the other knights."

Axel concurred. "The boy has other problems as well.

His family's disapproval was evident. Unless there is a change in his attitude, he will continue to struggle. Hopefully he figures it out. Unfortunately, some of us need lessons repeated multiple times in order to fully comprehend them."

Jurgen smiled. "True. It can be quite difficult to overcome stubbornness and adopt a more open-minded perspective. Since I wasn't sure if you were returning, I replaced your position and stored your things here." He gestured to a chest in the corner that contained Axel's meager possessions. "Take your gear to the Watchmen's barracks and report to your commander. You're dismissed."

He grabbed his belongings and was about to leave before Jurgen stopped him at the door. "It's good to have you back, Axel. I am glad everything worked out."

Axel grinned.

He left the keep and reported to Commander Leopold in the Queen's Curtain. Once again, he was assigned the night shift atop the northwest tower, a place he was intimately acquainted with. He left his trunk at the barracks and headed to the tavern. Since he'd arrived early, he sat at the bar and ordered a mug of brown ale as he took in the familiar surroundings. Little had changed in his favorite watering hole. The tables were still in need of repair, and there were additional cracks along the walls, but there was nothing more wonderful than this dark and dingy place. He was glad to be home.

While lost in thought, he heard someone sit beside him. Through his periphery, he glimpsed a BlackGuard's uniform and was surprised to see Basel. Axel nodded as they sat in silence. Basel shifted nervously in his chair and stared down at the bar. "I heard you returned," he said in a cracking voice. "I thought I might find you here. Gunter told me the chancellor ordered him to follow you to Verone. He was convinced you wanted to learn alchemy. He still hasn't returned, and I am getting concerned."

Axel took a long sip of ale and weighed his words. "What is it that disturbs you, Basel? That he hasn't returned, or that perhaps he will?"

Basel got a faraway look in his eye before he turned back to his mug. "When he wasn't making your life miserable, he directed his abuse at me. I looked up to him when we were young and honestly believed he was trying to strengthen me. Eventually, I realized he was a bully who enjoyed picking on those weaker than him. But at that point, I was already afraid of him and succumbed to his pressure to do things I knew were wrong. If I refused him, his eyes would get this deranged look before he started threatening me."

In hindsight, it made perfect sense. Gunter wasn't capable of being equal in a relationship. Whenever the focus wasn't on him, he would divert it his way. He'd tortured Basel, but Axel had been too consumed by his own hatred to notice. He looked Basel in the eye and said, "I don't think Gunter will bother either of us anymore." Their mugs clanked as Axel banged them together before taking a long draw.

Basel hesitated before doing the same. He conveyed his understanding with a quick nod. "Thanks, Axel. I'll leave you to your ale. I'm sure I'm the last person you'd want to talk on your first day back." After downing his ale, he stood to leave.

On his way out, Axel called to him, "Don't be a stranger."

Basel acknowledged him before exiting the tavern. Axel nursed his ale, taking small sips as he waited for his friend. Stefan arrived a short time later, and Axel ordered a round for the two of them. Stefan told him what had transpired since he left. Rumors circulated Axel had either been killed or deserted his post, but Jurgen and Stefan had kept them contained, preventing them from advancing beyond the BlackGuard. Axel had few friends at Frostgarde, so they were easy to dismiss.

When Stefan had finished, Axel conveyed a similar story to the one he'd given Jurgen and the king. Although he trusted Stefan as a loyal friend who wouldn't divulge his secrets, he chose to keep certain details to himself. In due time, he might consider telling others what he'd learned, but for now, he was still acclimating to everything.

Stefan took a long draw from his mug before looking Axel in the eye. "So, any regrets at seeing Ysabelle?"

Axel grinned. "Not at all. In fact, it was something I needed. It wasn't until I saw her again that I realized how much resentment still lingered. I'd always thought that if she had gotten her emotions under control, we would be married and have a wonderful life."

Stefan burst into laughter. "We can't all be made of stone."

That was the type of comment that typically irritated Axel. However, he now understood that each person's perspective was their own, and he had no right to judge them. How could he possibly know the unconscious thoughts that drove someone else's behavior? Things were simpler this way. "Traveling gave me time to reconsider the entire relationship. It dawned on me that I blamed others for my unhappiness and my stubbornness didn't serve me. I was trying to save Ysabelle from herself and thought if I could solve her problems, then our relationship would be healed. Instead, I tried to force my perception of the world onto her rather than attempting to view it from hers."

"That's wonderful, Axel. I've tried explaining that you were your own worst enemy. You lived in your own head and avoided the real world."

Axel chuckled. "I still live in my head, but I've stopped listening to everything it says. I thought it was protecting me, but it was the source of my problems. Now, instead of controlling my life, I use my mind to enhance it."

They finished their ale, and Stefan called for another round. "It sounds like you had one hell of an adventure. I don't know what prompted you to see things differently, but I'm happy you did. You've been cooped up here so long that you probably needed time away to clear your head. Now that you've moved past Ysabelle, have you given any thought to finding another woman?"

Axel hadn't thought of seeking another mate but wasn't opposed to the idea. He planned on seeing Winfrey once he'd reestablished his routine. "I hadn't really thought of it. It's a relief not to have to worry about such matters. I never realized how much Ysabelle was still on my mind."

"When you are ready, my wife has a cousin that would be perfect for you. She is not only smart but quick-witted, and has a figure that I'm sure you'll like," he said with a wink.

"Perhaps. I'm in no hurry, but if you want to mention it to Arin, I wouldn't be opposed. You never know where a door may lead until you open it."

Stefan clinked his mug into Axel's. "I'll mention it to her. Speaking of which, I'm supposed to see her tonight. I'm sorry I have to run, but I wasn't expecting you."

"Of course. We have plenty of time now that I've returned. I'll leave with you. It's back to the Curtain for me."

"I'm sorry about that, Ax. I know you hate it there. I'm surprised you haven't drunk more to cope."

Axel hadn't even thought about another drink. In fact, he had thought little about getting drunk since he met the alchemist. He smiled. "Thank you for being a genuine friend, Stefan. You made me realize that without resentment festering inside me, I no longer need to drown my sorrows. Oh, I was thinking next time we meet for a drink, we can invite Basel. He seems lonely without Gunter."

"Aye, good idea, Ax. I'll see you soon."

Axel headed back to Frostgarde to begin his first watch atop the Queen's Curtain.

# Chapter 28

## *First Watch*

A xel stood at the bottom of the stairs, the memory of what he'd believed was his final descent still firmly etched in his mind. He counted the steps as he climbed to the top of the Queen's Curtain: fifteen to the first landing, another fifteen to the second, and a final fifteen to reach the top. He banged his midsection against the wooden banister that jutted from the stairwell and chuckled to himself, making a mental note to be more careful next time. Instinctively, he knew he wouldn't make the mistake again.

The tower looked just as he remembered: a sturdy oak table, an assortment of ranged weapons adorning the wall, and a large firepit blazing in the middle of the room. Axel bid the Watchman on duty good night before adding a couple more logs to the crackling fire. After taking a moment to bask in the comforting warmth, he proceeded toward the battlement, ready to begin his preliminary patrol.

On this chilly evening, the full moon hung in the sky, casting its soft silver glow over the sea. A gentle breeze blew through his hair as he ran his hand along the sturdy stone wall, tracing the grooves time had etched into it. As he overlooked the amazing view before him, a sense of tranquility washed over him, unlike anything he had felt before. The sheer beauty of his surroundings seduced him, and he didn't understand how he had ever grown tired of it.

The salty scent of the sea filled the air, devoid of the repugnant stench of the harbor that seeped in during the summer months. Calm waters mirrored the stars above, shimmering in the moonlight like a beacon of hope. In the distance, the lights from the city illuminated the bustling taverns and brothels, distinct from this elevated vantage point.

As he gazed up at the stars adorning the night sky, he recognized his own meager existence within the expansive universe. Every light below represented a group of people, each carrying their own burden. One could never fully comprehend another's hardships. What would be insignificant to one could be an unbearable weight to others.

Even time itself lost meaning. Every fleeting moment was trivial in the grand scheme of things unless he chose to attach meaning to it. He wasted too much time putting undue importance on frivolous events. He resolved to embrace the present moment and appreciate the unique experiences it brought him.

As he rested his arms along the ledge of the stone

battlement, a deep sense of gratitude washed over him at how fortunate he was. He could now appreciate all the things he had taken for granted throughout the years. At Frostgarde, he led a quiet, uncomplicated life, filled with reliable friends and the prospect of a budding romance on the horizon. The oppressive manner in which the Koenigs governed was troubling and something to reflect on in the days ahead. The closure he had longed for obtained, he now looked ahead to what his future held. He slowly exhaled the salty air, relishing the sensation as it escaped his lips. He'd thought he hit rock bottom when he left Verone. But without falling, would he have had the courage to push past his self-limiting boundaries? Would he have realized he shaped his reality, regardless of the situation? The alchemist had taught him that by guarding his thoughts and consciously directing his awareness, he had the power to command his life.

In the end, it was so simple: master his mind and determine his destiny.

A smile graced his face as he gazed down at the world below, recognizing he had achieved his highest aspiration. He'd found peace within.

# About the Author

C.L. Embry is an emerging fantasy author, focusing on stories that revolve around themes of alchemy and mysticism. Drawing inspiration from his own experience with self-victimization and addiction, he felt compelled to write his novel and offer hope to others facing similar challenges. When not engrossed in a captivating book, he embarks on inspiring adventures, guided by the open road, in his RV. Originally from Southern California, he now resides wherever his journey leads him. Knightfall is his first novel.

***If you enjoyed this book, please consider leaving a review on Amazon or your favorite online bookstore.***

Printed in Great Britain
by Amazon